Tess

JOCELYN REEKIE

RAINCOAST BOOKS

Vancouver

Raincoast Books
9050 Shaughnessy Street
Vancouver, British Columbia
Canada, V6P 6E5
www.raincoast.com

In the United States:
Publishers Group West
1700 Fourth Street
Berkeley, California
94710

Raincoast Books gratefully acknowledges the support of the Government of Canada through
the Book Publishing Industry Development Program, the Canada Council and the Department
of Canadian Heritage. We also acknowledge the assistance of the Province of British Columbia
through the British Columbia Arts Council.

Edited by Barbara Kuhne
Text design by Ingrid Paulson
Typeset by Teresa Bubela

NATIONAL LIBRARY OF CANADA CATALOGUING IN PUBLICATION DATA

Reekie, Jocelyn, 1947-
  Tess

ISBN 1-55192-471-4

1. British Columbia — History — 19th century — Juvenile fiction. I. Title.

PS8585.E422T47 2002   jC813'.6   C2002-910547-1
PZ7.R2544Te 2002
Library of Congress Catalogue Number: 2002091847

At Raincoast Books we are committed to protecting the environment and to the responsible
use of natural resources. We are acting on this commitment by working with suppliers and
printers to phase out our use of paper produced from ancient forest. This book is one step
towards that goal. It is printed on 100% ancient-forest-free paper (100% recycled, 40% post-
consumer), processed chlorine-free, and supplied by New Leaf paper. It is printed with
vegetable-based inks. For further information, visit our website at www.raincoast.com. We are
working with Markets Initiative (www.oldgrowthfree.com) on this project.

10 9 8 7 6 5 4 3 2 1

Printed and bound in Canada by Webcom.

To my husband Bill, and my children
Stephanie and Curtis, with love.

In memory of my grandfather,
George Herbert Barr.

CONTENTS

❧ ONE ❧
November 1857
The Hunt

I REMEMBER how the exhilaration of the hunt made my breath come in quick little gasps until I forced myself to slow it down. *Breathe!* my mind-voice ordered. A single, shrill cry split the air. Save for it, everything except the mist was still. Slowly, I uncurled my trigger finger and wiped the water that was running down my cheeks off my face. Just as slowly, I rewrapped my finger around the cold blue steel. The warmth in my belly had long since seeped out of me into the cold rock I was lying on: my soft flesh was turning to a hard ridge of rubbery cramps. My arms and hands started to shake. *Keep still!* I told myself. I was used to the cold and the wet, but not the waiting. "Timing, lass," Father had said. "Ye maun be prepared and when the time is right, use it to your advantage."

Below me, the red deer stag's ears flicked back and forth. Its nostrils flared. It stood with its back legs bent like coils ready to spring. Its body froze in that position and for an instant it seemed to vanish into its surroundings. Then it raised its quivering nose to taste the air. I squeezed the trigger.

At the same instant the rifle cracked, the deer staggered; then it bounded into the forest behind it and disappeared from sight. I got to my feet. I had to look hard to see the branches of a small tree move. *There! It's hit!* Slinging my rifle over my shoulder, I ran back along the outcrop searching for a place to jump down. When another shot rang out, I flew.

✦

By the time I found them, my father had the stag loaded on the tough little dun-coloured pony we used to pack a kill.

"Ye canna track a wounded animal if ye break yer bones, Tess," Father said. I looked where he was looking. Below the hem of my skirt, the soft leather of my Hielan shoes was soaking up the blood running down my legs from the scrapes I had suffered when I'd slid down the hill after jumping from the outcrop.

"I canna track anything trying to run in these lang skirts," I said. "Next time I shall wear trowsers. Is it my shot halfway up the neck?"

"Aye, ye grazed him enough to give me a killing shot."

Above an opening in the trees I saw an eagle dipping in and out of view, swimming in the currents. Soon another came, and another. In a few minutes, I counted eight circling, swooping birds.

"They've smelt the kill," Father said. "Look here, lass; see how I've arranged the antlers so they will nae touch the pony's hide." I looked and saw how he'd put the deer across the saddle in such a way that no matter how the horse moved it would not be bothered by the rack. The pony stood quietly while Father finished tying on. Long ago any skittishness at blood-smell had been trained out of it. "Ye'll finish up," Father said.

"Aye," I agreed. Saying nothing more, he turned away. He went deeper into the forest, and soon, cushioned by the moss and needles on the forest floor, his footsteps could not be heard. I took hold of the halter lead and began to walk. At home I would unload, gut, behead and quarter the deer the way I had seen Father do so many times before. The offal would be put in tubs: the intestines would be used in making sausage; organ meats were cooked and eaten as they were, except the lungs, which would go into a recipe for haggis. Brains were deep-fried *fritôt*, or served creamed in a white sauce. Nothing would be wasted. The butchering would be a load of work, but it was the bargain I'd made when I'd begged Father to let me come hunting with him this morning. "I've nae the time to go at your pace, lassie, and to get the meat home both," he'd warned. "I maun get myself to the mines."

"If we make a kill I'll get it home," I'd boasted, though I'd never done it on my own before. Now he was gone, heading back to the border country where the mines were located and we would not see him home for months perhaps. I sighed. There was nothing to do but get on with it.

Two hours later I was at the bottom of the steep brae that led to where our ancestors had built Castle Dunharbar on the top of a knoll two hundred and fifty years before. The pony, knowing its box and a breakfast of oats were close at hand, tugged on its line and started up faster than I could walk. I dug my slippered feet into the dirt and tried to keep pace with it, but my lang skirt interfered. Stepping on the hem, I tripped and fell onto the scabs that had been forming on my scrapes. I lost the halter rope and the pony went on.

The skirt had caused me enough trouble for one day. Three swipes of my knife and the wool was cut off well above my knees. The air was cold on my legs but I liked the feel of it. I stepped out of the circle of cut cloth, tied it round my waist and headed up. When I trudged through the outer gate and headed for the stables and the meat room, the pony was standing by the meat-room door; the stablehand was untying ropes. He gave no sign that he noticed my strange costume, but helped me lift the deer and carry it to the cutting table.

"A bonny stag, miss," he said. "He will dress out at seven stone."

"Aye," I agreed. I was tired and tempted to leave the cutting-up to him, but I remembered the promise I'd given Father and said, "I'll butcher it." He nodded and led the pony to its box, where he would rub it down, feed it and then clean the tack of blood. I set to work.

Much later, washing the blood from my own hands and legs from a barrel of cold water before going into the house, I felt the warmth of satisfaction. I had helped to kill a deer and I had brought it home.

❦

The fire in Mother's room was glowing and danced canty lights of yellow-orange on the tapestries that hung on the walls. Tapestries she had made, full of deep, rich reds, heather purple, the green of fir tree needles, gold and silver-grey. The colour on the walls was a stark contrast to her own pale and hollow face. I had entered quietly but her eyes were open and she watched me come toward her bed.

"Tess. I'm glad to see ye." She pushed herself up and patted the covers beside her. I sat beside her as she bid. I saw her take note of my skirt and legs.

"I was hunting with Father and I slipped running down a hill," I said to reassure her. "'Tis only scrapes."

"Aye, ye'll heal," she said, "but your skirt will not. Money disnae grow on trees for ye to be cutting up your clothes, lassie."

Where a few short weeks earlier there would have been a hint of merriment behind her gentle reprimand, I now heard only tiredness. "I'm sorry, Mother, but it was so much in the way. I can make use of it in vests."

It was a few minutes before she said, "Tess, ye are thirteen and will soon be full grown. Tis time ye put aside the impetuousness that governs ye. Ye are being noticed."

"What do you mean, noticed?"

"Have ye nae seen Mr. James and Mr. McWhattle, the minister, watching ye?"

I laughed. "Mr. McWhattle is so fond of the whisky he walks with a permanent tilt, and Mr. James is older than Father. Let them watch someone else."

Mother shook her head. "They are both respectable men with very large holdings. Ye maun begin to think about keeping all good prospects open for your marriage."

I was horrified. "Marriage! I've plenty of time to think of that."

It was a long while before she said, "Perhaps."

Beads of sweat glistened on her forehead and just above her upper lip. "I'll let ye rest," I said. "I'll look in on Colin."

"Aye," she said. "Sweet wee lad. Tell Nanny to bring him in to me."

"This morning Nanny said his fever is still high and we are nae to go near him till it breaks and the contagion is past. If she brings him to you, is there nae a chance ye'll be reinfected?"

"I am beyond that, and I want to hold him," she said. "Tell her to bring him, Tess."

Misunderstanding her meaning, I said, "Aye, I will, Mother," and I went to do it.

TWO

Losses
Meeting Uncle Hammond

RAIN pooled in puddles at my feet. As was the custom, everyone from the parish was there. The miners and crofters with their families; the peers and lords and ladies. Perhaps three hundred people stood in rows and clusters inside and outside the picket fence. They were listening to my father's voice. I was listening to my heart beat as I stood beside the hole, watching my hands twisting one inside the other. I did not want to look at the four men lowering Mother's casket into the wretched hole, nor to raise my eyes and see Colin's tiny casket beside its muddy hole at the children's end of the graveyard. He would be lowered next. Father was saying the prayer for the dead but I kept hearing Colin's bonny voice, his cries of delight and giggling while he'd chased the chickens round their yard. He'd almost caught one. Was it only two weeks ago? He was such a bonny lad. He had the dark colouring and mellow, happy temper of our mother. They couldn't both be gone.

I held my ears against the graveside service. *How can Father keep on talking?* My own voice was lost somewhere inside my aching throat.

❧

The women of the parish swarmed through the house. They were putting out platters filled with food, carrying plates of food among the people, cleaning up empty trays and platters, bringing more food out. It seemed all anyone could think to do was eat.

When I said I wasn't hungry, some put a hand underneath my chin and lifted it so they could look at my face. I didn't know what they wanted to look at and I thought it rude. Then they'd say, "Ah, lass, you have to eat. Keep up your strength." Others said, "You must let it go, lass. Have a good cry now. No good will come of holding on to it." Still others preached, "The good Lord giveth and He taketh away and though we mortals might not know His wisdom, we must accept it, lass." They were people who had known my parents long: my parents' peers, who came from neighbouring estates and from town, as well as the miners who had come up from the Lowlands because of the respect they held my father in, and the crofters from closer to our home, many of whom had known my mother. Everyone wanted to be kind. All I wanted was to be left alone.

In the hallway near the kitchen, a man blocked my way and put a hand on my shoulder. I stood looking at my feet, wanting to be gone. "You must be Elizabeth," he said. "I've been told you'd grown up, and so you have." He didn't wait for me to agree or disagree but went right on: "Tis a terrible business the measles taking your two brothers last year, and flu taking your mother and young Colin this. And your Dad left with no sons after him, though I suppose with your mother gone tis a blessing of sorts not to have a wean running about. You ought look after your Dad."

His words jarred me out of my own thoughts. "A blessing? Who on God's earth are you, sir, to say such a thing as that? How could anyone believe such a thing as that?"

With an angry look on his face he came toward me. When his hand clamped around my arm I backed up in surprise and snarled through my teeth, "Let go of me, sir!"

The next thing I knew Cook was standing behind me crooning, "Hush now, lassie. Hush now. Tis only your uncle."

"She's hysterical," the man said. "I've seen it before. Your sex cannot stand up to strain. It raises the female blood to dangerous levels. Best have the doctor apply the leeches and bleed her before the excess makes her vessels burst."

My ears had stopped at "uncle." "My uncle?" I stared at the man. Yanking my arm free from his grasp, I moved farther away from him. Again he reached for my arm as if he would take hold of me and see to it himself that I was doctored with the leeches. I turned and ran into the kitchen. Mercifully, he didn't follow.

Cook sat me on a stool, brought me a drink and ordered me to swallow. It tasted earthy and bitter and burned my throat. I must have made a face. "It will do you good, lassie," Cook said. "Drink some more."

I could feel the heat spreading from my throat into my chest and stomach. The taste of it didn't seem so bad now.

"That man is nae my uncle," I said to Cook. "My uncle has been in the colonies for almost ten years."

"Aye," she said. "But tis your Uncle Hammond sure enough, come home. I heard tell he were come back some months ago, though we've seen nowt of him until today."

She busied herself taking pans of hot buns out of the oven, leaving me to quench my anger at whomever the man was by drinking the rest of the whisky she had given me.

When Mr. McWhattle, the minister, came into the kitchen, I watched him with a curious feeling of loose detachment, as if I were safe inside a cubicle with see-through walls. He tottered around the room, pausing to look at all the trays and meats, then, sniffing the air like a dog, he stopped beside a butcher's block covered with a plate of tarts and pies. He stuck a finger into a tart and withdrew a large wad of jam, which he put into his mouth. As he reached for a meat pie, Cook was on his heels, deftly stretching an arm round his girth to scoop the pie clear of him before he touched it.

"'Tis a lovely pie, isn't it, Mr. McWhattle. I'll bring you a slice in the parlour. Off you go then; I'm sure there's many oot there looking to be consoled by you." With a silly, crooked smile on his face, he turned and tottered out.

Cook huffed. "Saints protect us! Poking his fingers into pies! Sets he one foot in here again, I'll poke my fingers into his great, round doughy belly and see how he likes it. What are ye grinning at then?"

"You," I told her. "Someone ought to warn Pastor McWhattle his hot air filling is at risk of being popped. But I hope no one does."

"Oh lassie, isn't that exactly what yer mother would have said." And before I knew it, she and I were wrapped together in a corner of her warm kitchen, soaking one another's shoulders with our tears.

Long before the crowd was gone and the house was quiet again, I went to Mother's room. Her dressing table and stool were near her bed. Only a few months ago she had covered the stool with a square of her needlepoint. I touched the beautiful irises, roses, daisies and forget-me-nots she'd made, and smelled a summer bouquet. The scents, I knew, were coming from the glass bottles and jars that littered her tabletop. I sat on the stool and imagined I was sitting on her lap, as I'd done so often until not so long ago. An exquisite little cut-glass pitcher with a glass stopper in its top had been her favourite. I picked it up and touched the stopper to the hollow in my throat and to my wrist. I sat breathing in the delicate smell of lavender. Mother had had so many scents. Sometimes it was marjoram and thyme she smelled of. Other times her hands and clothes were full of a delicious mix of rosemary, basil and the desert odour of oregano. She grew herbs and flowers, milked their oils, and used them liberally. She had known how to flavour both herself and food.

I didn't realize how dark the room had gotten until Father came in carrying a candle. "Ah, here ye are. Are ye all right, lass?"

I nodded and he went to a fixture on a wall and, with the candle, lit the gas. A soft light dimly flooded a portion of the room. He stood where he was for a long time. Finally he said, "Ye look a lot like her."

I looked into the mirror. Mother's colouring had been all earth and sun: her eyes brown with little golden flecks in them, her skin a lovely coppery warmth, her lips thick and soft — the colour of ripe plums — her hair sleek, straight and black. A throwback, she said, to her ancient Egyptian ancestry. She always wore her hair tucked into a net. My hair, wild and whipped as the Scottish wind, was also black, but as always happened when I tried to hold it still with bows or ribbons, strands had escaped. My black eyebrows almost came together over the green-blue eyes Mother had always called jade. The rounded almond shape of our eyes was similar, I thought, but people said how Mother's eyes were like a baby's — wide open and trusting — and I knew mine were not like that. My skin was light and my lips looked stretched and bloodless. I could see few of Mother's features, and none of her tidy grace, in me.

"Ye've grown up well, Tess," Father said.

It was too much. *No!* I screamed inside myself. *I've not grown up at all!* I wanted to curl up in his hard, strong arms. I wanted him to hold me, and to rock me, and to sing to me as he used to do when I was small. I turned away from the mirror to reach for him, but he had turned toward the door. On his way out he said, "If ye'd like any of those bottles of yer mother's, you're welcome to them, lass."

I stayed in Mother's room among her things all night.

The man Cook had told me was my uncle was at the breakfast table.

"Ye remember your Uncle Hammond, Tess," Father said.

I didn't remember him at all, but I knew the story of him. He was Father's older half-brother, who had never married, and had left Scotland when I was just two years old. When I was six or seven, I had heard my father and my grandfather in an argument about my uncle, and though I didn't know what it was about, I recalled grandfather saying Uncle Hammond had gone to the colonies to expand the family's business opportunities.

Six years ago grandfather had died and Uncle Hammond, as the eldest son, inherited according to Scottish primogeniture inheritance laws. Father was put in charge of

Uncle Hammond's properties in Scotland. It had been almost ten years since Uncle Hammond had last been on Scottish soil.

I did a shallow curtsy and mumbled something proper, like "Hello, Uncle."

"Are you feeling better?" he asked.

"I'm very well, thank ye."

"I'm glad to hear it. We don't want a repeat of yesterday, do we?"

I wasn't hungry, but I made a show of taking some porridge and milk from the breakfast foods Cook had put on the sideboard. I didn't want Uncle speculating on my eating habits or on my future health.

Father waited until Uncle Hammond had gobbled two helpings of eggs and bangers, a bowl of porridge, several pieces of bread and butter spread with strawberry preserves and his third cup of coffee before he said, "Hammond has sold Castle Dunharbar, Tess. He's recommended me to the Missionary Board in the colonies, and he's offered us a room in his house there until we can find accommodations of our own. He's secured us tickets on a ship sailing three weeks from now from Liverpool to Vancouver's Island."

I blinked. "Leaving Scotland? Leaving Mother and Colin and ..."

"They'll no begrudge us a fresh start, Tess. Hammond is not obliged to make us this offer or to provide a roof for us. We'll owe him a debt of gratitude."

I did not feel one smidge grateful, and I turned the full force of my spite on my uncle. "If you dinna want Dunharbar, why daena ye give it to us?" I demanded.

My uncle's little bow mouth opened and closed, and his double chins shook before he said, "I believe hysteria has overtaken her again. As I told you yesterday, Iain, you must have her bled immediately. For her own good."

"I am not hysterical, Uncle. You've Glensamonie Castle as well as this, and the mines, and all the lands." Father tried to interrupt but I ploughed on. "Why should we be left with nowt and be beholden to ye just because my father was born second? Why won't ye give Dunharbar to us?"

Uncle Hammond's face had turned purple. "You allow her to speak to her elders in this manner, Iain? To speak at all on matters she knows nothing about?"

Giving Father no room to answer, I jumped to my own defense. "I ken the laws well enough, Uncle. Mother said Scottish inheritance laws are wrong. I'm only asking that ye give us what ye clearly dinna want."

"Tess, that is enough!" Father said sharply.

My uncle wiped his mouth with his napkin, got up from the table and walked stiff-legged from the room. Father kept his place. He was holding the table with both hands and his face and neck were mottled with colour. I recognized his fury, but I didn't care. I kept up my tirade. "'Tis not fair, Father. Uncle Hammond has nae been here for years, and ye've done all the work. Why must we leave?

What about Cook and Nanny? And Sampson, and the other horses? We canna just — "

A low growl issued from my father's throat: "Stop now!" I stopped, and realized both of us were shaking. Father visibly took in breaths. A vein was throbbing in his temple and the knuckles of his hands were white. Finally he said, "Ye are but a lass and ye will obey me in this. No matter what ye think ye ken, ye will nae put yourself above your uncle, or me, again."

Hot tears stung my eyes. "But I love Dunharbar," I said. "I dinna want to go away from it and from Mama and Colin and Wallace and Earl. I dinna want to leave everything I know."

Without warning, his whole body seemed to sag, as if he'd been deflated. The lines that had been cut into his face on either side of his mouth in the past few weeks deepened. There were also lines etched into his forehead. He suddenly looked old to me.

"We dinna have a choice about this, Tess," he said, sounding very tired. "I'm counting on ye to be brave."

I hardly heard the words. My father's defeat reached into me and tied my innards in a tight, smouldering knot. I would, I told myself, never forgive him that defeat. I didn't answer him. Instead, I wiped my lips with my napkin in the same manner my uncle had done, and I left the room.

A few days later, I said a tearful goodbye to Cook, who had been discharged by Uncle Hammond. She was going back to her home in England. Nanny and the other servants had already gone.

In the days that followed I was forced to go through the entire house, helping Father to sort our belongings and to assess what could be taken with us to the colony, and what could not. Uncle Hammond warned Father that missionaries were on the move a lot. He said the New World was a rough country and we would have no place for, and no opportunity to use, many of our things. We would be better off to sell them. The money would allow Father to repay him for our tickets, as well as to have the necessary funds to make a new start. An auction was arranged.

Almost all of Mother's beautiful tapestries, our furniture, the china, the crystal and Grandma's heirloom silver — all were up for bids. I was not much attached to the larger furnishings or things that in my ignorance I thought could easily be replaced. But two little double-handled, silver baby cups that had been passed down for generations and that I had used, and then Wallace and Earl, and lastly Colin, wouldn't bear parting with. Nor would Mother's precious lucifers. Father did not trust the little lighting sticks to be safe. People had been poisoned by using an earlier kind that had been made from white phosphorous, he said. He had told Mother to throw them away, but she had lighted the fire and the lamps with them often and had found them very convenient and safe to use. She kept them in a bottle made of thick glass, which I wrapped along with the silver cups in a pillow case I had embroidered for her birthday when I was six. Uncle had allowed only one wooden box for trinkets, so I put these into my own trunk.

When I had to sort through Mother's personal things and decide what could go with us, my throat closed with anguish. Twas as if I maun divide *her* into parts and decide what parts of her to keep, when it was the whole of her I wanted. Her smells were in her dresses, her petticoats and shawls; her delight in pretty things was in her jewellery. But few of those things could be taken. Uncle Hammond said the jewellery would be lost or stolen. It was better as hard cash. As for her clothing, I was already taller than she had been and I showed every sign of getting even bigger. I took only what had been her favourites, including some very old Hieland clothes of my grandmother's that Mother had kept and carefully preserved.

The day of the auction, I was up before dawn. I wrote a note for Father saying not to worry, and I tucked a small parcel of mutton, bread and cheese into my plaid. I took Sampson from his stall. I did not return to the castle until long after dark. I refused to light a candle or to look into any of the rooms, going straight to my bedchamber, where I crawled under the comforter and fell instantly asleep in the cold dark.

The next day all the horses were taken away.

From then until the day we left for Liverpool, I walked and ran Dunharbar's lands. I spent entire days roaming up and down the braes, splashing through and sitting by the burns and rivers, tromping through fields of heather, skirting the bogs, breathing in the forests. Often I went to the little graveyard by the kirk and sat beside Mother's grave. I talked to her. Told her of my sorrow. I asked her to make me strong, as she had been. I had no dreams, except that someday I would come home.

THREE

IT was raining when we got to the Mersey. It was not the first time I'd been in a city, but it was the first time I had seen so many people in one place. Crowds of emigrants, barterers, carters, dockworkers and sailors jostled one another in the muddy streets and on the docks. I saw strange costumes and heard languages I hadn't known existed. All of Europe, it seemed, had come to Liverpool. Father said that thousands had already left from here for the New World and thousands more were waiting to go. We were dressed more like English than like Hielanders, with woollen coat and cloak, and stiff, English shoes in place of Hielan slippers. Father said the shoes would protect us better from the city filth. But I'd drawn the line at an English bonnet and had my own tam on my head.

We shouldered our way down Salt House Dock, walking in front of the cart Father had hired to carry our two trunks and two boxes. The sheep and chickens we'd brought to be killed and eaten during the crossing, and those we were taking all the way to the New World, had been earlier given to a husbander to be put on board our ship. Often we had to stop and wait while the carter, a brown-skinned man with a turban on his head, prodded his mule. I was so assaulted with new sights and sounds that I had to concentrate on moving through them, and for a short while the heaviness that had settled in my chest was forgotten.

Boats, large and small, wooden and iron, were moving in the harbour or were tied beside the docks or anchored in the bay. Black smoke rose in puffs and billows from the stacks of tugs and steamers. Ships' whistles sounded and the songs of men rowing dinghies back and forth from the docks blended into the cacophony of commands and pleas being shouted by those who were ordering work done and those who were seeking it.

Above the noise of the people and the ships, there was a mournful sound, like banshees wailing their laments. It was the wind, howling past the bare masts and through the chains and rigging of the ships. It made me shiver while the cold did not.

About two-thirds of the way down the wharf, Father walked to the edge and looked over it at a small boat that was bobbing in the choppy, black, sudsy water ten feet below. The boat already held trunks, boxes, casks and ten men. Father addressed a barrel-chested man dressed in a blue jacket and wide-legged trowsers, who seemed to be in charge of the sailors manning the oars. "Is this the ship's boat for the *Borealis*?"

"It is, isn't it," the man answered.

Closest to the bow there were two gentlemen in stovepipe hats and greatcoats, and behind them sat two more with rounded bowler hats and shorter coats. A remarkably big man with the bushiest red beard I had ever seen was sitting by himself nearer to the stern. He had on a short, thick jacket with ravelled sleeve ends and a tattered hem, trowsers with holes in the knees and other tears, and a filthy hat with a low crown and broad brim. The part of his face that could be seen, and his beard, were streaked with dirt. By his appearance I thought he must be poor.

"I'm Iain Macqueen and this is my daughter, Elizabeth," Father said. "We've passage on the *Borealis* to the Fort Victoria colony."

"I be Dermot, sor. Will ye ever come down then into the boat," the sturdy sailor said.

"We have chests and boxes to be loaded."

"Aye, sor. Send them down, and will you ever be quick about it. Don't meself and the lads 've many more trips to make back and forth."

"Aye," Father nodded.

The driver of the cart produced some rope, which Father had to buy, and Father made a rope harness. He tied it to a chest. Dermot caught hold of the hundred-pound chest while it was still above his head, and with an ease and steadiness I did not appreciate until I had my own feet in the boat and knew how badly it was rocking, he carried it forward and stacked it on top of a box.

"All right, herself, come down," he ordered me.

There was a rope ladder hanging down the side of the dock. I could see no other way down. "On that?" I said.

"Unless herself would prefer to jump for it, which I don't recommend, do I," he said.

I had climbed trees but rope ladders were new. It was a shaky business to get myself down it, and then I could not find the boat with my feet. I had to be convinced to let go of the ladder and drop several feet. I stood, teetering for long moments, and then stumbled toward the stern. The big man held out a hand to steady me and I sat on the bench beside him. Father had no trouble getting himself beside me, even though our boxes and chests left only the narrowest of passages for him.

The ship we were being rowed toward looked much smaller than most of the ships around us. It was squealing on its ropes and chains as it rolled from side to side in the wind-whipped waves that were crashing against it. I couldn't imagine how a boat that looked like it could carry anyone across a vast ocean like the Atlantic. "How big is this *Borealis*?" I asked.

"She's seven hundred thirty-four tons," Dermot called over the noise of the harbour.

I didn't know what that meant. "Is that how much it weighs?" I asked.

"No, colleen, it's the amount she carries in her holds."

"My name is Tess," I said.

"Aye," he said. Then, as if he understood my worry, he added, "You needn't fret, colleen. She's the grandest sailor that ever did cross the seas. Jesus, Mary and Joseph, won't she outsail the *Marco Polo*, which under command of Bully Forbes made a record run from St. John to Liverpool in fifteen days."

There was nothing in his speech to comfort me except the length of time he'd given for the journey. "Fifteen days? Is St. John near Fort Victoria?"

"Nowhere near, lass. Fort Victoria is clear on the far side of the Americas, isn't it, and then farther still because tis on an island, not on the mainland of New Caledonia. St. John is on the near side, in New Ireland."

"How long will it take us to get to Fort Victoria?" I wanted to know.

"Himself and Neptune willin', perhaps four months."

"Four months? Aboard that?"

"Aye."

My heart sank. I couldn't comprehend going that far from home. I looked at the ship again and at all the boats coming and going around us. "Will there be many other people coming with us?" I asked.

"Would ye ever run out of questions, Tess?" Dermot asked.

The way he said it made me laugh, and when I did, Father chuckled, too. It was the first laugh from him I'd heard since Mother and Colin had died. I was lulled into silence, but I still thought about the ship. It could carry more than seven hundred tons. It seemed a lot. Were there great lounging saloons and dining rooms on it such as Uncle Hammond had said were on the *Leviathan*, which he was crossing on when it was finished being built?

Now that we were getting close to it, the *Borealis* did look much bigger. The top railing of its deck was fully thirty feet above us, and the boat was rocking so hard our oarsmen were working up a sweat to keep us from being drawn under the ship's side when it rolled away, and then from being smashed by it when it came back toward us. There were two ropes hanging loosely down either side of what looked like steps that ascended from the water to the railing. Each time the ship rolled toward us, the ropes dipped down into the water. Each time she rolled away, they dangled several feet above our heads. I had not considered we would have to climb up the side of the ship to get aboard. "Is that how we're to get on it?" I demanded of Dermot.

I saw him flash a wink at Father. "Well, me darlin' girl, an angel such as yourself will fairly fly up that." He ignored the sour look I gave him and said, "It is a grand adventure. When I give the word, take hold of the ropes and jump. Don't jump before I say now, or won't you be falling into the sea. Grip the ropes tight and pull yourself up."

The oarsmen worked to get the dinghy close enough for us to be able to reach the ropes. Father volunteered to go first. He landed well enough when he jumped, but as he climbed the small steps I could see the wooden soles of his shoes kept him from getting a good purchase. I decided barefoot would be better and removed my shoes. I said I'd go next. When Dermot yelled, "Now, lass! Jump for it!" I leapt and landed on the third step. When he saw my bare feet, Dermot laughed, "Ah, Tess, is it not a first-class sailor we'll be making of ye?"

I was struggling to hold on and wasn't sure I'd even make it to the top. From watching Father I'd gained no clear idea of how much strength it took to pull oneself upward by the ropes, and by the time I reached the rail I was tired. A seaman's hands took hold of me and pulled me through a gap in the rail onto the gangway. "Just to your right a few steps, Miss, and down the ladder to the main deck," he said. I started to move and was given another surprise. Because of the motion of the ship, a queer sensation of unbalance, such as what a babe might feel in trying to take its first steps, spread through me. I couldn't seem to trust the place I put my feet. I took hold of the low railing and was relieved to make it to the ladder and then down to where Father stood on the main deck.

We waited for the next passenger to come up but there was shouting and confusion, and then a sort of cage I hadn't noticed till then started to unwind from its place up tight against a wooden arm. Below it, sailors pushed against the arms of a turnstile. They chanted while they walked in a circle and the cage was lowered to the water. A few minutes later, the sailors reversed their direction and changed their song and the cage started to come up. When it swung over the upper rail, we saw it had a gentleman in it who had lost his hat and was dripping wet. The cage was set down on the gangway and one sailor unlatched the gate while another helped the man come out. The poor man's face was screwed up in pain and he held one arm tightly to him with the other and was led away on the deck above us.

Later the captain told us the man had dropped into the water twice while he was trying to embark, and that when he fell the second time he was jammed between the dinghy and the ship and his shoulder was dislocated and his arm broken. So he was in sick bay, where the ship's surgeon was attending to him, and in the morning he would be taken back to shore. The captain was sorry to say the man's trip had ended before it had begun.

One by one the other men successfully embarked and joined us on the main deck, where we waited for our boxes and chests to be hauled up the side of the ship, and then for the captain to appear on the quarter deck and tell us we could go below. When he did, a mate appeared and bellowed, "Ere! Look lively, boy!" at a skinny, dark-skinned lad who was a full head shorter than I.

The lad straightened from his job of bending heavy rope into a neat coil. "Aye, sir?"

"Show Mister and Miss Macqueen to the aft cabin, larboard."

"Aye, aye, sir." Turning to us, the boy asked which were our sea chests. Father pointed, and with one continuous movement the boy bent, swung one onto his shoulder and stood. Without a backward glance, he started on a course through a maze of ropes, boxes, chests, spare spars, animals' cages, ship's boats and sailors. He moved so swiftly we could not keep up. Far ahead of where I was, I saw him disappear into a low, closetlike structure in the middle of the deck. When I got there, I looked down a steep set of wooden stairs with rope handrails. I could not see the bottom of the stairs, which were cloaked in darkness.

As I climbed down, the air took on the musty, mouldy odour of decay. The gratings on the deck above me admitted only narrow bars of wet light that were surrounded by shadows and blackness. The creaking and groaning of the ship's timbers as the *Borealis* rolled to and fro made me wonder if she was breaking. I felt as if I was lowering myself into a smelly, wet tomb.

At the bottom of the ladder I saw a narrow passage lit by candles in glass bulbs set at intervals on the walls. "You'll have to bend, sir," our guide said as Father came down. I turned toward his voice, which came from the other side of the ladder, and he stepped forward out of shadows. The lad no longer carried Father's chest.

"How far below the main deck are we?" I asked.

"Six feet," he said, sounding proud.

The exact depth of a grave, I told myself.

He led us aft. When he opened the door to what would be our cabin, I peered through dim light provided by a grate that made up part of the cabin's roof. There was a narrow bed on my right, a hammock on my left, and Father's chest against the wall across the room from the door. The chest took up fully one-third the width of the floor, leaving very little space for us to walk. Neither the bed nor the hammock looked as long as Father was tall.

Father touched the small of my back and we stepped inside. In order to close the door, one of us had to move. I ducked under the hammock. Two iron rings were bolted to the wall behind the door. One ring held a small tin basin, the other a small tin pitcher. On the wall above the rings there was a glass globe with an unlit candle in it. Below the pitcher and basin a small dresser stood bolted to the plank floor. These, plus the hammock and the bed, were all the furnishings.

At Castle Dunharbar there were sixty rooms, the least of which was four times the size of this. Overwhelmed at the prospect of spending even one day in this dank, dark, tiny space, I cried, "Father, the entire cabin is nae bigger than a closet! How ever are we going to live here for months?"

"Tis small," he said. "The ship's main enterprise is cargo, lass, not people. She's scant accommodation for passengers. But we do have a cabin, and one with light and air. Some of the passengers will be much worse off."

There was a knock on the door and Father opened it to the boy, who said, "Yer mess were number one, Sir, in the wardroom on t'upper deck." He touched his cap and vanished.

"Mess?"

Father explained. "Our dining room."

"Oh." By now it didn't much matter to me where we were supposed to take our meals. My stomach was getting queasy and the knot inside me had returned. I couldn't think about food, but I wanted to get out of this gloomy place so I followed Father when he went out of the cabin and headed back the way we'd come.

Like the space between the main and middle decks, where our cabin was, the ceiling of the wardroom brushed Father's hair, even when he stooped. The support beams were even lower and he had to duck when going under them. For light, there was a row of windows on the port side and lamps hanging from the beams. A long couch was built into the wall under the windows, and horsehair chairs and low tables were scattered about the middle of the room. All of these were bolted to the floor. Right now the seats were empty except for one chair that was occupied by our ragged companion from the dinghy.

He'd removed his hat and jacket. A mass of red curls had been hidden by his hat and now fell below his ears. The curls, combined with his beard, gave him an enormous red halo. He wore a faded black wool shirt, open at the neck. The sleeves rolled to just below his elbows revealed forearms that were as big around as my father's calves. He leaned forward with his elbows on his knees as if they were a table, reading a small volume he held. His feet, clothed in a sort of boot I'd never seen before, were the biggest I'd seen. I thought he must be poor indeed and wondered how he'd managed to be a first-class passenger.

Father said, "Good afternoon, Sir."

I looked away.

"Hello," the man answered pleasantly. "You must be Mr. Macqueen."

"Aye, I'm Iain Macqueen. I'm afraid ye have the advantage of me, Mister ..."

"Jock," the man said. "And the young lady is Miss Macqueen."

Manners forced me to answer. "Aye. Elizabeth Macqueen, Sir, but most call me Tess."

He smiled. "Happy to meet you, Mr. Macqueen, Tess." And then he returned his eyes to his book. I was glad that he seemed to want to keep to himself, as I much wished to be invisible right then.

There were three doors on the starboard side of the wardroom and one in the long wall at the back. Father went across the room to a door with #1 marked on it and I followed him. We looked in at a room no bigger than our cabin. Three of the walls were covered with racks, some of which held an assortment of plates, bowls, mugs and cutlery. In the centre of the floor was bolted an oval table with a sort of gutter cut down its middle. When I asked, Father said the trough was for bowls of food and where we would put our mugs to keep them from sliding off the table. I began to fear for the safety of a ship that needed its furniture bolted to the floors and walls, and a trough cut into the table. Father started back to the door we had come in. I went to the couch and sat and he turned back to me. "I'm going for a turn on the decks, lass. Do ye want to come?"

"Nae, Father, I just want to sit."

He looked surprised, but said nothing and went his way, leaving me to mine. When he had gone, I pulled a notebook and pencil from the leather purse that hung suspended from my belt.

At Dunharbar, I'd spent whatever time I wasn't doing lessons or learning needlework or music, out of doors. I had never been the great reader Mother had been, nor had I kept a regular diary, as she had. But when I went through her things I had read her diaries and I had determined I would carry on her tradition. Every day I would write something of the day in a notebook. Since I'd made the promise, I'd been so tired at night I had managed to scribble only a line or two before falling asleep.

Now, I wrote a page and a half describing what I'd seen of the dark, cramped, noisy, smelly ship. I wrote brief descriptions of the men in the dinghy, the captain, and the lad who had shown us to our cabin. The descriptions suited my roiling stomach and my mood — meanspirited, all of them, even about the poor man who had been injured. I saved the ragged man till last, but I couldn't think what to write of him. Perhaps because he was here in the room with me I was afraid my un-Christian thoughts might carry right over to him. I gave up and put my notebook away.

I sat gazing out the window, dreaming about how I could get off the *Borealis* and make my way back to Scotland and Dunharbar. We were to be in port until the following day, when we would leave on the change of tide. Perhaps it was possible for me to escape before then. Perhaps the new owners of the castle would take me in, as an orphan or a servant. Anything, even being an urchin on the streets of Edinburgh, would, I thought, be better than this. At least I'd have the city to wander. I was startled when the giant spoke to me.

"Would you like a bite to eat, Tess?"

I saw that he was unwrapping a cloth that had cream-coloured biscuits and dark crackers inside it, and another that had cheese, and said, "No, thank you."

"Ah." He reached into a pocket of his jacket and brought out another parcel bound in cloth. Inside it were little packets wrapped in brown paper. He selected two, got up and crossed to me. "These are meadowsweet and dill, Miss. If you boil meadowsweet in water and drink the water, the tea will help settle your stomach. If you make a tea from the dill, it will calm your stomach and your nerves." He didn't wait for an answer from me but set the packages beside me on the couch.

While I knew I ought to thank him for his trouble and for generously sharing what looked to be meagre supplies with me, I did not. I got up, leaving the packages where he had put them. "Excuse me," I said. I tried to march out of the room on legs that still had no understanding of the movement of the sea. I lurched rather than marched out to the upper deck.

Outside, I was delighted to hear female voices coming from somewhere. I rushed to the net rail and looked down at the main deck. A group of lasses and women were being marshalled together by a short, round lady whose voice was much taller than her person. I went quickly to the ladder and climbed down it backwards, but before I had reached the bottom and turned around, the group was gone. Still, I was glad to know there were other females aboard.

Father said the captain had invited us to supper, which was served at 6 p.m. At 5:45, we were ushered through the wardroom to the chart room, and through the chart room to the captain's cabin. His quarters occupied the whole of the ship under the poop deck, and were by far the roomi- est and best-furnished I had so far seen. The walls were polished mahogany. Everywhere, around the doors and on the beams and bulkhead, there were elaborate carvings coloured with gold and silver leaf. On one side there were two smaller rooms partitioned off the main with heavy velvet draperies, and on the other a curving stairway led both up and down, promising even more space. A bank of windows along the back wall let in light and air. I wished I were sleeping here.

The table in the centre of the room was covered with a snowy cloth, and set with silver, crystal and china of the finest quality. Like all the furniture on the ship, the table was bolted to the floor. The chairs, though, were movable.

Father and I sat down with the captain and five other men, one of them the ragged man. Except for his size and clothing, which was clean but the same style as that he'd worn before, I would not have recognized him. He'd shaved his beard completely off and his hair had been cut short. His skin was clean and smooth. He looked a great deal younger than he had looked before. *He's not more than twenty,* I thought. Taking each man's hand as they introduced themselves, he shook it and introduced himself to them as he had earlier to us, saying only, "Jock." No surname was given. His hand was warm around mine as he smiled and said, "Miss Macqueen."

I replied only, "Sir," with what I hoped was a smile, as my stomach was now very queasy and my mind largely employed with trying to quiet it.

The food was as sumptuous as our surroundings. Split pea soup, roast pork, ham, pork pies, leg of lamb, roast chicken, cheeses, fresh bread, currant pudding, baked apples, grapes and melons, all being put before us by two stewards. Wine and tea were also served. And after all was eaten, Drambuie was ordered by the captain from his supply. I was able to eat only a little of the feast. The food rolled around inside my stomach much like the ship was rolling in the sea. I unwillingly thought of the packets of calming teas the man named Jock had tried to give me. Would I had taken them!

During the meal the captain told funny stories of his journeys, and several men spoke about frontier politics, and of establishing businesses in the colonies in such a climate. A man named Mr. Rake said he was going to the California gold fields to make his fortune.

Jock, who had been quiet till then, said, "There aren't many fortunes left in California gold. The interior of British Columbia is where the new strike is."

Mr. Rake took exception. His chest puffed up. "I have read the *Emigrant's Guide to the Gold Mines*, Sir. There are riverbeds, and I quote: 'paved with gold to the thickness of a hand' and 'twenty to fifty thousand dollars of gold' can be 'picked out almost instantly.'"

"That book has made a beggar of many a man," Jock said. "Even at the start of the rush it was not that easy, and there's been eight years of thousands of men crawling over every ridge, river, stream, creek, field and forest in an area hundreds of miles wide and long. There isn't a rock that's been left unturned. The area is picked out, and the worn-out claims are being worked by the Chinese because they're willing to break their backs fourteen to eighteen hours a day to get two or three dollars' worth of flakes. The white prospectors have moved on. Gone home, or they're on their way to British Columbia to try again."

"You sound as if ye've been there, Sir," Father said.

"Since '52."

Still bristling, Mr. Rake said, "One can see you've been badly discouraged, but not all have had your kind of luck."

The captain laughed. "His kind of luck. I should say not, Sir. He's the luckiest scoundrel alive. Jock was only a whelp apprentice of thirteen when he arrived at San Francisco aboard the *Argonaut* in '52. The fever was at its height. The *Argonaut*'s captain and crew saw fit to jump ship, and so did Jock. Within a year, Jock had three good claims in Emigrant Gap. That's drained by three forks of the American River and, that, Sir, is where the richest gold find in history occurred.

"But don't be fooled, tis not entirely luck that got Jock his gold. There's danger in prospecting. Besides the brutal work of it, many a man would take a gun and shoot down a lad what's found a good claim. If a man escapes being shot, there are blackguards hired to shanghai any able-bodied men they can lay their hands on to replace crews sorely reduced by the call of the gold. The navy have been so hard hit they yearn to stretch the necks of any that jump from their ships." He turned to Jock, who sat on his right, and said in a somber voice, "Take notice, Jock, they've no pardoned any man who deserted, no matter if twas six years ago. They'll hang ye yet if they get their hands on you."

So now I knew my estimate had been close. He was nineteen.

Mr. Rake glared at Jock. "You, Sir, are a felon."

"Hah!" the captain barked. "A felon? In the early days of the rush, a man could work up at the mines for as little as two months and come down with three thousand dollars in his pocket. A sailor takes all of twenty-one years to earn that kind of money! I've laid me own eyes on a report where one boyo summed it all up when he wrote: 'The struggle between RIGHT and six dollars a month and WRONG and $75 a day is a rather severe one.' By the time Jock's ship got to San Francisco, more than five hundred ships were lying at anchor, rotting where they lay for want of a crew. Would it seem most sailors decided $75 a day was what was right for them? What would yerself have done, Mr. Rake?"

"I, Sir, would have held my post."

"Well," Captain Allan replied, "I dare say ye'd be an outstanding exception, Sir."

"Are ye no worried about your own crew giving in to the temptation in British Columbia, Captain?" Father asked. "We'll be very near that colony at Fort Victoria."

A laugh rolled out of the captain's round belly. "No, Sir, I'm not. Jock's got our lot purchasing shares in everything we make. They've got their gold with no risks, and no price on their heads. They've nowt to gain by jumping our ship."

All at once I saw the resemblance between Captain Allan and Jock. For all their differences in size and shape and dress, they had the same red hair, the same noses with hooks that almost turned them into beaks, and though Jock's way of speaking was vastly different from the captain's, the two had the same inflections in their voices. The captain looked by far the older and I thought Jock must be his son.

My thoughts were interrupted by Mr. Rake, who was looking at Jock with pale, cold eyes. "Perhaps you will not always be so lucky, Mr. Allan," he said to Jock. "However long it takes the navy to catch up with them, deserters are often found, and when they are, they're justly punished."

My father said, "As ye well ken, Mr. Rake, there are navy men with a talent for applying unjust punishment. There's many a sailor with more than enough just cause to desert."

The man bared his yellow teeth and leaned toward my father. "As I well know, Mr. Macqueen, there's more than one deserter in this room."

The man's reply held a bitter rancour I did not understand. It spun my aching head and the spinning whirled downward to my stomach so that I had to excuse myself and hurry from the room.

I raced to the outer railing, where I, and two others who had likewise left the table, vomited the first of many offerings we would make to Neptune. I looked down into rushing, pounding water and listened to the shrieking wind, and vomited some more. I couldn't go back to the table in the captain's room, and I didn't want to go below, so I stayed hanging onto the rail until I was chilled to the bone. When I finally felt my stomach was quite empty, I went to the cabin. Although I thought it was impossible to bring up anything more, the stench, and my despair, caused me to spew up burning bile. I was so dizzy and wretched I could not stand. I had to go to bed. And we were still in port. "Whatever am I going to do when we get out to sea?" I wailed out loud. Thus I gave up plans of my escape.

Father came down at ten o'clock to tell me the captain said the northeast wind was good; if it held it would get us well on our way on the morrow. Father looked not a bit sick — a sin I added to my catalogue of sins he was committing, in spite of the fact he had brought me hot drinks of tea and soup, little of which I wanted.

FOUR

All Bets Are On
Where Tess Meets Gabrielle

THE next morning I woke in answer to the ship's surgeon's knock. At supper the captain had told us we would be knocked up by the surgeon at six o'clock every morning for prayers. In that way, the captain said, the surgeon, and then he, would daily learn the state of health of all aboard. The captain liked to keep himself informed.

Calling a "Thank you," I sat up as best I could. The candle above the dresser was lit. Father was already gone. Unused to moving about inside a hammock, I struggled to turn out. Father had bade me take the hammock, because with the grate above us the bed would soon be wet, he said, and it would not dry as the hammock would. There was cold salt water in the pitcher by the basin. I washed myself in it before I got dressed.

Outside, I could see that everything was changed. As I jerked my way aft toward the ladder to the quarter deck, the wind drove the rain hard into my face. Above my head, huge square sails were billowed out and taut. Ropes creaked and screeched. The bullocks in their pens in the ship's waist were bawling and a cock inside a cage was crowing. Moving hills of angry clouds swept across the still-black sky. We were no longer in the harbour. I wondered how we'd gotten out. The waves were even bigger here than they had been there. I had to hang onto everything I could to get across the main deck.

There was only one other person besides Father in the mess. A man who had a sharp face but a bulbous, red nose, and who had been introduced at the captain's table as Mr. Samuel, smiled as I sat and said, "Ah, Miss Macqueen. You'll want some of this." He passed me a plate of kippered herring. As soon as I looked at it I was forced to run ahead of the man's laughter out to the ship's rail, where I again delivered the little liquid that was in my stomach to Neptune. I went back to our cabin and stayed there for all of that day and part of the next. All I wanted was to be on land. Christmas dinner consisted solely of hot tea.

By suppertime the third night I felt well enough to eat some soup and the next morning I was starving. I couldn't wait for breakfast and hummed "My Bonny" as I washed and dressed.

Even though the day was dark and there were white-caps on the ocean, everyone from our mess who had been sick was up and moving. Six other men, my father and I crowded around the oval table. There was no elbow room and barely enough room for the steward to come and go as he brought the usual porridge, kippered herring, hard biscuits and pots of coffee from the galley and put them on our table.

It seemed I was to be the only female in the mess and my thoughts turned to the group I had seen that first afternoon. "Father," I said, "the day we came on board, I saw some lassies and ladies. Where are they?"

"I dinna ken, Tess."

"Oy, those're on the orlop," Mr. Samuel said.

"What is the orlop?" I asked.

"The deck below the gun deck, Miss."

"You mean two more decks below our cabin?"

"That's right, Miss."

"But where do they eat?" I wanted to know.

"Them eat where they sleep. They're kept to theyselves."

"But there canna be air nor light down there. If they dinna come up, they'll be ill."

"No need to worry yourself about the likes of they, Miss," Mr. Samuel said. "Them're a different sort from us."

How are they different? I wondered. They were passengers, like us. They had to have air and light. Also, they were female. "Then I shall have to go and find them," I said.

Father surprised me. "Nay, lass, you will na."

"But I only want to ..."

"I'll nae hae ye wanderin' about this ship, and that's an end o' it," he said.

I could not fathom why Father would be concerned about me wandering such a small place as the *Borealis*. It was not one one-thousandth of the lands I had roamed at will. But I could not protest against him in front of an audience, so I said nothing more. All the same, his dictum chafed.

⚬

The sixth morning, bright sunshine livened up the ship. After breakfast, people and animals were moving about on all the open decks. Sailors were holy-stoning the fo'c'sle deck, turning the planks white with their sand and salt-water wash. Some were polishing brass fittings while others moved high up in the rigging to tend to this or that. The armourer had his forge set up in a corner of the upper deck. I stopped to watch him for a while, then looked over the net railing and spied the women and lassies from the orlop on the main deck.

They were strolling in twos and threes, chatting among themselves. Most were dressed in torn and filthy clothing and their feet were bare. A few had shawls they draped over their heads to protect their ears, shoulders and arms from the bitter wind. Another few were dressed in decent though worn clothes, and had shoes. The short, round lady who seemed to be in charge of them had on a proper coat, hat and boots. She was walking with Mr. Samuel.

One wee lass was by herself. She had neither shawl nor shoes, and her frock was made of thin material such as what English ladies wear in summer. Her lips looked blue from cold and I saw her shiver, but she was smiling. She was the smallest of the group, and her wee face brought back Colin's happy child's voice and images of Mother. I ached for my family. I ached for more connection, both to past and present. I started for the main deck.

My foot was on the last step of the ladder when a mock battle began between the captain's large, black, shaggy dog and a goat that had been sleeping in the sun. The dog poked its nose into the goat's side and then leapt back, bowing and wagging its entire body so hard it seemed it would shake its lolling tongue right out of its head. The goat did not respond, so the dog moved in and nipped an ear. That got the goat to its feet. It ran first one way, then the other. Seeming to make up its mind, it rose on its hind legs. Its front legs pawed the air. Dropping down, it galloped at the dog, which jumped sideways like a matador to avoid the horns aimed directly at its face. Still running, the goat raced up a large coil of rope, exploded into the air and twisted mid-flight to come down again facing the dog, which was jumping up and down like a child skipping rope. Its bushy tail waved a feathered challenge high above its back. The goat stopped, folded its legs, and dropped to the deck. With a mighty yawn it shut its eyes. The dog jumped forward and back, whining, bowing and wiggling its encouragement, but the goat stayed where it was. Not to be denied its fun, the dog trotted over to a grate, where it sniffed a large pig from its hiding place behind a tarp. The pig squealed and broke, and the dog raced after it. Both were headed straight for the wee lass, who seemed unable to move.

The dog knocked her to the deck; the pig wheeled in a tight circle and ran over her legs. The animals tore aft a short distance, then the pig suddenly turned and charged back. The lass was only starting to sit up. When she saw the pig coming at her again, she began to scream. I was closest and got to her and waved my arms and shouted. The pig veered and raced past, the dog hot on its tail.

Without thinking, I lifted the lass off the deck and held her to me, as I would have done with Colin had he been hurt, and I felt her stiffen. I set her down. "My name's Tess," I said. "What's yours?"

"Gabrielle, mistress," she said so softly I had to strain to hear her.

The animals were coming back. With a cry she grabbed me round my waist. I had only time to grab a ratline and pull us up before pig and dog thundered through the spot we had occupied and raced on, scattering a flock of squawking ducks that had been waddling after them. By now everyone on deck was cheering on the contestants, placing bets and howling with laughter. The captain, too, had come from the poop to join in the fun.

Round and round the pig went, followed by the dog. Then, suddenly, the pig ran up the coil of rope and launched itself over the rail into the blue, white-tipped sea. Abruptly, everyone went silent. Then a great shout went up. "Pig overboard!" and amid a new round of bets, the captain ordered the helm put round. A ship's boat was quickly lowered with two sailors in it, who were soon in pursuit of pig. Gabrielle and I were down on the deck again, joined with the company that was leaning over the rail, laughing and laying bets, this time gambling on how long it would take for the sailors to recover the animal.

Pig was a champion swimmer, able to run through water faster than the men could row. New bets were called and matched on who would give up sooner, pig or man. The pig was rank. Every time one of the sailors got a hand on him, he bit and squealed and fought. It took twenty minutes before the "rescue" was completed. And still pig's stamina was not run down. Back on board the ship he charged the human closest to him and the man barely escaped being tromped. The bets were now on who would cage the pig and how long it would take.

A dozen men were needed before he was surrounded and forced to turn into a large wooden crate. They slammed the front gate closed and pegged it shut before he had a chance to turn around and run back out. The captain said the entire ship would have roast pork for supper. The ship had been turned back on course.

Gabrielle's small hand was clasped in mine. Her earlier reluctance to be touched by me had been abandoned when, giggling at the antics of the animals, she'd pressed her wee body against me as we leaned against the ratline ropes. We had both been thoroughly engaged with the entertainment, cheering and laughing with the rest of the crowd. Once or twice I'd said something to her, but she had not replied. Now I looked at the red and bluish marks forming on her bare shins where the pig had run across them. She stood firmly on her legs and I didn't think there was any worse hurt than bruises. I started to ask her if she was feeling all right when one of the women from her group appeared, and with a brief nod to my "Hello," led the lass away. Before I could say anything they had rejoined the others and the whole group from the orlop rapidly went down the companionway leading to the middle deck. A little shocked at the suddenness of their departure after we all had joined in the fun, it took me a few minutes before I decided to go after them.

When I stepped off the ladder into the gloom, there was no one to be seen in the passageway, and nothing except the usual noises of the ship to be heard. An eerie feeling was beginning to settle in me. I wondered at the elusiveness of the women who were living literally right underneath my feet. I couldn't understand why I was seemingly being isolated, kept apart from them. I thought it all very strange.

FIVE

A Good Ship Sunk
Rendezvous on the Fo'c'sle deck

I WENT to my cabin. At home, Mother had often taken me with her to deliver packages of our things outgrown to the crofters' cottages, or she sent packages with father for the miners. I was mindful of the end of December weather, and of the lass's cold flesh. I thought of my own warm clothing, and knew I had a shawl at least that I could give the lass, if she wanted it. It was a good reason to go in search of her. I knew well enough now where they were housed. I found the shawl I wanted and wrapped it in brown paper.

Filled with frustration at Father's refusal to allow me the freedom of the ship, I'd pestered Mr. Dermot about its layout until he had unwillingly described it all to me. Forward of the ladder on this deck that went up to the main deck, there was a hatchway and ladder going down. But Dermot, too, had warned me away from exploring. "The hatches to the lower levels is sometimes closed up tight without notice," he said. "Ye wouldna like to be down there when that happens, Miss, in a black and nasty hole with no hope of anyone hearing yer screams for help, yer carcass chewed on by the hungry rats until there's nought left of ye but your puny white bones." I said I was sure the rats would prefer oatmeal, cheese, biscuits and the like to me, but I knew rat bites were not to be taken lightly.

If I went to the orlop on an errand, it could not be thought wandering, I told myself. And with the clement weather, the hatches were not likely to be closed unexpectedly. I would go straight down, find Gabrielle and give her the package, and come straight back up.

Without any trouble at all I found the ladder and went down it as far as the gun deck, where I stopped. Here, the globes were far apart and the light dim, but I could see the large piles of canvas Dermot said were in the sail room. The crew's quarters were on this level, aft of the sail room, and aft of their quarters was another bulkhead that led through to the purser's room and storerooms. I waited for a moment to see if any sailors were about, but heard only the usual ship's noises. Below me, the steps continued down into what looked like total blackness. That was where I had to go, to the fo'c'sle platform, which was the forward part of the orlop deck. I needed a candle. As quickly as I could, I stepped off the ladder and retrieved one from a globe. Then I descended to what Dermot had told me was the bottom of the ship except for the deep holds.

The fo'c'sle platform was not completely black. There were lighted candles along the walls, though they were so few and so far apart I could barely make out shapes. Huge piles of ship's cables lay along the side. I could smell the wetness, mildew and mould. I could also smell the bilge water that slapped against the hull under the planking of the deep holds. Dermot said a great deal of the ship's slops went into the bilge. The smell of that, at this level, was a cloying, choking stench. I struggled to get air. I would never get used to trying to breathe in this, I thought. I could only imagine what it must be like in the holds themselves.

The ship's noises were far louder here than they were where I lived on the middle deck. Beams creaked and groaned, barrels shifted and strained against their ropes, and when the ship rolled to starboard, a stampede of noise thundered across the decks somewhere above, behind and in front of me. When we rolled to port, the thundering noise was followed by the clang of metal bashing metal like a clashing thunderbolt. The second day I'd lain seasick in my hammock, I'd heard a muted version of the thundering and the clashing. Father said it was the ship's guns rolling backward across the gun deck until the ropes that held them were as taut as they could go; then the guns rolled forward until they smashed their barrels into the metal rings of their ports. I'd asked father why the ship had guns and he'd said that though merchant ships didn't carry as many as man-of-war ships, there were pirates on the open seas, and a trader never knew at which port he might need to protect his ship. I wished I hadn't asked. Down here the noise was deafening and I knew it was a sound those living on the gun deck and the orlop had to endure every time the sea was not as smooth as glass.

I stepped off the ladder, took two steps, and caught sight of a rat scurrying between some barrels. For a few minutes I was afraid to move. For the first time I blessed the stiff, bootlike English shoes that had replaced my Hieland slippers. Thinking of Gabrielle's bare feet made me shudder. Slowly, I started toward the canvas bulkhead that separated the fo'c'sle platform from the orlop deck. Random barrels jutted into the passage. Being mindful of rats that might be living in the cracks between them, I carefully worked my way around them.

The thundering of the rolling guns hid the sound of footsteps. When someone grasped my arm from behind and spun me round, I jumped. "Ere, my girl," he said, though not roughly. He was not holding me hard, so I raised the candle to see him. His curving, drooping black moustache, his sunken, oily, pockmarked cheeks, a huge, beaky nose and eyes that popped so far out of their sockets they seemed as if they'd soon fall right out of his head, made me gasp involuntarily. "Where does you think you're goin'?" he asked. I was frozen, lips and tongue included.

"This here's no place fer you," he said.

That was all it took for me to answer back. "I'm looking

for a wee lass that's down here," I said. "If it's a fit place for her, surely it's fit for me as well."

"Aint. What's your business with her?"

"I want to give her this," I said, holding up the package I'd brought.

"Give it me," he said. "I'll see she gets it."

He wasn't going to move. There was nothing I could do but hand it to him. "Her name is Gabrielle," I said.

He took the package and stepped around me so the only way I could go was back toward the ladder. "You aint allowed down here. Keep to the upper decks, my girl," the man ordered. He watched while I walked back to the ladder, and waited until I'd started up it.

By the time I reached the middle deck, my anger at being continually stopped from meeting the only other female passengers aboard the ship was a fury. Determined to make Father give me a satisfactory explanation at last, I sought him out.

He was on the quarter deck, at the ship's wheel, in conversation with the captain and Jock. Jock was at the helm. Impatiently, I stood to one side waiting for a chance to speak to Father. Though Jock was not straining to make his voice heard, his words carried easily above the wind. "It's the worst hurricane and the biggest story of the decade, John. For weeks after, there were reports from broken ships that limped into harbours all up and down the coast. And countless accounts given by the survivors were written in all the newspapers. You must have read some of them in the *Times*."

"Newspapers've no interest in giving accurate accounts, laddie. I've no the time for them. How many from the *Central America* survived?"

"The women and children and forty-four men were taken off her by the *Marine*. The *Ellen* spent half a day tracking back and forth through the wreckage and a large area around it, but she only found forty-nine more. More than five hundred passengers and crew went down."

"What about the gold?"

"All sunk with the ship."

The captain looked stricken. "A king's treasure — lost," he said.

"A treasure, Sir?" Father asked.

Jock said, "Most of the *Central America*'s passengers were fresh from the gold fields, or Californians rich from the gold business. Many of them had their entire wealth with them in bars, coin, gold dust and raw nuggets. Plus she was carrying a large consignment of gold bars bound for the government of the United States. Over a million dollars just in gold was registered on her cargo manifest, and not half the wealth that was aboard her was registered. We had a considerable sum in bullion in her hold."

Five hundred people drowned! "I beg your pardon, Mr. Allan," I said. "Was this terrible storm very recent?"

"It were September 12th the night the ship sank, three

and a half months ago, weren't it, Jock?" the captain said.

"Would there be a storm like that this time of year?" I wanted to know. "Would this ship sink in it if there was?"

The captain looked at me. "Och, lass, dinna worry your fine head about any storms. The *Borealis* has weathered many worse as that were, and this ship's as strong as the day she were set afloat. Stronger than the sorry excuses for boats they're building now. I'd bet my life on her agin any sea or blow."

"I think we're all betting our lives on that, Sir," I said, and the men laughed.

After a long moment my father said, "Will you recover your gold, Jock?"

"She went down two hundred miles off the Carolina coast. We were insured, but with so many really big losses the insurance companies will fight, and we'll only get a small portion of the worth. No one will recover what they lost."

"'Tis a tragedy," my father said.

The captain sighed. "Aye, Sir, tis a great tragedy indeed."

I could almost see and hear the people drowning. It was devastating. Feeling my eyes beginning to water and my lip to quiver, I turned away and went to the wardroom where I sat on the couch and took out my notebook. I wasn't able to write. I held it only, closed my eyes, and tried not to think. But neither the *Central America* nor my deeper grief could be blocked. Five hundred people lost. *Oh Mother!* The afternoon and night were long and cold.

❧

Well before it was time, I woke. My breath was turned to steam. No light was coming through the roof vent, only blackness. I needed to get up. The floor was frigid. I hopped from foot to foot while I searched for my slippers, and with a sigh jammed my feet into their sheepskin warmth. I felt my way along to the dresser, reaching for the cloak that hung on a hook Father had put up on the wall.

The tween deck lights were extinguished every night at 10:30 for safety from fire. The passage was inky but by now the creaking, groaning and muttering of the ship had an almost comfortable feel, and I could walk the pitching decks as easily as I could cross a Hieland meadow. The privy for officers and passengers was on the starboard side of the fo'c'sle deck. The portside privy was for patients from sick bay. The crew hung onto the bow chains on whichever side of the ship was most protected from the wind and leaned their bottoms out. In a rough sea this could be dangerous, but the method was clean and had been used for centuries, Father said. Contrary to their name, the tiny huts provided for our convenience had walls on only three sides, which gave little privacy, so I had decided early morning, when few were about, was the time I preferred to use ours. I went quickly to the stairs and up them to the main deck.

Though fresh snow covered the decks, the clouds had disappeared. Overhead, the stars shone. A fat white moon sat on the horizon, marking the edge of the world. The moon was melting, flooding a silvery path of mercury that attached itself to us, and drew us by degrees toward it. As the ship rose and plunged in the rolling sea, phosphorescent spray laced the dark with diamonds. The night was full of light. The clear beauty of it gave me such a perverse longing for the winter mists of home that I would have turned back to the hatchway and the darkness below decks if I'd not heard female voices on the fo'c'sle deck. I had not previously met anyone on the fo'c'sle at this hour, and a growing excitement gripped me. Perhaps, at last, I would meet the women from the orlop in circumstances that would allow some time for talk.

They were standing in a line on the starboard side. They spoke in low tones and I could not make out their words, but I saw some of them take notice of me as I stepped from ladder to deck. I couldn't see Gabrielle. I took my place at the end of the line and said "Good morning" to the smallish woman in front of me. She acknowledged me with a turn and dip of her head, but kept her back to me. I thought perhaps our business gave her some reserve. I was wondering how to overcome her reluctance without being rude when I saw a lass who looked about my age come out of the line ahead, and was surprised when she walked back to me. She stopped a few feet away and, facing me, said in a breathless, halting voice, "Please to excuse. Thank you much for Gabrielle." She made a lifting motion with her hands, "You save from boar," then pointed to her shawl, "give her cloths. Thank you." When it was out, she breathed as if she'd gotten a great weight off her shoulders.

I smiled and said, "She's a bonny wee lass. She's all right, then?"

The girl smiled back, showing beautiful white teeth, and cocked her head in a way that said she didn't understand. The line moved several paces and she went back to her place.

Warmth crept through me as I thought, *They weren't ignoring me! They don't know my language!* Where were these women from? Where were they going? How came they to be on this ship? They looked so very poor.

The line was moving quickly and I realized the women were disappearing one by one down the forward hatch, which descended to the galley on the gun deck and then down to the forepart of the orlop. With their leaving, my chance for any conversation was going, too. I tried to think. *What was the accent of the lass who spoke to me?* "Pardon, Miss," I said to the woman in front of me. Again the slight turn. "Do you speak English?" I asked. She shook her head, but this time she didn't turn away. She continued to stare sideways at me. I touched my chest. "I'm Tess," I said.

She turned her head when someone called to her and I saw we had advanced to be the only two remaining in line. She nodded curtly one last time and walked away. To give her some privacy, I walked to the rail and searched the sky in four directions. There was no hint in any quarter of the grey line hovering over the water that signalled the beginning of sunrise.

I listened to the wind whistle in the rigging. I heard the water slap against the hull and felt the motion of the ship. The rise and fall of the bow as she cut swiftly through the waves was now no more disturbing than a rocking chair. It reminded me of riding my favourite horse, Sampson. I smiled at the thought and turned back to face the privy. It was empty. Here and there sailors could be seen: dark, shadowy forms clinging to the rigging or scuttling over the decks as they went about their work. I sighed. It seemed I was surrounded by shadows.

But at least I had a hint. The lass who'd come to me must be someone who was close to Gabrielle. She seemed to care for the lass. And she knew some English. Perhaps she'd learned it from Gabrielle, who, now that I thought about it, also had an accent I couldn't place. Or perhaps Gabrielle had learned from her? I realized the wee lass had only said the one thing to me, her name. But she had seemed to understand me. Well, at least one of them knew some English. Perhaps the women would be here again the same time tomorrow morning. I would come earlier. But what if they weren't? What could I do?

❧ SIX ❧
The Plan

I T had been two days since I'd seen the lasses last, and the whole of my energy since then had been spent thinking about how to meet with them again. The halting English of the one lass and the others' inability to understand me had hinted at a plan. Now, as I came wide awake in the dark, the plan took shape. How often when I'd complained of being kept indoors for lessons when I wanted to be out had my mother told me how important it was to be educated as well as one could be. How often had I and my brothers been told by Father that we would each spend time on the continent, being educated in things we would not learn at home. There were few things my parents held in greater esteem than education. We were going to a country where English would be spoken, and the lasses did not speak it well. What if I offered to teach them? Surely Father could not object to that. I could arrange to meet with them in, perhaps ... the wardroom, or the mess when it wasn't being used.

Father was up and gone. Almost as I thought the question, *What time is it?* salt water poured through the vent in the cabin roof and soaked the bottom of the bedding in my hammock. The crew had begun their daily washing of the decks. It was 5:00 a.m. I rolled out of bed and yanked Father's coverings from his bed just before the stream rained down on them. I stowed them in his chest. No use to remove my bedding now. It would be wet until there was a day fair enough to tie it in the rigging and blow it dry.

It was another hour to the captain's morning prayers, and an hour after that till breakfast, when I could ask Father about my plan. I could go back to bed. Ugh. Wet bedding or a thin wool plaid? Which would keep me warmer? I decided on the quilt and blankets. The crew had moved past our cabin roof; the worst of the wetting was over. I climbed back into my hammock, pulled my feet toward my chest to a somewhat drier spot, covered my head against the lesser drips, and was soon asleep.

There was no opportunity for me to talk to Father at breakfast. Afterward I asked him to walk on deck awhile with me. Although it was a blustery morning, the fresh sea air was far more welcome than the confined spaces of the ship. My head was crawling with the vermin I had learned inhabited all such vessels as this, and there were large red welts on my stomach, chest and arms where some of them had found parts of me to test. I wanted to take off all my clothing and stand naked in the salt spray flying over the railing of the fo'c'sl deck. The hard rain would provide a rinse. But of course it couldn't be done. I scratched at my itchy scalp and complained, "I want a tub full of steaming water to bathe in."

"Aye," Father agreed, "but there are nowt but wee buckets on the *Borealis*."

"Well, sometime this morning I'm going to ask Cook to heat a bucketful for me and use it to at least soak my head."

"Aye. Dinna throw it out. I'll use it after ye."

I loved water and often dreamed of the lochs and burns of home. When I was five, I'd ridden my pony into a loch and learned to swim by holding to his mane and floating with him as he swam. Every summer since then I'd spent part of every day in water. In winter, in spite of Nanny's dire warnings that we'd catch our death, Mother had insisted on us being bathed every other night. She said when she'd lived in China as a little girl the Chinese upper classes regularly bathed, and no one died from it. It was human filth and vermin that brought illnesses, she said. Cook grumbled about pneumonia while she heated the water, and when I was little, Nanny whisked me into the tub, soaped and scrubbed me, and had me out again in less than a minute flat. When I got older and started pushing myself underwater and holding my breath, she threw up her hands, told my mother it'd be the death of me sure, and she wanted nothing to do with it. Henceforth she would not be responsible. I'd been delighted to be left alone in the bath. Now, the thought of plunging my head into a bucket of hot water and holding it there was so delicious that only my thoughts about my plan kept me from going right to Cook to see about getting it. We climbed the ladder to the fo'c'sle deck.

"Father, I want to ask you about Gabrielle and the other lasses. Dae ye ken if they'll be on the *Borealis* with us all the way to the colony?"

"Aye, lass. They will."

"Dae ye ken anything about them?"

"Mr. Samuel has said they are from Russia and they're in his care until they reach the colonies. Ye must not concern yourself with them, lassie. They're being looked after."

"But I have an idea about them. A few days ago some of them were on this deck when I was here, and one lass came and talked to me a little. I knew her accent was foreign and she didna ken much English, but she knew some, Father, and she was very gracious and seemed to want to be friendly to me."

"Did she?"

"Aye. She thanked me for looking out for Gabrielle that morning the pig knocked her down."

"Ah, that were a gallant act, lass," said Captain Allan, who had come up to us unnoticed. "Fancy a lassie hauling up the rigging with a wean clutching at her skirts. Would that half the sailors I've commanded were as active as yourself. It must be in the blood, that, eh Iain?"

Notwithstanding the flattery, and the heat that rushed up my neck and cheeks, I sighed. This ship was so small one simply could not walk about it, or talk to anyone on it, without being interrupted. "Good morning again, Captain. It's kind of you to say it about my helping Gabrielle, but the truth is there's almost no weight at all to the wee thing. It didn't require a sailor's strength to carry her." Since I had his attention and he showed no sign of departing so I could continue my conversation with Father, I decided to enlist him. "I've been thinking about Gabrielle and her companions, Captain, and I've a plan about them. I'd be grateful for your help with it."

"Have ye noo?" he laughed.

"Aye. Father says they're going all the way to Fort Victoria with us, but they're Russian and don't speak very much English. So I thought I might meet with them two or three times a week, if they've a mind to meet with me, and I could teach them more English. Would ye ask them if they would like it? And would we have permission to meet in the wardroom or in our mess when it's not being used?"

The captain shook his head. "Nay, lass. Passengers from the orlop deck are not allowed above the main deck."

"Oh. Well, we could meet on the main deck when the weather's fair, and in our cabin when tis foul." I saw him throw a guarded look to my father. "Tis a long voyage, Captain, and it would mean a great deal to me to have the company of some of my own sex through it," I explained.

"I canna gie my permission," Father said.

"Why not?"

"They're nae the sort of lasses for ye to mix with."

I was shocked, and I blurted, "Why ever would ye say that? Gabrielle's a dear wee bairn. And the lassie that spoke to me is the gentlest of girls. They are only poor."

"Ye ken nowt aboot their circumstances, lass."

"What aboot them? We are all on the same ship going to the same place."

"There is nowt to argue about. Ye'll nae meet with them."

I was incredulous and unwilling to let it go. "Mother would never forbid me it," I said. "And were ye nae my father, she would counsel me against forming an opinion of the lassies, having no direct experience of them myself. 'Never judge another by another's words,' that's what she said whenever she heard gossip. 'Ye must decide yourselves whom ye'll have in yer life and whom ye will na.' Ye ken it was her way and ye never disagreed with her."

"'Tis another time and another matter, daughter, and tis long past time ye faced the fact your mother's no here."

I caught my breath and stared at him. The aching blackness of my mother's absence scorched my throat and burnt my eyes so that I didn't see his pale white pain. In that moment, Captain Allan, too, disappeared in a haze of hate and disappointment. "My mother is more here than you are, Sir! What about missionaries!" I shouted. "Do men of God shun people because they are of a different class?"

"You've sorely overstepped your boundaries, Elizabeth. Go below and stay there until ye have come to your senses."

"*My* senses! All right, I'll take my leave, but I'm hard in this, Father, and I tell it fair. The lassies and I canna avoid each other all the time we'll be aboard this ship." Without waiting for a reply, I turned on my heel and went.

I started down the ladder without looking first to see Mr. Rake was coming up. He backed down, and when I stepped off the bottom rung I saw that Mr. Samuel was there as well. I made a decision on the spot. "Excuse me, Mr. Samuel, might I have a word with ye?"

Mr. Rake frowned while Mr. Samuel's tongue made a little clicking sound.

"T'will take only a moment, Sir."

Mr. Rake said, "Miss Macqueen, if children must be seen at all, they are certainly not to be heard."

"Aye, Sir. My mother often said how terribly it was to be regretted her bairns were such a noisy brood. But tis about wee Gabrielle and her companions, Mr. Samuel, and tis you I must speak with because Father says you're in charge of them until they reach the colony."

"Your father's right enough. I am."

"I spoke briefly with some of them this morning. They dinna ken much English, do they?"

"They're Rooskies after all, Miss," Mr. Samuel said.

"Aye. So I thought I might meet with them, if they wish it, and teach them. Captain Allan says they must not come above the main deck but we could meet there for the lessons, or in their quarters, or in my own cabin."

He jutted his pointed chin. "Those'll be learned all the English they needs to know when they needs to know it, Miss Macqueen."

"Excuse me, Sir, but how will they learn it?"

"From them that has use for them. Good morning to you." With curt nods, the two men began to climb, Mr. Rake following Mr. Samuel.

Before they reached the top rung Mr. Rake brayed a nasty laugh and said, "I'll wager ten pounds, Mr. Samuel, you'll not find any that have use for that lot. They are so rude in both appearance and manners I doubt even a bordello will take them in."

"It's been a time since you was in the colonies, Mr. Rake. There's hundreds of men what have not seen home nor family for years. What are starving for the comforts, so to speak, offered by the weaker sex. It'll be no different on Vancouver's Island than it were in Australia. No, Sir. Hammond Macqueen knows what he's about. All these'll be snapped up, and we'll be begged for more."

The last of that was lost to me. I supposed Mr. Samuel had meant the women would be taught, when they went into service, by their employers, which brought another idea into my head. I ran up the ladder after the men. When I cleared my throat they looked round, startled to see me close. "Excuse my interrupting ye again, gentlemen, but I couldna help but overhear Mr. Rake's observation. Would Gabrielle and the others not be better able to find good employ if they know English when they arrive in the colony, Mr. Samuel? If I instructed only one of them in English, couldna she in turn teach all?"

A hard light oozed into his small eyes. His thin lips stretched into the misshapen grimace that was his smile. "Mmmm. There's something in that, Mr. Rake. Better quality goods, higher paying *employers*. Higher paying employers, more profit for the man what supplies the goods, eh, Mr. Rake? What do you say to that?"

"Indeed, Mr. Samuel," Mr. Rake said.

"All right, Miss Macqueen. You can 'ave one for one half-hour a week. That one what you snatched from the pig. She's the youngest of the lot. Won't give me no trouble."

"Thank ye, Mr. Samuel. She and I could begin this afternoon ... uh ... that is, if Father agrees to it as well as Gabrielle. I confess Father is not in favour of my meeting with the lasses. But I'm sure that when I tell him ye agree my teaching the lasses English will be helpful to them, and to you, he canna continue to refuse it."

I'd never heard a sound as awful as Mr. Rake's chuckle nor seen eyes glint as Mr. Samuel's did. I was suddenly extremely uncomfortable in the two men's presence. But it was too late. I could not withdraw the offer and I very much wanted to have contact with the lasses.

"I'm sure as I'll be happy to explain to your father that it will be most helpful, Miss Macqueen," Mr. Samuel said. "I'll fetch the girl to and from her lessons myself."

I was taken aback. "Would ye be present during them?" I asked.

He didn't answer for some seconds and I was afraid he was considering it. "No. I'll 'ave her repeat to me all what's said. All, Miss Macqueen. I'll be checking up."

I had no doubts about Gabrielle's abilities and told him so. "She's a lively wee lass, Mr. Samuel. I'm certain she'll learn her lessons very well. Ye'll have no cause to regret your decision, Sir."

"It's both her and *you* what I'll be checking on. There's to be no talk except what's needed to learn her useful English. I'll have no uppity ideas put into her head. Is that clear?"

Mystified about what he would consider "uppity" and not useful, but feeling like I should hold tight to what I'd gained, I said it was.

"Good."

"Shall you speak with Father this morning?"

"As soon as I lay eyes on him, Miss Macqueen."

"Thank ye, Sir. Good morning, Mr. Samuel, Mr. Rake." In spite of a nagging reservation about exactly what it was I had just done, inside myself I skipped. Surely my father could not hold onto his objections when the lass's guardian himself was so in favour of my proposal.

SEVEN
Matters of Race and Station

I WENT down to the main galley to see about some hot water for my hair. The cook's assistant said he would put some on the fire after the huge pot that held the pea soup he was making for dinner had been taken off. When the water was ready, a boy would bring it to my cabin. I thanked him and went to my cabin, where I busied myself remaking Father's bed and pulling things from our trunks to check them against the constant damp. Doing that reminded me this was the day our boxes would be brought up from the hold, too, as they were once a week, for us to get things we wanted from them, or to air the contents if the weather was fair. So far I hadn't detected any signs of mildew in the trunks and I was thankful for it.

When the boy had brought the water, I kept my head in the pail until I was quite dizzy from hanging upside down, then wrung my hair and wrapped it with towelling. For a few minutes I pranced in front of the looking glass I'd hung up on the wall, fancying myself. I moved the towel to my shoulders to keep my back from getting wet and fixed my hair in different styles.

What would the Indians on Vancouver's Island look like, I wondered. I had seen pictures in books. Would they look the same as that? In Britain, Hielanders were different from Lowlanders and Lowlanders were different from the English. And within those divisions there were dozens of dialects spoken throughout the country. Everyone was different from the Welsh, who spoke another language altogether, and Father said they prided themselves in not being understood. Would there be various Indians? I decided there would. Would they speak different languages? If the Indians had only different dialects such as existed at home, I thought I might learn to understand most of them all right. Everyone going to this new country would have to learn new languages, I thought, but especially the emigrants who did not ken any kind of English at all. In that, I supposed Gabby and I would have an advantage, because Mother had said often how easily the young learn languages. She regretted, she said, that adults had not the same facility. Occupied as I was with my thoughts about language, and about how I would approach teaching Gabrielle, the forenoon slipped away.

I went up for dinner in anticipation that Mr. Samuel would have talked with Father by now and arrangements would be complete. Thinking this gave me a terrible feeling of apprehension, though I couldn't say why it should. I was actually relieved to find neither Father nor Mr. Samuel was at the table, and after cordial greetings to and from those who were seated, I kept to myself throughout the meal. After declining to have our boxes brought up on the main deck in the rain as there was nowt I wanted from them, I spent most of the afternoon in the wardroom. I tried to occupy myself with writing notes in my diary while keeping an eye on the door to the chartroom, lest Father came through it, but I did not see him until supper.

His absence caused me to think that, small as the *Borealis* was, it seemed easy enough for one person to keep out of the sight of another. I wondered if that would be true if a thorough search was conducted.

At supper one of the gentlemen began a conversation about English politics, bringing up the subjects of trade and war. The latest war for the English had been the English-China war, which had ended but a few months earlier with the English capturing Canton.

"The Chinks in Canton is now marching to proper English order," Mr. Samuel said. He went on to espouse many noncomplimentary opinions about the Chinese, and said he had been there to see them throw up a flag of truce. "English might will win out wherever we finds opposition from inferior races," he said.

"Sir," Father said, "one race is not superior to another because it has the might to force its will upon the other. Many great races have been extinguished by peoples whose greatest accomplishment is the blood and death of war."

Another man said, "Mr. Macqueen, are you not going to an English colony to conquer the savages living there and turn them into God-fearing Christians to save their heathen souls?"

"Nay, Sir, I'm not. I'm going to the colony to earn a living I no longer have in Scotland. If I can do that best by offering a Christian view to the Indians, that is what I shall do, Sir. If they give up their heathen practices in favour of Christianity, they'll have a better life no doubt, but tis they who'll decide what beliefs they'll follow. They'll no be conquered by the likes of me."

"Pah. It's long proved the coloured races is inferior to the European and have to be told what to do," Mr. Samuel said. "What are Niggers and Chinks when they's put next to the English? Nothing, that's what." This was said as the Chinese steward who served our mess came in to bring us a pudding made by the Chinese cook. "Tis the same with Indians. At Fort Victoria they relies on the English someat as dogs relies on their masters. A coloured brain, sirs, is as small and feeble as a woman's."

Several men, in obvious agreement, leapt into the talk, giving me no opportunity to voice my outrage. Disgusted, I excused myself with little notice.

It was after 11:00 when Father came down to the cabin. He moved quietly, perhaps thinking me asleep. "There's no need to be careful, Father," I told him. "I've been lying awake waiting for ye."

He was surprised. "Have ye? I've spent the evening in Captain Allan's quarters. He and Jock asked after ye, lass, but I told them ye maun be tired as ye'd retired early. They were sorry not to have your company."

"I should have liked to enjoy their company, too, Father, but I was vexed hearing Mr. Samuel's views and I couldna bring myself to stay one more minute among the men. It has given me reason to regret something I've done, and I've lain awake waiting for ye to confess it."

"Och, a confession. Is it a murder you've committed?"

"Father!"

"Well, short of murder, lass, let it wait till the morning. I'm very tired and I've a mind for sleep." He blew out the candle and I heard him getting into bed.

"Please, Father. I'll not sleep if ye won't hear me."

He sighed. "What is it?"

"Did Mr. Samuel nae speak with ye this morning?"

"I've not seen the man today until supper, and after supper I was happy to be invited out of his company."

"Aye."

"I've no the patience for a game of guessing, Tess. Go to sleep now."

"I'm sorry. Tis no guessing game I want. If ye'll hear me oot, Father, I'll abide by what ye say at end. Tis a promise."

He sighed and remained quiet and so I went on. "After you and I parted this morning, I met Mr. Samuel on the ladder and I ... I told him of my desire to teach the lasses.

He was not in favour at first, but then he reversed and said it would be a service to him were I to do it. Please Father ... there's but little more. I've been thinking on't all the evening and I've asked meself would I undo the request if I could. I widna. Since I was a wee bairn I have heard you and Mother say education is a blessing that should be had by all. If that be true, can helping Gabby and the other lasses to learn English do other than good?"

"Tess, ye are no worldly. There are things ..."

"Ye've said it yourself, Father, I'm grown. Mr. Samuel says I may have one half-hour a week with Gabby. She's a winning lass and I know if I teach her she can pass it on to the others. Please Father, will ye give your permission for it?"

"I'll say this, ye've learned to argue like your mother."

At this I began a quiet crying. "Mother used to say I was as stubborn as you. I miss her so much."

"Aye, lass. So do I." He was silent a while before he said, "All right, I'll advise Mr. Samuel I'm in favour of it. One half-hour a week. Quiet you now."

I was quiet, but I slept very little.

❦ EIGHT ❧
Gabby's Secret

I T was our third lesson together. Gabby came into the cabin and settled herself on Father's chest, which was her usual chair. I sat across from her on mine. She moved stiffly, as if her legs or feet were paining her. Her body, always thin, looked even thinner, yet her exposed joints looked swollen. Dark shadows made her blue eyes recede deep into her thin face and her cheekbones stood out sharply. Her appearance had been altering weekly and I could not keep quiet about it. "Gabby, ye are so thin. Are ye ill?"

She made a rolling motion with her hands and said, "Sick of sea."

"Oh dear. Seasickness is frightful. Mr. Allan has some teas that are helpful for the stomach. He offered them to me but I didna use them. I'll ask him for them and pass them on to ye."

She looked at me, her eyebrows up. It was a habit of hers, and I guessed it meant I had babbled far too much and too quickly for her to get any of my meaning. Which was a habit of mine. During our first lesson she had demonstrated no knowledge of English, save answering her name. The words of that particular question, I thought, would be very familiar to her because she would have been asked it many times during her journey. So I had proceeded to teach her English in much the same way as it would be learned by an infant in my own country. Her present confusion was a reminder I must go slowly.

"Tea," I said again, and touched the pot of tea that sat on a tray on the floor between us. I rubbed and smoothed my stomach. "Good for your stomach." Then I picked up a tin of ordinary tea, opened it and had her look, saying the word again. I handed it to her and she quickly replaced the lid and tucked the tin into her plaid. I'd had Cook bake a cake for me that morning and I passed her the plate, saying, "Cake." She took several slices and tucked these also into her plaid, not keeping any out to eat at the moment. It was her usual way. I'd learned to offer her only what I was happy to have her take away with her.

"You maun eat something, Gabby," I said now. "Ask Mrs. Motherwell to get you lots of soup and bread from Cook. Bread is very good for your stomach." Her usually quick eyes looked dull and almost veiled when I said this, and so I took up my notebook and on a blank page drew pictures of a teapot, a cup filled with liquid, and a loaf of bread. Then I labelled them. "Teapot. Cup of tea. Bread," I said, pointing to the pictures.

She repeated what I said, adding, "Good for stomach."

She had made the association. I smiled and handed her the book and my writing lead. She traced the letters, repeated the words, turned the page over and did the words and pictures from memory. She missed some of the letters but knew it immediately and tried again, getting it right the second time. I was delighted. "Good!" I said. I drew a star beside her efforts, then tore the page from the book and gave it to her.

The lesson I had planned for that day fitted in with the *t* for tea. Turning to the page of the notebook where I'd written the alphabet at the top, I circled the *a* and *c*, which we'd done before, and the *t*. Then I wrote "cat" and drew a picture of one crouched down on its haunches, its tail low above the floor. Next I wrote "rat" and drew a picture of that some distance in front of the cat. The next picture was the cat again. Now he had a very round belly (which I labeled "fat"), and was licking his chops. Underneath all this I wrote, "The fat cat et the rat." Gabby laughed her little squeal. She took the book and repeated what I'd done and we tore out that page, too.

As if they'd been a nestling bird instead of paper, she brought the pages from the first two lessons from a fold in her plaid and added the new pages to the others. I had given her a lead of her own to take away the first day, and now I saw she'd covered every inch of white space on the old pages with letters, and that they were very dark and thick, as if they'd been traced over and over again. Just as carefully as she had brought out the pages, she refolded them and returned the bundle to her pocket pouch.

By then I knew it was time for what had become our usual ending. I poured two cups of tea, handed her one and again passed the plate of cake. "Tea and cake," I said.

Smiling her shy smile, Gabby took one piece and put it on her saucer. "Thank you, Mistress," she said. She sat holding her cup and saucer, letting her eyes travel the room.

"I like Nadia come here," she said. "Nadia together with me since Russia, when I sold for rubles. Man say he take us to Vladivostok, get more womens, go to Sitka, in New World. We don't go there. We go in boat to place he call Rangoon. In Rangoon he die. Chinaman take us in junk to Canton. Many ships; many flags. Nadia say flags from many countries, maybe we go to see whole world. Mr. Samuel come, take us from junk to other boat. We go to Liverpool. We don't see whole world, only boat and water. In Liverpool we stay in house, all womens there. I work in kitchen, scrubbing, scrubbing. Nadia not work kitchen but she come and look at me each day. We are friends."

I was breathless and for some length of time all I did was look at her. Finding my voice at last, I started, "Gabby ... what ... how did you —"?

A hard, staccato knock on the cabin door made her jump. I sat still, almost too dumbfounded to move. The knock came again. Our time was up. "One moment, please,"

I called while Gabby set her cup and saucer down, put the remainder of the cake into the pouch in her plaid, and arranged the folds so no outline of any of the hidden things showed. A third knock and Mr. Samuel's "Open up in there!" made us both move toward the door.

As she lowered her finger from her lips, I opened the door. "Oh, Mr. Samuel. We were just having a wee drink of tea. Here she is," I said as Gabby darted past him and started down the passage, still with the queer stiffness in her gait I'd noticed when she came. "See you next week, Gabby," I called after her.

"See you next week," she repeated gaily and we both laughed as she kept on moving away, keeping herself far enough ahead of Mr. Samuel to be out of his reach. And then they disappeared in shadow.

Closing the door, I leaned against it. My thoughts whirled inside my head. For three weeks I had treated her as if she were an infant learning her first words. And she had played along, doing the repetitions I asked of her, sounding like a child testing sounds. Looking back, I realized that even when she looked as if she had not comprehended what I said to her, when an action was required, she had always done what I wanted her to do. Equally clear was the realization that Mr. Samuel was as unaware of her ability with English as I'd been. I was certain that if he had known he would not have allowed our meetings. Why had she kept her knowledge a secret? Where had she learned the language? Did all the lasses housed on the orlop deck speak English or understand it as well as Gabby did? That morning on the fo'c'sle deck, the girl in front of me had genuinely seemed as if she did not understand what I was trying to say to her. Now I wondered if she, too, had been pretending ignorance.

The only thing I knew for certain was that Gabby had decided to reveal herself to me today. I had somehow gained her trust. She had asked me with a finger to her lips to keep her secret, and I must respect her wish, at least until I'd had a chance to ask her what it all meant.

E VERY morning at prayers, the captain asked the
Almighty for the continuing good fortune of his,
and of all merchant ships. Thus far in the journey,
we had had great good luck. In the Bay of Biscay
we'd been blown about with no more say in where we went
than a stick caught in river rapids. But the blow was mercifully short and the captain said we'd lost nowt but time
and two shredded sails. From there we had nothing but
good winds and running seas until we came to the Gulf
Stream, where we sailed from bright sunshine and calm
water into short, steep walls of sea that lifted us high and
slammed us down with a fury that seemed designed to
break *Borealis'* back. As suddenly as we had sailed into the
notorious strip of ocean that Captain Allan said knocked
every ship about, we pushed through a black curtain of
rain and crossed the invisible barrier that marked the other
side, and were out of it. The captain ordered the sails shaken
loose again. So we spread our wings and flew.

In the horse latitudes, scrambled winds and weather kept us humbugging about for several days before the sails were able to catch and hold a fresh wind that carried us south and west. The captain had put as much sail on her as she would carry, and we'd relished days of doing fifteen knots or better. One day, we reached nineteen knots and then it truly did seem as if we were flying. Everyone on board cheered the speed.

Now, we were coming to the Horn. The way orders were being given, the sharp haste of the sailors, and an end to any patience on the part of the bosun and the mate raised in me a feeling of foreboding. I tried to shake it off.

I stood next to Father on the fo'c'sle deck, wrapped up in my cloak, muffler, mitts and boots. All the crew were occupied at unbending old sails and getting up new. "Three new topsails, new fore and main courses, new jib and fore-topmast staysail with a complete set of new earrings, new robands and reef points, along with new braces and clewlines, fore and aft," Father said. I was astonished to hear his commentary. I knew hardly half the names of the sails, and far less of the rigging.

"How do ye ken all that's being done?" I asked, but before he could answer the captain's shout went up.

"Haul the topgallant studding sails! Clew up topgallant studding sails! Haul the lower and topmast studding sails!"

All hands sprang to action and Father and I looked over our shoulders. The southwest was filled with a bank

of mist that blocked out sea and sky. The captain was bel-
lowing orders at the mate and the mate was roaring at the
crew. "Haul down!" and "Clew up!" were shouted over and
over and sails came down faster and faster. Sometimes
two sails dropped at a time. When they had finished, the
men slid down the rigging to the decks and stood there
waiting, watching the bank grow darker and bigger as it
drove for us. The whole ship seemed braced in wait.

The first blast of snow, sleet and wind hit and heeled
the ship on her side by forty-five degrees, her yards and
rigging snapping and cracking as she went. I grabbed the
weather rail and watched in horror as the topmost masts
bent so far they were almost hoops. The forward part of
the ship plunged beneath a huge sea and water poured
over the decks. Father and I, pulling ourselves along the
weather rail toward the wardroom door, were soaked. Into
the noise of the screaming wind, the whining, snapping
rigging and the pounding sea, a medley of new orders
went up. "Close-reef the fore-topsail! Furl the main! Lay
aloft there, you mizzen-topmen, and close-reef the
mizzen-topsail! Haul out to leeward! Taut hand. Knot
away! Two reefs ... two reefs!" the mate bawled and the
crew shouted back, "Aye, aye, Sir!" from the yards one hundred feet above the deck. Father and I made the wardroom
door, and he left me there. I passed what remained of the
afternoon trying to read a book that had been left on a
table, but spent most of the time looking for someone to

come in so I could ask about our progress, and how much longer this would go on.

Supper was an affair of trying to hold onto rolling cups and sliding plates. Not much food was swallowed. Passengers who'd not been sick for months were turning pale and leaving rapidly to go below.

In the middle of the night, I gave up trying to sleep in the fierce racket and determined to dress and go back to the wardroom, where at least I might find company. Father had not come down. But I discovered when I got to it that I could not get up the ladder. A cover had been put over the hatch and fastened down. I went back to my hammock. Unlike Father's berth, which was part of the pitching, rolling ship, the hammock at least hung vertical no matter how wildly the ship danced. I could lie in it with a sense I would not be thrown out.

All night I waited. The ship, being hammered by water, sounded as if it was crashing into rocks. I could hear shouting and the pounding of feet, and the boom of yards being lowered or falling to the decks. Below me were the thunder of rolling guns and the lightning-cracks of metal on metal when the guns smashed into their ports. One of our sea chests broke its lashings and slid to and fro, punishing the cabin walls. Shortly after that the metal basin and pitcher came out of their iron holders, and then the drawers of the little dresser came flying loose. It was a night of crash and bang. I worked to get out of my hammock and stumbled around for what seemed a very long time trying to catch and secure things as best I could. I was very grateful when, at eight o'clock, the hatch opening to the main deck was finally released.

The sleet and hail had stopped, but the heavy seas continued running high. The decks were covered with snow. I had to haul myself along the windward rail and hang on for life when a towering sea broke over the bow, and swirling foam and water came over the lee rail and set the waist awash. A sailor holding his pot of tea that was half his daily ration was at the end of the windlass on the fo'c'sle deck when the sea broke and carried him aft. The stern lifted and the water ran forward, and he lay sprawled upon the main deck. I watched him, afraid to take my eyes away lest he be gone when I looked back. The bows came up, the ship rolled, and the sailor was on his feet, moving steadily on. His teapot was filled with nothing but green seawater now. He laughed about his loss. Knowing sailors were allotted but two pots of tea a day, I did not think I would have been at all cheerful in his place.

On the quarter deck the captain was still shouting orders at the mate, and the mate still shouted at the crew. The sun had been up an hour by then, but there was no warmth in it. I saw men clinging like monkeys to the rigging and the spars, banging their hands against the sails to get their fingers warm enough to try to tie knots in ropes that had been stiffened to straight, unbending, icy pipes. I wondered if any of the officers or crew had slept that night.

Father was in the wardroom. So was Jock. Both were dripping wet. Jock was addressing two stewards, telling them to get a pot of coffee to the captain and one to the mate. "And tell the cook I'll be down directly to pick up pots of coffee and hot chocolate for the seamen," Jock said.

The steward's eyes bugged large when he replied, "Aye, Sir." I did not know his reaction was because seamen's needs were not usually thought of by part-owners of a ship. I thought twas fear made his eyes look like that. My heart beat faster.

Father said, "Tess, ye should have kept yourself below."

"I didna want to be shut up in the darkness and the wet. I prefer it here," I said.

Dermot stepped inside the door, bringing with him a cold, wet blast.

I spoke to Jock. "Is it a hurricane we're in like the *Central America* was?"

He hesitated, and my concern deepened. Dermot piped up. "Ye've nae need to fret, lass, Captain Allan is a bluenose man."

"What, pray, does that mean?"

"It's a sailors' school in Nova Scotia where only the best get in and then they are made better," Jock said. "Those that get through are respected round the world."

"Ye remember what I told ye of Bully Forbes, colleen?" Dermot asked.

"Aye. Ye said he set a record from St. John to Liverpool and that the *Borealis* would outsail his ship."

Jock laughed. "Derm's not fond of Bully Forbes. But the man's a sailor. His hobby is pushing ships to records. He also sailed the *Marco Polo* from Liverpool to Sydney in record time. When he got there, he said that voyage had made the world take notice, and he boasted that on his next voyage HE'D MAKE GOD HIMSELF TAKE NOTICE. I'll go his boast one better. My brother doesn't have to summon notice. God himself could not outsail John Allan."

"Sweet Jesus, may the saints not strike us all down dead for your blasphemy," said Dermot. But there was pride in his voice, confirmed when he added, "But tis part true. Haven't I served ten years under the Skipper, and don't I know he was always as canny a seaman as ever commanded a ship. Not that I'd tell him that meself, mind. Sure and he disnae need me own opinions to stretch his ego at all."

Jock and Father laughed. "Cookie'll have the hot drinks ready," Jock said, making for the door. Dermot and Father followed on his heels.

All three men seemed to crackle with excitement, Jock flashing the greatest share. Thinking of him, I remembered our cook's adage about foolish young men when she was complaining about one of my brothers: "If a rift appeared in front of him were he out for a gallop," she used to say, "he would spur the horse to jump, no matter the distance across." In this case, I thought the complaint might apply to Father and Dermot, too. I bit my lip and sternly told myself there was nothing to be afraid of, but silently I started to pray.

Through the day I kept mostly to the wardroom, preferring the snatches of rushing air and light to the sludgy darkness below decks. In the afternoon the wind and hail and sleet of the day before were repeated. All I could see when I looked out the windows was undulating, heaving, ominous water. Hail beat against the glass, and rain sheeted it. My sea legs threatened to leave me. For the first time since the beginning of the voyage, I was nauseated. All hands were often wanted on the decks and Father stayed occupied outside at whatever work there was. Left mostly to myself and unable to either read or write, first chance I got I asked the captain if there was something I could do.

"Bless ye, lassie. Ye would be very welcome in the galley. Cook's taken ill and his assistant has taken over, and he's in need of an assistant himself. Hot food and drink are a great comfort to us all."

At home, Cook had taught me some things and Mother others, so I thought I could manage. Little did I know that preparing food in a tossing ship was far different from working on the flat, motionless surfaces of a land-bound kitchen.

I had only one hand to use for measuring, cutting, mixing and otherwise carrying out the new cook's instructions. I had to use the other hand to hold myself upright, clutching hard the nearest bolted piece of furniture. While I learned this trick of one-handed cooking, I wasted more than a little of the purser's supplies.

It was now I learned about the different menus on a ship. I knew well enough that three pints of water, minus what was wanted in the galleys for soups and other cooking, were rationed to each person every day. Since the beginning I had had to save fresh water from my daily allotment if I wanted it instead of seawater for washing clothes or hair. The ship's water was laced with vinegar to keep it clean. It made my hair shine, but it tasted awful. No one drank it straight. Ale and porter could be purchased by the tween deck passengers from 10:00 a.m. to noon; wine and spirits could only be gotten by those who had obtained permission from the captain. Otherwise, tea and coffee were the drinks.

I had thought food, like water, was the same for everyone. It wasn't. I was about to spoon quantities of rice into the tubs, called kids, that went to each crew's mess. The new "Cookie" stopped me. "No lice in sailor kids. That one salt meat. That one hard biscuit! Salt meat, biscuit, that their supper. No lice! Only lice fi'st class, cabin. Sailor no lice."

In our mess we'd been served bread and biscuits, oatmeal, rice, eggs, good pea soup, cakes and puddings throughout the voyage. Fresh-killed meat or fowl, including chicken pie, was served for as long as it was available, and salt meat was substituted when the fresh was gone, along with cheeses and potatoes. As well, we'd had fresh fruits and meats when the captain stood in to Lisbon and then to Rio de Janeiro to take on supplies. "How can they work if they're fed only cold meat and hard biscuit?" I demanded.

"This good ship, Missie. Lucky sailor have oatmeal, soup, salt meat, ha'd biscuit, tea, lime juice. Duff on Sunday. Potato sometime. Sailor wo'k. Captain not have *sogers* his ship." Then he cut off some of each crew's ration of salt meat and set it aside. "Fo' Captain's dog," he said.

If I thought the crew were badly fed, the women on the orlop were hardly fed at all. Cookie said once a week they were given rations of flour, tea and sugar, measured into containers brought by the purser. That and lime juice were all they got. "They'll starve to death on a diet such as that," I said.

"You don expec Captain give same to pipple who give less for passage and to pipple who pay mo?" he said. "They wan mo, they buy."

"Who cooks for them?" I asked.

"They cook. Wan pudding, cake, they bling to galley befo noon; I bake. We don cook fo them."

I had never thought Gabby might have so much less to eat than I did. I had never thought about it at all. If I had, I would have supposed she and the others could do as Cookie said and buy food from the purser. I had a vision of Gabby averting her eyes when I brought out fruit, or her mouth watering when I offered her cake. I had not heeded those things before but now they weighed on me. *How could they buy food? They are so poor. They must all be so hungry!*

Cookie jolted me. "Make bled. Mo wo'k to do." I poured ingredients into a large bowl, and returned to my thoughts while I mixed, folded and kneaded.

Father and I had brought flour, butter, brown sugar, salt, soda, cheeses, baked suet cakes with fruit and cured with brandy, a little wine, and single malt scotch with us in our chests. We had also brought four wethers and a crate of chickens for eating, and four ewes and two rams to be kept alive for breeding when we arrived in the colony. The wethers were gone and so were the chickens. We were, however, certainly in no danger of starving. I determined to ask Father if something could be done to supply Gabby and her friends with more food.

But I didn't see him that night, and the following morning breakfast was a game of catch and gobble as mugs and bowls of food jumped out of the trough and slid from side to side and end to end on the pitching table. Cutlery and coffee ended on the floor, along with one of the gentlemen who loosed his hold on the edge of the table at an injudicious moment and found his chair instantly upended. Mr. Samuel said the hatches to the lower levels of the ship had been battened and that those who were housed on the orlop would stay there until the hatches were opened up again.

The storms came each afternoon and piled on top of the constant gale. By the third day the seas were running so high, and we were pitching and tossing at such a rate and shipping so much water, all Cookie and I could do was boil water for tea and heat soup for supper. We struggled to keep the galley fires lit. It was then I lost my sea legs altogether. I became so ill I had to retire. The battened hatches prevented me from getting to my cabin. I stumbled to the wardroom, where I lay on the couch, or on the floor, spewing almost constantly. A crewman came in from time to time to mop up the mess. Father came, briefly, and washed my face and told me I would be all right.

The weather worsened. I could think only of my wretched stomach and head. I silently and fervently begged the Almighty to please, please wash me overboard to join the fishes. Of course I didn't venture onto the deck to actually let Him do it. I spotted an albatross bobbing in the horrible sea, but I failed to appreciate the beauty of it then, having no liking for anything about the place and time.

We inched round the Horn.

I had lost all track of time when Jock came in. I didn't recall seeing him since I had taken refuge here. I was sitting in a horsehair chair, holding onto the arms of it.

"We've come through with only some sprung spars," Jock said. "We can thank John for that. Your father's been a workhorse and we're grateful for his help, as we are for yours, Tess. Cookie's assistant isn't given to praise, but he has said you were a great asset."

For two days I had been far more a hindrance than a help. The praise embarrassed me and I didn't know where to look. "Is the storm over then?" I asked.

"Aye. She's blown herself down to a regular hurricane. The sea's as calm as milk slopping in a pail."

I looked through the window, gulped, and quickly turned my head away. All I could see was rolling, churning water. No sky was visible to fix my vision and stop the heaving of my stomach.

Jock saw my look and laughed. "Green's a colour that suits you well, Tess. It almost matches your eyes."

His tease turned my embarrassment to annoyance. I was not, at all costs, going to let him see me retch. Forcing my chin high, I asked, "Are the companionways open?" I much wanted a change of clothes.

"Only the forward hatch has been opened so Cookie can get supplies from the stores. As soon as he's satisfied, it will be closed until we're out of the blow."

I couldn't get to my cabin from there, and I didn't consider going anywhere else. Jock took his leave and went through the door to the chart room. I had wanted him gone, but now I felt very alone. I looked out the window, trying to see his "milk-pail" calmness, but my eyes were met with what looked to me like mountains of sliding water. I could detect no lessening of tumult. However, I was inclined to join him in thanking the captain for getting us through the worst of the storm, even if I did feel it likely I would remain queasy for the rest of my life.

When the messes had been returned to a regular order of dining hours and the diners had returned to the messes, I asked Mr. Samuel if Gabby could come to my cabin the following morning. He informed me the orlop passengers were still recovering from being seasick and it would be some days before Gabrielle was fit to meet with anyone. She, and the others, were being looked after by Mrs. Motherwell, he said.

I suddenly recalled my promise to Gabby the last time I'd seen her. "Oh dear, I had forgotten. When last we met I told Gabby I'd ask about some special teas for her," I said. "I shall do it immediately and take them down to her. They're a help for seasickness and the others will be glad of them, too."

"If you insist, Miss Macqueen, hand them to me and I'll pass them on to Mrs. Motherwell. Them as what are below are 'appiest left to theirselves, if you knows what I mean."

"I'm acquainted well enough with that desire," I said, remembering how I'd felt lying in the wardroom. "I'll speak to Mr. Allan as soon as I can. I would very much appreciate it, Mr. Samuel, if ye'll ask Mrs. Motherwell to tell Gabby how much I miss her, and that I hope she is well soon. And to express to all the lasses my wishes for their quick return to health."

"I'll do that, Miss."

"Thank you, Mr. Samuel."

We had three days of beating into headwinds before we caught a fair wind and ran before it, leaving the Cape and the albatrosses far behind. But far off the coast of Peru, we sailed into the doldrums, and we sat.

"A regular dead muzzler," Captain Allan said.

It had been discovered after the storm that all the remaining food in the ship's larder had been more than halfway spoiled by seawater, and now in the heat it was spoiled further. The entire ship was put on short rations. It had taken only one meal of soggy biscuits and cheese and cooked apples for me to revise the captain's statement about the state of the food. In my estimation, it was not just halfway ruined; its ruin was complete. When our boxes were brought up from the hold, I learned that what remained of Father's and my provisions had suffered the same fate, so I could not ask him if we might share our food. For the first time, I began to experience the ache of real hunger. *And if I'm hungry*, I thought, *what of Gabby and the others?*

The next day I again asked Mr. Samuel about seeing her. He said she'd taken a turn for the worse, but Mrs. Motherwell had had the care of many more young ladies in her career than she wanted to remember. The girl would be fine, he assured me, but she must not be disturbed just now. He would not relent and I was forced to occupy myself with other things to fill the time.

Father's and my clothing was full of mould. Some was even starting to rot. I soaked and scrubbed it, and hung it up on lines strung about the main deck. Every deck except the poop was covered with bedding, clothing and mattresses hung to air. I spent some time watching the ship's armourer. He even let me try my hand at shaping a few small ornaments, but the heat of his forge was overpowering and I could not keep long at it at one time. Once or twice I sat in on the seemingly endless games of cards being played; however, after a very few rounds I grew restless and excused myself. I sat in the wardroom or on a deck under whatever little shade I could find, trying to bring my diary up to date, but it seemed my account of what was happening was becoming as tedious as the heat, and I gave it up. I watched the glassy sea, hoping Mrs. Motherwell or the lasses would appear.

The most fortunate thing about these days was the amount of time the sailors had to sit around the windlass spinning yarns. Not continually occupied now with taking in and putting out sails, they were able to spend the full dogwatch hours of four to six o'clock in the afternoon in their favourite occupation, which was each trying to outdo the others in telling the most outrageous tale. I sat as close to them as courtesy would allow, and listened. One fellow in particular told stories in such a manner as to make the goosebumps rise on my skin. Deliciously affrighted, I sat spellbound while he talked of his days aboard a merchant ship that plied the silk-trade routes, and spun yarns of pirates in the South China Sea and of the imperial majesties of China and Japan.

His stories were not like my mother's. She had talked about the strength of the Chinese people; of their love for and fidelity to family. She had told me how in their ancient knowledge they had many kinds of wisdom we knew little of. She had also spoken of cruelties she couldn't countenance, such as binding little girls' feet, which caused the children years of indescribable pain and deformed their limbs forever.

The sailor's stories were of warlords and mighty clashes and court intrigue. Whenever he finished a tale, he would ask for payment by saying, "Did ye know, lads, that fishermen would come and bargain with storytellers such as I to take one on their boats, and they paid wi' half their catch and a good drink? Ante up now, boys." And some would pour part of their daily measure of rum into his cup to keep him going.

One morning when it was so hot even the captain had unbuttoned his coat, the ocean, touched by the yellow sun, sparkled like blue diamonds. It was by no means the first time I'd seen this pretty sight, but now I licked my chapped lips and it seemed I could almost taste cold, refreshing ice on my tongue. I stripped to my petticoat, climbed over the rail and down the side steps to a lower platform, and jumped off to have a swim. The water was a glorious heavenly blue and filled with light, and best of all, wonderfully wet as it closed over my head and streamed away from my nose as I blew bubbles of air. I kicked back to the surface, rolled and floated, and dove downward again like the porpoises I'd seen playing near the ship. Clear, clean water flowed all over and around me. I pushed against its weight with all my limbs, but I felt free of any weight at all.

"A MAN OVERBOARD!" someone called and I looked up to see the ship was a little distance off and moving farther.

I stroked and kicked and waved to show them I was fine and not to think I'd fallen overboard; then I swam toward the ship. I was moving, but the ship was going faster than I. I tried harder. I knew now the sea was not glass-smooth, but was moving in long, gentle swells, carrying the ship on its silky rollers. I sputtered when a swell smashed against my face. A small alarm stung me. *What if I can't catch it?* I buried my head and windmilled my arms as fast as I was able.

Something was making a clamour. I raised my head and heard a cheer and saw someone toss a line and buoy toward me. It took several tosses of several different lengths of line, but finally one came close enough for me to grab. "Tie it round your waist!" someone shouted. I did, and hand over hand they hauled me aboard, and the ship's boat that was partway lowered was hoisted up again.

Father fumbled to untie the rope around me. His face was pale but his voice was livid when he said, "Have ye taken leave of your senses, girl? Of all the fool things anyone could do. If they hadn't pounded on the hull to make ye lift yer head ..." For once I bit back my retort. I knew I had been very lucky.

"I'm sorry, Father," I said. "I shall always tie a rope around myself when I go swimming in the future. That way I'll be kept up with the boat."

"Ye'll do no such thing," he said, his face even frostier than it had been. I couldn't think he was telling me I was forbidden to swim, but it didn't seem an appropriate time to ask him to clarify what he meant, so I stayed quiet until he had gone away.

Jock was at the helm, wearing a grin as wide as a hyena's, and I realized I was partially undressed. My cheeks began to burn. "Did ye swallow a mackerel sideways?" I shot at him; then cursed myself for being childish, instead of clever as I'd meant to be. Without giving him another glance, and fancying I was moving with the proper restraint and decorum, I retrieved my frock. Keeping on, I walked toward the forward ladder while I pulled the dress on over my wet petticoat. Somewhere off to one side I heard a sailor say, "Did ye see that body, laddie? Strong and lithesome as a big cat."

Another replied, "Shut yer face. She'll not look in yer direction, ye stupid bugger, and if ye know what's good fer ye, ye'll keep yer eyes to yerself."

I knew I should be outraged, but in a secret part of me, I blushed with something close to pleasure. It wouldn't do. I doubled my pace. I would go down to the orlop deck and discover for myself how Gabrielle was doing. She'd been ill for far too long.

❦ TEN ❧
Mrs. Motherwell's Paranoia
Captain Allan Tightens Ship

STOPPING briefly at my cabin to tie my wet hair up and fetch the only apple we had that had somehow escaped from being soaked, I was soon on my way to the forward ladder on the middle deck. Mr. Samuel was coming up. I moved into the shadows, but I could not avoid him. "You are not going below, Miss Macqueen," he said.

"Aye, Sir. I want to visit Gabrielle. I've a story to tell her that I think will make her smile. I also want to take her this," I said, holding up the apple.

"She'll have no use for stories and fruit. She's not like to last the hour, though I doubts she'll be going to a better place. I'm off to fetch the surgeon. Come with me away now."

I was stunned. "No, thank ye, Mr. Samuel, I'll not go back. If Gabby is so sick, then I willna leave without seeing her. How can she be so ill? There maun be something to be done for her." I moved away from him.

"It's my permission what allows you to see her at all, Miss Macqueen, and I'm withdrawing it."

"Then I shall have to visit Gabby without your permission."

"Nay, you'll not."

"What would ye do to keep me from it, Sir?"

"Oy, there's dire consequences to them what thwarts authority. I has only to call an officer and you'll ..."

"Call him then, Sir."

Seeing he could do nothing with me, he stomped off. He was hardly out of sight before I continued down. Long before stepping off the bottom rung, my senses informed me I was coming into a most unholy squalor.

The women were housed aft of the carpenter's stores in the foremost part of the deck. Their quarters were defined by bulkheads made of canvas sheets. In the canvas wall facing me, there was a rectangle cut for a door. The natural light that filtered down the ladderway through the grating and glass skylights in the upper deck was lost when I stepped through that hole and into their room. The odours of vomit, human waste and unwashed bodies were choking. I pulled my wet handkerchief from my sleeve to put it over my nose, but stopped when I discerned there were eyes in the dimness watching me.

The lone lamp hanging from the centre beam barely lit the room. On either side of a narrow passage, wooden platforms built one above the other lined the walls. Three platforms to a side, each about five feet wide and placed close enough above each other that a full-grown person would not be able to sit up straight between them. There was a sucking noise under my feet when I stepped forward. I looked down and saw a brownish swill running side to side with the rolling of the ship. I wanted out of that and thought to climb up on a platform, and turned to the one closest to me. What I saw there made my stomach clench so hard I thought I would be sick. I swallowed hastily and forced myself to take a breath.

Four lasses lay side by side on a thin, bare mattress that was covered near their heads with vomit, bile and blood. They were all thin and sweating. Their clothing was filthy, streaked with vomit and blood; the lower part soaked with the effects of loose bowels that could not be controlled. Three of them had their eyes open; one appeared to be asleep. None of them was making any noise. It seemed to me I was looking death in its face. "Oh!" I said, involuntarily putting my hand to my mouth. *Oh! Oh! Where was Gabrielle?* "Gabrielle?" I said out loud.

"On top bed," someone said. I thought I recognized the voice and squinted into the gloom.

At the aft end of the room, in front of the mouldy canvas back wall, a huddle of three lasses stood in a small space close to two boxes standing on their ends, and one tin pail, the room's only furnishings other than the platforms. All of those lasses had their eyes on me, but I didn't recognize any of them. Still, the voice had been familiar.

"Nadia?" I asked, thinking one must be Gabby's friend. "I've just seen Mr. Samuel going to fetch the surgeon. He has told me Gabby is very ill."

"Is scurvy." The speaker was a girl I thought could be Nadia, but if it was, she had changed mightily. The lower part of her face around her mouth was puffy; the upper hollow. Her eyes were huge and sunken under a bony brow.

I had heard the pride in Captain Allan's voice when he'd said how he had taken a lesson from James Cook and because of that man's knowledge and practices there had never been scurvy aboard the *Borealis*, or any ship under his command, because lime juice was given regularly to everyone on board. I thought also of the fruits and breads I had given Gabby during our lessons, and I was certain Nadia must be mistaken. "Surely you mean tis the effects of being so seasick she's suffering from."

"Not seasick," Nadia declared. "All here have scurvy. You give food to Gabrielle; she give to us," Nadia said. "We not knowing she only keep so little for herself and so she is most sick."

A rough voice outside the canvas called, "Where's the patient?" Then, "Holy Mary, mother of God! I'll not come into no stinkin' hole such as that!" And with that the sailor disappeared.

Looking at Nadia, I said, "I shall get help for you all, but first may I see Gabby?" Nadia nodded and pointed upward on the starboard side.

I climbed up the berths. Gabby was lying by herself, still asleep in spite of my and the sailor's noise. Being as careful as I could to not disturb her, I manoeuvred myself onto my side beside her. Her face was swollen almost beyond recognition. I touched her head and then her neck. My fingers made dents in her skin that stayed. She was on fire. Her chest rose and fell in quick, shallow breaths. The joints in her wee arms and legs and feet looked an agony of swelling. Gently, I wiped her sweating face with my damp handkerchief.

She opened her eyes and stared unseeing at the ceiling and made noises, but could not seem to open her mouth.

Frightened, I tried to calm her. "Hush. Tis all right, Gabby. Tis me, Tess. Shhh. There's a darlin' girl. We'll get you well. I'm going to get Father and we'll take ye out of this," I said, just as another burly sailor came into the room and peered into the berth.

"Up you go, then, girlie," he said, and picked Gabby up and put her over his shoulder. She cried out from the pain of being moved, but he carried on up the ladder with her.

"I'll be back," I called to the others as I went after him. I followed him to the forward bulkhead on the middle deck.

Not unkindly, he prevented me from going farther. "No one into the sick bay without the doctor's say-so, Miss." With that, he opened the door to a room and closed it behind him, leaving me outside. "Christ in heaven!" I heard the surgeon say through the door. "Put her on that bed.

Let's get a tube into her. And get a pail of water, man!" I went immediately in search of Father and found him in the wardroom, playing whist with Jock, Captain Allan and one other passenger.

Jock spied me first, and seeing my visible anger, started a banter. "Is that steam rising from your collar, Tess? Could be you need another swim to cool off."

I hardly heard him. By now the entire table was facing me and as I did not know whom to address first, I harangued them all. "I've been to the orlop deck to look in on Gabby, and I have never seen anything so awful!" I almost choked remembering it. "All the lasses forced to live in that horrible place are ill. They have the look of starving, but Nadia says tis scurvy that they're sick with. Gabby is so ill, Mr. Samuel has told me she's like to die!"

"What's all this, then?" Captain Allan sputtered.

"Mr. Samuel didna want me to go down to her. I disobeyed him, and ..." I felt myself begin to shake and fought to keep back the tears. Crying would do nowt to help the lasses. "You maun do something. They are terribly ill. They maun have good food and medicine and clean quarters or they will die!"

It was then the unfortunate Mr. Samuel came into the wardroom. Seeing all eyes turn on him, he immediately wheeled, but Captain Allan put a forceful stop to his retreat. "Mr. Samuel, Miss Macqueen is reporting there is illness among your charges. Please accompany me to my cabin, Sir, and we'll sort this out."

"Tis all right, Captain. The doctor's come and taken the girlie what's ill to the sick bay. I've just come up from giving orders to Mrs. Motherwell about the others meself."

"All right, Mr. Samuel? I should say tis not. Miss Macqueen has said the wee lass is close to dying and all the lasses are ill with scurvy. Scurvy, Mr. Samuel. How in bloody hell could there be scurvy aboard my ship? I shall have the surgeon up to explain it to us both, and also why he has not reported it to me."

Mr. Samuel bent his head in a pleading gesture sideways. On his face was an anemic smile. "Oy. Well, now, Captain, tis per'aps possible the doctor weren't knowing it. Mrs. Motherwell's been meetin' him on the middle deck of a mornin' and makin' her report on all those in steerage to him there, keepin' him from all the trouble of goin' down below like. It were not for her to know how sick the girlie were, Cap'n, for it's God's truth that girl's a first-rate malingerer. Complained of this and that since I first laid eyes on 'er, when anyone could see she were as healthy as meself. And I knows well enough from past experience the affections of those what takes on the care of her kind is often trifled with. Oy, there's no truth whatever in 'em, no Sir, there's not. So poor Mrs. Motherwell could 'ardly take it to heart when the girl complained, likely thinkin' the child would recover herself soon enough, as she always 'as in the past. It were only this morning Mrs. Motherwell brought the matter to my attention. I waited until the doctor made his examination before bringing the matter to you meself, Captain. To save you worries what ought to be carried on me own broad shoulders like."

The captain stood up. "Come with me, Mr. Samuel. Now!"

There followed a scandal, the details of which quickly travelled through the ship, gossip being an even more regular entertainment than gambling for those aboard.

It was said Mrs. Motherwell had developed a paranoia about scurvy. She said she'd been told all who undertook the journey to the New World contracted it if all they had to avoid it was one bottle of lime juice a day, and she claimed her fear of getting the disease must have put her out of her right mind. That was why she'd hoarded for herself all the lime juice that was given her by the purser to share among the lasses. She also had other fears that must have further depressed her right mind, as it was found she had kept back part of the lasses' rations and sold what she hadn't eaten herself to sailors wanting more to eat. In her defense, she told the captain that she and Mr. Samuel had meant to use the money gotten for the food to help secure good positions for the lasses when they reached the colony.

As for not reporting the sickness, she claimed Mr. Samuel had forbidden her to do so. She said that when she knew it was so severe it must be reported to the doctor at once, she had made Mr. Samuel come below and look at Gabrielle for himself. Her intervention, she said, was why

Mr. Samuel had finally summoned the ship's surgeon, and that was what had saved the girl.

The filth, she said, was a result of the order Mr. Samuel had given at the first sign of illness a month before, forbidding the lasses to leave their quarters except very infrequently to empty their pots. He had been relentless in enforcing this, Mrs. Motherwell said, no matter how she pleaded with him to allow them at least a little air each day.

The horror of the lasses being kept below all that time, with only enough to eat as would not keep a gnat alive, forced to relieve themselves in a corner of their quarters because their pots were full and they were not allowed above deck to empty them, made my head pound. Many of them had suffered terrible dysentery and they were all too weak and sick to be able to keep up with the effort required to clean up the effects. And no one did it for them. While I, ill only a few days, was so well cared for. I was not new to prejudice against the poor, but this was cruelty I had never seen. I, too, had had a part in it, disregarding as I had how much time was passing without seeing Gabby. For want of enough food and a simple vitamin — among people who could give her both — she might have died. It did not bear thinking about. My throat was filled with a hard lump. Hot tears burned down my cheeks.

Dermot said Mr. Samuel refuted Mrs. Motherwell's testimony, and gave us Mr. Samuel's story. Mr. Samuel said he had relied on Mrs. Motherwell, trusting that with her qualifications she would look after the girls properly and give him an accurate account of their condition. He claimed she had daily calmed him with assurances their illness was not serious, and that he had only taken the precaution of confining them to their quarters until Mrs. Motherwell could report there was no fever among them, because he wanted to make sure no sickness was spread to others on the ship.

Derm scoffed at this. "Tis more likely the man did not 'trouble' the captain about the poor lassies because he thought he and they would be put ashore in some port other than Fort Victoria while they recovered, where he might sit idly by for months waiting for other transport, paying the cost of their food the whole time."

"But he kenned they were being starved," Father said.

"Bah, he claims no knowledge of that," Derm said. "Didn't he put all the blame for it on the lady in 'is employ. Didn't he say he never believed a lady could commit an act so black, so foul."

"What are they eating now, then?" I demanded.

"Do na trouble yer pretty head about that, colleen. The captain has ordered good soup and the juice of mashed raw potatoes given them to counteract the scurvy. They must start slowly so the food will stay in their stomachs."

"Is it the truth, then, that Mr. Samuel didna ken they were going so hungry?" I wanted to know, for I could not fathom it.

"It boils down to Mrs. Motherwell's word against Mr. Samuel's word," Jock said, "and that makes a difficult job of finding justice for the captain. I do not envy John his position."

"What will happen?" I asked.

Dermot answered, "The captain canna let stealing go unpunished, nor the concealment of sickness that might have put us all at risk be it a different one than twas. Tis the order of the ship at stake, lassie. There'll be a penalty to pay."

Jock said, "My brother is not a hard man, but Derm's right. And where the safety and the reputation of the *Borealis* are at stake, John is proud."

Once again I thought about how it was possible for a place as small as a single ship to have so many secrets. I hoped the penalty inflicted on Mr. Samuel and Mrs. Motherwell would be severe.

That evening all who were fit enough to be there were assembled on the main deck. Captain Allan stood above us on the quarter deck and spoke. His voice was not quite steady, but it was clearly heard by all. "My duty as the captain of the *Borealis* makes me responsible for all souls that are aboard this vessel," he began. "I apologize to God and to you that I have failed in carrying out the full measure of my responsibility, and the result is abhorrent neglect acted on a group of passengers it were in my hands as well as God's to protect. On my oath, I shall have no repetition

of anything like it on any vessel I command! And I shall
do what is necessary to set this abomination right.

"All crew on watch below will immediately commence
to scrape, mop and holy-stone the orlop deck until it
shines white, and twill be kept in that condition. By God
it will! All mattresses and clothing that have been fouled
will be thrown overboard. We shall take up a collection of
clothing and bedding to replace what will be lost to the
lassies."

There was a murmuring of assent. *I and Mrs. Motherwell
are the only ones who can do aught about replacing female gar-
ments,* I thought. *Mother's clothes that are too small for me, can
I give them up?* I knew Mother would never see another
person go without something she had an abundance of. I
had cloth, too, for making new dresses when the old were
outgrown or worn out. My thoughts were interrupted by
the captain continuing to speak.

"Mr. Samuel, your compliance in the shameful treatment of your charges cannot be proved, but at the least ye
are guilty of gross neglect and ye will go below with the
hands and get down on your knees beside a bucket of
water, Sir, and scrub. Ye will repeat the exercise every
morning. In that manner, you will easily keep yourself
acquainted with the state of the lasses' health and the
fitness of their accommodation. Is that understood, Sir?"

Mr. Samuel, whose face was the colour of ripe berries,
could do no more than bow his head in answer.

"In the matter of their rations, Mr. Samuel, I order ye to purchase supplies from the purser to feed them well enough to ensure their complete recovery, and to prevent any recurrence of this illness. I promise ye I will regularly require an account of your purchases. There will be no unnecessary deaths aboard my ship!"

He then turned his attention to the second culprit, who stood beside Mr. Samuel, twisting a handkerchief in her hands, sobbing. "Madam, it has become clear to me during my and Mr. Clement's examination of ye that you suffer from a delusion that was caused by misinformation ye received about the disease of scurvy, and that that delusion has caused ye to fear unnaturally for your own vitality. It is a greater pity that your fear led ye to endanger the well-being of those in your care by unnatural acts of theft and negligence against them. However, I do na find any cause sufficient to condone the heinous theft of rations meant for them who were at your mercy for their subsistence, or to allow it to go unpunished. You will have ten strokes for it, and may God help you." At which news Mrs. Motherwell slumped in a dead faint. She was revived and then was hauled to the mizzen-mast by two sailors who supported her under her arms. There she was tied, and her dress was torn open to expose her back.

Thinking I wanted to see her justly punished for what she had done, I stood where I was, and then when I knew I did not want to see any more of it, I could not move away. For a long time after the flogging I had nightmares of her welted back and her screams, and mixed with this terrible scene were the horrible scenes of wasting, writhing children.

❧

Gabby was recovering in sick bay from her ordeal. After a week, I was allowed to visit her and I asked the doctor if I could take her up on deck for a bit of air.

"She's fit enough for that," he said. "Do her good."

The day was very fair and we found a spot to sit in the lee of the pinnace. We sat in companionable silence, looking at a sunlit sea, until Gabby said, "Is lovely here. Not like my village."

"Tell me about your village, about your people, Gabby."

"We are serfs. Planting, farming. But village get too hot, too cold; we go other place. When we go other place, we are becoming troupe. Some sing. Others dance. Peoples like to see us. Pay us rubles and we have some monies."

"Oh! Mama used to tell me wonderful stories about gypsies that went from place to place singing and dancing and doing tricks on horses and all sorts of things. She saw them every summer when she was a wee girl. Are your people Rom, Gabby?"

She nodded. "We are Rom. Papa say long ago Tsar say we farm, so we don't go place to place. We go anyway. But since Russia is having war with Turkey, Tsar Alexander say no more we can go around country because maybe we are spies for Turkey. Before when Russia is having wars only mens who drink too much vodka and mens who get in trouble, and some children from families where are too many children, must go to war first, but Tsar say all peasant mens must fight with Turkey. Many from my village are killed. My papa is hurt. He cannot work. Mama cannot provide. She say I must go away from village. Away from Russia. Man give her rubles for me, she give me to man." Gabby turned her head aside. Her small fist came up to her wet eyes. "I not see Mama again," she whispered.

My chest filled with a thick ache and I put my arms around her and held on tight. "Oh, Gabby."

We clung together, fighting our separate loneliness. Then a still calmness seeped through the thin cloth and the skin between our bloodflows, and warm pleasure surged through me. I felt Gabby's taut muscles relax a little. The silence between us seemed as beautiful and as fragile as the wariness of a doe being offered grass by a human hand. I waited, unwilling to break the calm.

After a while she drew away and asked, "You teach me more, yes?"

"Of course I will, as soon as you're fit enough. But Gabby, ye speak English very well. Did the people of your village speak it?"

"No. Nadia teach."

"Do ye all speak it then?"

She shook her head. "Only Nadia."

"Mr. Samuel disnae ken you and Nadia know it."

"We don't tell him."

"Does he no hear ye teach the others?"

"I am saying only simple words when Mr. Samuel listen. Nadia saying nothing."

"But why?"

"Nadia say is better for us we don't talk English in front of other peoples. She say if we don't talk, peoples will talk more in front of us."

I laughed. "Like you were spies," I said.

"No," she said solemnly. "Spies are shot."

I didn't know what to say to that, and saw that she looked tired and wan. Reluctantly, I realized it was time to take her back. "We maun go," I said, and she obediently got to her feet.

At the door to sick bay I told her I would come again as soon as I was let. I blew her a kiss. She blew one back to me. She went inside and I turned and found myself almost face to face with Mr. Samuel and Mr. Rake.

"Gentlemen," I said, starting to go past. The two of them remained where they were, blocking my way. Mr. Samuel leaned closer to my ear. The hairs on the back of my neck bristled with his nearness. "Very pretty, Miss Macqueen, I'm sure. Ye've learnt 'er yer uppity ways well enough. But ye'll have no hand with 'er on Vancouver's Island, will ye."

He shifted and I brushed by the pair.

"Don't let us keep you, Miss Macqueen," hissed Mr. Rake.

My heart did not stop pounding for several minutes after I was back on the main deck. I had not expected Mr. Samuel to be friendly with me after I had gone against him, but I had not thought he would threaten harm to any other on account of it. Had he threatened to harm Gabby? I didna ken, nor kenned I what I could do about it if he had. I resolved to be careful of him.

Father and I were supping at the captain's table when, in general conversation, I said how glad I was Gabby and the other Russian girls had recovered so well, and wouldn't it be a good idea for Gabby and me to start our meetings again. Father's disgust at what had happened to the lasses had shifted his position in favour of them. He readily approved. The captain said he thought it could not but benefit the lass. Mr. Samuel, therefore, could not with grace refuse.

In the weeks that followed, Mr. Samuel was more tight-fisted than ever with Gabby's and my time together. He did not allow us a minute past the half hour he had set. But now when the lasses came up on the main deck to take some air, Father did not prohibit me from joining them, and I thus had more time with Gabby and began to know a little about them all.

Gabby flourished and was filling out. She proved to be a lively sprite who loved to play practical jokes. More than once I was a laughing audience to her antics, which found targets among the crew, her fellow passengers and myself. In that, I was reminded of my brother Earl. Every day I grew more fond of her. Nadia, too, was a friend to me, and so it was we three who were most often seen together when we promenaded on the deck. Nadia was quiet, saying little except to ask questions of me. When I questioned her, she was very good at turning the subject back toward me or to something else. I was glad to have someone to tell stories of home to — of my mother and my brothers, for it helped them stay alive in me.

❧

The ship was off the coast of Oregon and we were strolling on the deck. The talk was of our destination. We were close to it. Anticipation had started to rise. "What do ye dream of in the New World?" I asked the other two. Both were silent so long I thought they mustn't have heard. Then Nadia said, "There is Rus' story. Was told me by my Babushka. Is story about person famous in Russian stories, Ivan.

"Ivan ploughing land, but he stop to dream. Ivan like very much to dream. He is dreaming he sees hare standing in tall grass and he is thinking, Good luck for me. I catch that hare. Get monies for him. With monies I get sow. Sow have dozen piglets. Piglets grow big, have litters, same as sow. I kill pigs and sell meat. Monies I get make me rich to get married. I have two strong sons, Vasha and Vanka. They are growing up and working for me, and I am sitting in sun on porch, shouting at them. 'Go easy, boys! Do not whip horses like that. Take care of them, they take care of you.' Ivan is shouting at his dream sons and waving his arms at them. Hare is frightened and runs away. Away with hare goes Ivan's sons, Ivan's wife, one hundred fifty-six piglets and one sow."

Nadia looked, for a moment, so hopeless that my heart was wrenched and I protested. "But that story only means we maun work to fulfill our dreams, not that we shouldna dream."

"I will work," she said. "Gabrielle will work. Mr. Samuel say we work five years to pay monies for passage."

I was stunned. "That cannot be."

She looked at me in a way I might have thought showed pity. "Kachka, Abez'iana have prospect to marry. Maybe husband pay for passage. All who not have husband will work."

I could not believe a child as young as Gabby would be held ransom. I had imagined she was being brought to the colony to a family who wanted a child. Nadia was emphatic, yet I did not want to believe it was true.

Gabby said simply, "I dream we are always being friends."

"Oh, Gabby, I promise we shall be. We shall all visit each other as often as we can." I meant it with all my heart. I had no idea how glib that promise would prove to be.

Father confirmed Gabby and the others would have to work as Nadia had said, if they were emigrating as indentured servants. An indentured servant, he said, was brought to a new country on the promise he or she would work for a number of years to repay whoever paid the passage. Part of their wages went toward the debt until it had been repaid. He said Scottish miners had emigrated to Vancouver's Island that way.

To me, it sounded like a return to serfdom for Gabby, and I railed. "She didna have any say in what happened to her. How can she be laden with a debt when she had no part in the making of it? 'Tis unfair."

"Nay lass. 'Tis a system that allows the indigent to relocate to somewhere they might make a better life. The wee girl will no doubt be taken in by a family and do some small work for them."

We were a family. I loved Gabby and I would dearly love having a little sister. It was on the tip of my tongue to beg Father to let us take her, but I knew well enough twas not our own house we were going to. I knew, too, that we were in debt to Uncle Hammond for our own tickets, and that Father had never been able to abide owing money to anyone. Still, I held the hope in my breast, not daring to tell Gabby or anyone of it, lest the telling made it disappear as had Ivan's hare.

EVERYONE was out on deck, chattering and straining our eyes to see. When we were just outside the entrance to the harbour, Captain Allan ordered the guns fired four times to alert the authority to send us a pilot. The booms, the rise and fall of voices, sounded like a party and everyone aboard the ship was celebrating now. One hundred and thirty-four days after sailing from Liverpool we were coming in to Esquimalt.

For the past few weeks the sailors had been busy. *Borealis* was newly painted, her sails and rigging had been checked; her lines unroved and roved until not a string was out of place. The masts gleamed with a fresh coat of tar. When the boat was shipshape, the sailors had overhauled themselves. They had filled tubs with water, trimmed their beards and moustaches, or shaved completely, and scrubbed their skin until they'd removed so many layers of colour they were now light brown and rosy-hued instead of almost black. Their hair was shiny clean. This morning they had all put on their best togs. Now, with nothing to do but change the sails as necessary, they were free to walk about and talk.

Father was off somewhere with the captain. I was on the main deck, beside Gabby, with Nadia on her other side. All of us were also dressed in our best clothes. Nadia was pretty in a yellow frock. Gabby had chosen a red plaid that had been made for her. Its cheerful colour suited her well. I had on Mother's tartans, which I discovered fit me after being so long at sea.

Some of the other lasses were wearing dresses of Mrs. Motherwell's that had been made down to fit them. Two had new-made skirts from gabardine and sailors' shirts turned into pretty blouses. They were clustered together close to us, talking so fast in their native tongue I couldn't make out a word. "What are they saying?" I asked.

Nadia clucked. "Abez'iana and Kachka thinking of big weddings they will have. The others want to find husbands, too." She shook her head. "They foolish women to think only of men."

"Ye don't want to be married, Nadia?"

"First I become very rich. I have business; make much monies."

I laughed at the shining in her face. "What sort of business will it be?"

She teased, "I not tell what or maybe someone other do it first."

"Jesus, Mary and Joseph!" Dermot burst in behind us. "There'll be no getting close to a hot-water bath for a week or more with all these boats ahead of us."

Jock, who was with Dermot, said, "They're coming for the gold."

"Is like harbour at Canton," Nadia said.

Dermot said, "'Tis rumoured there's to be a war with the Yankees over the San Juan Island. It must be true. Will ye look at all the navy ships."

Jock laughed. "The navy don't come here to fight. The hottest action they see here is the Sunday horse races at Beacon Hill, and of course the parties given by Fort Victoria's finest. There's many a young officer spends his days here escorting the daughters of the best houses on rides through the countryside. They spend their nights dancing with the daughters at balls and parties, and on Sundays there's the showing off for the daughters, laying larger wagers than they can afford at the horse races. Of course, there are at least thirty willing navy men for every daughter, which some would say gives the daughters a decided advantage." When he said this, he looked at me and then at Nadia with laughter in his eyes. She returned his smile and I pretended not to notice, but I had, and I felt a pang of something I couldn't name.

Dermot sighed. "Thirty eligible men for every eligible woman?"

"At least," Jock said.

"Ah me, won't it be a shame indeed if such welcoming young ladies fail to notice a fine figure of a man such as meself because I'm not wearing a navy uniform nor had a proper bath."

"You?" Jock teased. "You old sea dog. If I know you, you'll moor yourself in the nearest grog shop, and you won't come out till they roll you off the stool and out the door."

"Well, now," Dermot said. "I might have meself a pint or two."

"Just take care to keep enough of your wits about you that you don't come to with your head bloodied, lying in irons in the belly of some ship you don't want to be aboard," Jock said. "Both the navy and the merchants know a good crewman to shanghai when they see one."

It was too close to a compliment for Dermot. He remembered he maun shout orders in his most ornery voice to sailors who were working at lowering yards, and he went up the ladder to the fo'c'sle deck to do it.

No sooner had he gone than Mr. Samuel appeared to hustle the orlop lassies away. "Come, come young ladies. The captain is placed us in the second boat. Come away now."

I embraced my friends, all of us vowing we would see one another again soon. Having little clear idea of the country, I thought Fort Victoria was not London or Liverpool: it would not be hard to find them. Jock was near me still. I turned to him and asked, "Will ye be going to find gold in British Columbia, Jock?" I held a wish he would because then there was the possibility he would visit the island from time to time. And we would no doubt be travelling around the country with Father in his missionary role.

"No. The prospector's life served me well while I was engaged in it, but I've finished with that."

I was disappointed. "Oh. Will ye be going back to England, then?"

"From time to time, but not to stay. John is the one attached to England. I've grown accustomed to this side of the world. There's great opportunity for shipping on this coast and John and I've decided to expand. I'll be based here and I hope —"

Captain Allan came up with two men and interrupted him. "I must beg your pardon, Miss Macqueen," he said, bowing, "and take Jock from ye. Come on, laddie, time to help the customs men make an accurate count of the cargo."

Jock laughed. "Duty, Tess. I hope I'll see you after you are settled."

"Twould be a pleasure for both Father and me, Sir," I answered happily, and with a nod he was away.

I left the deck and went below and circled slowly round our tiny cabin, and a strange thing happened to me. I looked at Father's berth and at my hammock. At the dresser, basin and pitcher. The candleholder bolted on the wall. The two hooks Father had put up and left. I had lived in this room for months and yet it was so alien to me that I might never hae been in't before. My feeling was gone dull.

There were no more days and nights to wait, no more storms or doldrums or fresh winds to sail through. I would hear no more sailors' yarns, nor spend evenings in the wardroom with the other passengers laying wagers on the size of fish someone would catch for breakfast. There would be no more lessons here with darlin' Gabby. But there was neither poignancy nor fervour in my thoughts about those things. It was as if I had not been, and was not now, connected to anything at all.

I looked in the mirror above the dresser and retied the bright green bow that held my hair, put my tam firmly back on my head, and slowly made my way back up the ladder. The decks were all but deserted.

I looked over the side to see the last ship's boat waiting to depart. The sailors and Dermot were dapper in their white duck trowsers and bright blue jackets. Father had a sparkle in his eyes that belied his straight-set mouth. Suddenly the feeling inside me gushed back to life. My brain shouted, *Make haste!* Quickly I climbed down to join the others. At the last second Jock came over the side of the ship and heaved himself in with us.

The pinnace joined the flotilla of ships' boats carrying passengers to and from the landing dock. Our quarter boat, which had the orlop lasses, Mr. Samuel and Mrs. Motherwell in it, was far ahead of us. A thick fog was rolling in, but I could see the landing and a walkway that led up the hill to three little houses at the top. Everywhere there were people, goods and luggage.

There were many different groups of people, and I was curious about them. "Jock," I said, "those men with the guns and knives tied to their belts look someat like ye did when I first saw ye at Salt House Dock. They have so much hair!"

Jock laughed. "Aye, they're prospectors. They keep their hair to keep them warm."

"There are so many of them! And look at the Indians — they are, aren't they, there, squatting on the beach?"

"They are."

I was surprised at how they looked. I had expected them to be dressed in woven-bark capes and skirts, or animal skins, like the ones I'd seen pictures of in books. Instead, the women had tartan shawls or striped blankets pinned around their shoulders and many of the men had on shirts and trowsers underneath old navy coats or blanket shawls. Also, the ones in books were straight and proud-looking, while the group on the beach sat hunched and huddled together near the water's edge, just watching everything.

A sudden shout rang out. It was Mr. Samuel at the dock. "No one lays a hand on these here women now! Get back! You lot'll have your chance!"

The scene in front of us was awful. As Mr. Samuel prodded the lassies up the dock, men fell in in front of them, beside them and behind them, leaving them with very little room to move. Most of these men were dressed like Europeans, wearing jackets and trowsers, white shirts and hats. Like the prospectors, they had a great deal of facial hair, but unlike the prospectors, a number of these had their beards and moustaches neatly trimmed. One or two clean-shaven men stood out. Mr. Samuel shouted again and the lasses, heads bowed and clinging to one another for support, made slow progress. The men dogged their every step.

"Why are they being so rude?" I asked. "Why won't they let the lasses pass?"

"They're settlers in need of wives," Jock said, just as the pinnace reached the dock.

"Up wi' ye now, colleen," Dermot said, and ushered me forward and helped me out of the boat. I stood nervously shifting my glance up the walkway where the lasses and men had gone and then back to Father and Jock, who were setting our luggage on the wharf.

"There they are! That's Macqueen! And that man's Jock Allan!" someone yelled. "Bloody deserters!" Startled, I looked up the ramp and recognized Mr. Rake striding down it at the head of a group of marines. Mr. Rake pointed at my father and at Jock.

Jock immediately called "Away!" and the men at the oars instantly obeyed, lowering their oars and pulling with a will, whereupon the uniformed men began to run toward us on the wharf. One very young man sprinted ahead of the others and got to the landing first. He immediately dropped to one knee, aimed his gun and fired.

I screamed and flew at him and knocked him into the water. He splashed, submerged, and then came only part-way up. He hung just below the surface, working his arms in the feeble way of one who doesn't know how to swim. He stared up through water at me with eyes the size of saucers. I stared back at him, refusing to extend even a hand in his direction. One of his mates dropped to his belly, draped himself over the edge of the wharf with his heels held by another, and poked the butt of his gun into the drowning man's forehead. It was some time before the drowning man became aware he was being poked. When it seemed his lungs must implode for lack of air, he grabbed the stock and was pulled up.

I then revived my purpose of preventing anyone from shooting. I ran up and down the landing shouting at the top of my voice for them not to shoot my father, dodging in front of the marines and causing great confusion. Mr. Rake and Mr. Samuel, who had come back down, each tried to catch and hold me. But I would not be stopped. Suddenly a man who had just arrived at the landing put himself in front of me and said with great authority, "Miss, be quiet and stand still." He surprised me into doing so.

His bearing was very erect and his voice was like a foghorn. He had a large, open, clean-shaven face, except for a fringe of black beard that wrapped around his chin. His forehead was high, his mouth generous and his dark eyes filled with concern.

Turning his attention to the marines, he said, "Are you mad, gentlemen? Do you not see that the harbour is filled with innocent people who might be struck by a stray shot or by a ricochet? Your target is not likely to be the victim of your poor aim. In any case, you are driving this child into a frenzy. Surely no matter what crime her father has committed, you need not shoot him in front of his daughter as if he were a stray dog. Does this colony not run itself by British law?"

The leader of the military men came forward. "Citizens such as yourself, Mr. ..."

"Alfred Waddington at your service, Sir," said the man.

"As I was saying, Mr. Waddington, citizens such as yourself have no business at all interfering with Her Majesty's Navy."

"It is my business when the actions of Her Majesty's Navy affect me directly, Sir, and I must caution you that if you continue in this manner I shall be forced to bring charges against you." It was then he held up his left hand, from which blood dripped.

The officer did not appear impressed. He snapped an order at his men. "Get after the devils!"

"And hold your fire!" Mr. Waddington added. To me he said, "Do you have other escort, Miss?"

"Nay, Sir. But my father has not committed any crime. Mr. Rake ..." I turned about, looking to him for an explanation of the outrage, but in vain. He was nowhere visible. "I shall wait here for my father to come back."

"I fear that would be most unwise, Miss."

"I has a gang of ladies and a governess with me," Mr. Samuel said. "I knows her father very well, us having come all the way from Liverpool on the same ship. I'll take 'er."

"Fine," Mr. Waddington said.

"No, thank you," I said. "If ye are familiar with Fort Victoria and will direct me to a lodging place, Mr. Waddington, I'll wait there for my father."

Mr. Waddington was firm. "I have just arrived this very day with the intention of making Victoria my home, Miss. I have been before on business, but since news of the strike has gotten out in the world the town is changing daily. It has grown well beyond the palisades of the fort and we are but two among thousands of newcomers, many of whom will be only passing through. It is a rough, frontier town. You will be better going along with a gentleman and governess you know."

"Miss Macqueen," Mr. Samuel said, conducting me ahead of him with a sweep of his hand.

By now the pinnace was obscured by fog, and many boats manned by men in uniform had left the shore. Frightened and heartsick, I went with Mr. Samuel up the hill and through the crush of men into one of the houses at the top. There were two rooms inside, one with two officials seated behind desks, the other packed with at least fifty people. The lasses and Mrs. Motherwell were crowded into the far corner in the second room.

Since the day she had been flogged I had only glimpsed Mrs. Motherwell a few times from a distance, and she had been bundled in coat and muffler, no matter what the weather. I hardly recognized her. She was wrapped in a heavy shawl, but one could see her dress hung on her. She was no longer round and had almost the aspect of a frightened, cornered animal, standing as far from the others as was possible, in a sort of crouch, and picking at the front of her skirt. Long pieces of her hair, usually knotted in a tidy bun, bristled out from under her bonnet in all directions at once. She seemed to be staring at nothing at all and did not reply to my greeting. Feeling uncomfortable, I took a spot near Gabby. The place was stifling. Mr. Samuel took some cards from a pocket of his coat and went outside. I wished with all my heart that Father, Jock, Gabby, Nadia and I were back on board the *Borealis* with Captain Allan and Dermot, safe at sea.

When Mr. Samuel had done whatever needed to be done, he ushered us up to the road where a wagon with four mules hitched to it had been loaded with our belongings. The lasses and I climbed into the back, and Mrs. Motherwell was handed onto the seat. Mr. Samuel was occupied for several minutes giving out cards to men in all directions and saying something to them, but it was the driver I was watching. He had checked the wagon wheels and the traces on the harness. He had walked along the line, patting each mule on its rump. Now he was going from mule to mule, putting his mouth against the outside ear of each one of them, and loudly hollering blasphemies. The animals stood absolutely still, their ears barely twitching as each was yelled at and then passed over for the next. When he'd finished this, the driver took the reins and climbed aboard.

"Get on up thar, you sons of Satan!" he yelled. The animals dropped their haunches lower to the ground and leaned into their collars. The traces came taut with their effort as they pushed and strained, and slowly, with a sucking sound, the wheels came up out of the mud and started to roll.

The driver leaned close to Mrs. Motherwell, smiling a rotten-toothed grin. "Can't get nothin' outa them mules less you sweet talk 'em first," he said. "Sweet talk 'em proper, they'll pull two, three ton up a forty-five-degree grade. Pull right over a cliff if'n you ask 'em to do it. Learnt me thet runnin' freight up the Sierra Nevada. Yessiree, nothin' works harder'n a mule what's been talked to proper, ner balks more'n a mule what's been neglected. Sorta like a woman," he added. Mrs. Motherwell continued picking at her skirt and reacted not at all.

Gabby exclaimed at a field of grasses carpeted with blue, white and butter-yellow wildflowers. I drew my legs up under my skirt and wrapped my arms around my knees and watched the passing country: the forests — huge and green-dark; the land — wild and granite-hard; the acres of newly cleared, fallow fields that suddenly opened on either side of the road, their rocky soil littered with massive stumps still bleeding sap. To me it looked a raw, unfriendly place I'd come to.

I HAD been at Mrs. Trump's Boarding House for three days and was seated at the breakfast table with Mrs. Trump and ten gentlemen, also boarders. Gabby and the other lasses had been taken somewhere else that first afternoon. I didn't know where.

"What sorry ting dis be? Not one bite done been gone off'n dis here plate." I jumped. I was still not used to Primrose. At home our servants came and went unobtrusively. If they spoke to us without being spoken to first, it was with a degree of deference. Even at the friendliest of times they would not have been familiar in the manner of this servant, who was as black as dusty coal. She was standing beside and slightly behind my chair, now holding the plate of food I had not touched for the last five minutes.

"You kep et like dat, you gwine be skinny as a wore-out banjo string," she declared. "Aint no good bein' skinny cause firs' man what comes along to pluck you is gwine break you right in half." Reaching forward, she put the plate back in front of me. "You bes' be eatin'. wha's on dat plate, Missy. We gwine be filling you up and put some flesh onto dem sorry bones o' yourn."

I hadn't thought I was "skinny" as she called it, but I looked down at my waist. Where my belt had fitted me perfectly when I left Scotland, it now had a long tail to be tucked in.

"Law sakes, child," Mrs. Trump chimed in. "Primrose is quite right. Ywal aint et enough to keep a bird alive."

Some of the men smiled and I blushed. I stared at the plate Primrose had dished full of fried potatoes and turnips. There were pieces of ham and some other charred meat on the side. Dutifully taking a piece of potato on my fork, I looked at Mrs. Trump. "Uh ... I should like to hire a buggy after breakfast to take me to Esquimalt to inquire about my father, Mrs. Trump. Would ye tell me where I might find one?"

"I'll call Lukas to bring the cart and 'comp'ny you myself, child."

"Oh, I wouldna take ye from your establishment for that length of time," I said.

"Law sakes, it's the very least a body can do for a poor girl what's been left all on her own. Specially when her daddy's been accused of a terrible crime."

I stiffened. "My father has committed no crime at all, Mrs. Trump. If anything, a crime was committed against him when he was attacked and fired upon without warning.

And I should like it very much if ye would call me by my given name, which is Tess."

"Course I will. Now et up all your vittles, do," she said as she broke a piece of stale bread and mopped egg off her plate with it.

One of the men said, "I'd 'preciate some fresh bread and butter, Primrose."

Primrose sniffed. "Lawdy, caint nobody kip 'nough flour to kip up wid bakin' 'nough to feed ywal what're rollin' in here. An' der aint 'nough cows on dis whole islan' to make butter'n milk fer ywal neider. So don' be talkin' t'me bout fresh dis and fresh dat. Aint none."

Not knowing what else to do, I pretended to eat. The gentlemen quickly finished their meals and excused themselves to attend to their various enterprises. Some told Mrs. Trump they would be leaving this morning and would settle up with her at her convenience. She told them she was quite ready to take care of them, and also left the table. Primrose started clearing dishes and eyeing my plate, which still had a great deal of food on it. I brought up another matter.

"Primrose, when I came here with Mr. Samuel he also had several other lasses with him. Do ye ken where they have been lodged?"

She stopped moving. "Miz Sam'l?"

"Aye. And a matron and a group of Russian lassies. The youngest is seven years old and I've told her I will visit her, but I don't know where to find her."

"Aint sayin' I knows."

I studied her. "But ye ken?"

"Aint messin' wid business what aint none o' my affair an' dat's dat."

Her strange reluctance gave me a stab of unease, but I said nothing more. By the time I had gone back to my room for a light wrap and was ready to go, Mrs. Trump and Lukas were waiting to begin the drive to Esquimalt.

A man seated at the desk in the building I'd been in that first day directed us to another of the buildings. Mrs. Trump said this was called Hospital Hill, and these buildings had been intended to house men who might be wounded when the British sent ships to fight the Russians in the northern territory the Russians occupied, called Alaska. But when the British got to Sitka the Russians had evacuated the place, leaving everything behind them, even personal belongings, Mrs. Trump said. So there was no war and these buildings had never been used as a hospital. Now, she said, the Americans were going to buy Alaska from the Russians. The British had had their chance, but they didn't want it.

I recalled Sitka was where Gabby had thought she was being sent when she had been bought. She would have gone to a colony of her own people there. Twas strange indeed, the quirks of fate that had brought us to places we had never thought we'd be.

An officer informed us Father and Jock Allan had surrendered earlier that morning and were being held in yet another building, but they could not be visited as both were being kept incommunicado until their testimony could be taken at hearings which were to be held in due course. The officer did not know when I would be able to see either of them. "I'd wait two days afore trying again meself, Miss," he said.

Beside myself with worry, I petitioned again just to be allowed a few words with Father, but got nowhere. Feeling weary and fatigued, I said I would return, and left.

More ships had come in and the road was again filled with people and conveyances. "Goodness, the place is fairly crawlin'," Mrs. Trump declared. "With all these coming, it will be no time at all before Victoria is as full of people as San Francisco. Law sakes!" she gasped, "Nekid as a jaybird and proud as a pres'dent! You'd think he'd know better with all us white folk about. These heathens do take so long to become anything like civilized."

I turned my head to look and saw an Indian walking on the far side of the road, going in the same direction as we. He was not a dark brown, but a copper colour; had a medium height with legs no longer than my own, and a powerful-looking upper body. He was wearing a large, floppy black hat. Nothing else. To me, from behind, he looked the way the Indians I had seen in books looked. Straight and proud. Mrs. Trump stared and then suddenly remembered me. "Don't look, child. Turn your head away. And this a public road! Law sakes!" She ordered Lukas to gallop the horse so we would leave the Indian behind us, but I managed several backward glances.

I now began to notice some things I hadn't seen on the first trip. At various stages along the sides of the road there were little groups of Indians, all with a sameness about them and an air I could not define. In each group there were three or four females and one man. In each, one of the females stood just at the edge of the road while the others crouched near her, and the man stood a little way down a path that led into the bush or trees, watching the women and girls. All of the men's heads had a curious conelike shape — slanted backward in the forehead and very pointed at the top. Some of the women's heads also had this shape, while others were ordinarily round.

Every now and then travellers stopped at these groups, and when they did, the male Indian would come rushing up the path, and speaking and gesturing to the traveller, seemed to strike some sort of bargain with them. Then the travellers would accompany one or more of the females down the path into the trees. I observed this ritual half a dozen times, becoming more and more curious about the meaning of it. "Who are they?" I finally asked Mrs. Trump, pointing out one such group we were coming to.

"No one at all," she said crisply. "Put them right out of yer mind. Law sakes, with all the excitement I almost clean forgot. Here I was wonderin' what kind of entertainment would be best this evenin' and all the time there's a lovely play to be performed right at our own theatre. That's what we'll do, we'll attend the play."

"That's very kind of ye, Mrs. Trump, but I don't think I ..."

"Nonsense, child. A play's just the thang to lift the spirits up." And she looked as if the matter had been settled.

Farther on we drew abreast of two men dressed in thigh-high boots, coats with tails and top hats. They were carrying carpet bags. "Aft'noon, gentlemen," Mrs. Trump said.

"Aft'noon, ma'am," both replied, touching the brims of their hats.

"Thought I recognized my own countrymen," Mrs. Trump said. "If you don't already have lodging, gentlemen, I'm the owner of Mrs. Trump's Boarding House, the best boarding house in the colony, if I do say so myself, and aint I jest had rooms come available this very mornin'. This here's Miss Elizabeth Macqueen and she's a guest of mine. I'm sure she'll tell you about the quality of my rooms."

I was not put to the test. One of them grinned, "We've bin hearing as how there aint a room to let anywheres in Victoria and we'd be obliged if you have one with a bed. We'll be stayin' about a fortnight."

"Oh, I assure you I have a room," she said. She said nothing about a bed.

"Consider it taken, Mrs. Trump." Extending their hands one at a time, each gave his name.

"Well, now, I can offer you a ride right to my own door for 50¢ each; 25¢ for your bags, and well worth it to keep those fine new boots out of the mud," Mrs. Trump said. "Lukas, stop the cart so the gentlemen can git in. Where ywal from, then?" she asked when they and their bags were in the cart.

The men said they had come up from Los Angeles for talks with the Governor about obtaining a supply of timber from this area for a new sawing mill they had opened there.

"Well, you can see for yerself there's plenty of trees in these parts for that, and people willing enough to make a profit from them. But I can tell you you'll do a lot more business if you talk to Americans about yer idea, gentlemen, because Americans has so much more energy with enterprise than Canadians has." That settled, she asked them if they would care to attend a play that evening to take their minds off business. They said they would be delighted to partake of the performance in the company of ladies such as we, and there seemed now no graceful way I could escape going.

The one-room theatre was filled from floor to ceiling with the murmur of people's conversations. We were seated in the upper balcony. I was on Mrs. Trump's left, while the gentlemen sat on her right. Mrs. Trump was explaining who in the Fort had been responsible for building the theatre. That led her to disclose who had "piles of money made from land speculation and the like."

Conversation stopped when the band that was seated in front of the raised platform stopped tuning their instruments and started to play "God Save the Queen." The audience stood, sang and sat, and a boy carried a placard announcing ACT ONE across the stage.

A man dressed in top hat and tails marched out to where a chair and a table with a mug and plate on it had been put. The "gentleman" sat down and began to pretend he was eating and drinking. When his back was turned, a "fairy" came out and stole his food and drink. The gentleman accused someone in the audience of the theft and removed his table and chair to a different spot, where the eating, drinking and theft were repeated. Again a member of the audience was accused. It continued thus until the whole audience was shrieking its innocence and pointing frantically at the fairy, who managed to elude the vision of the gentleman every time he turned. Finally, a man in the audience who was being accused of the theft bolted out of his seat and gave chase to the "real thief." It was a very acrobatic chase, ending with the fairy being caught, much to the satisfaction of the audience.

ACT TWO started with a man with a black face singing, "Where are you going, my pretty maid, pretty maid?" Suddenly he swung round, revealing his other half was made up as the maid, who replied to the question in a high falsetto. The singer's dexterity in changing his image and his voice from male to female delighted the audience, which clapped and cheered each time he turned. I was swept into the rollicking good humour.

ACT THREE was a variety of hornpipes and Hieland flings, which were danced so becomingly by the actors that my own feet twitched. The performance ended with a round of rousing songs.

During the walk back to the boarding house, Mrs. Trump described and criticized past performances at the theatre. Echoing what Jock had said on the deck of the *Borealis* when we were coming into Esquimalt, she talked, too, about dances and parties held on the ships and in peoples' homes, until I began to think that attending balls, parties and the theatre were the main occupations of all the people living here. At home we had rarely had such entertainments. Our days were filled with various chores and outdoor activities, and when night came we were tired enough to spend the greater part of it in sleep. This night, it was three o'clock when I finally went up to bed, which made the night much shorter. I was grateful for that because the play had been but a temporary distraction for me. As soon as I was alone in my room my thoughts went back to Father.

THIRTEEN

The Hearings
More Secrets Are Revealed

PRIMROSE was unhappy with me at breakfast. So anxious was I to be gone to Esquimalt to see my father, I could swallow almost no food at all. Finally giving up on her efforts to bully me into eating every morsel on my plate, she surrendered to my state. "Miz Trump busy but she say kip my eye on ywal. So thet's what I'm gwine be doin'. Don't be thinkin' ywal goin' to anywheres thout ol' Primrose cause I's comin' an' tha's all." Again, Lukas drove.

At Esquimalt, Primrose and Lukas waited in the cart while I went down to the same building I'd been in the day before. The officer informed me I could be present at Father's hearing, which, he said, was to begin shortly. I was angry and grateful at the same time. Angry I might have missed the hearing if I'd waited two days to return, as the officer had said yesterday; grateful I was here. My spirits picked up when Captain Allan came and I learned he was to be a witness on Father's behalf.

Another officer showed us into the hearing room and directed us to sit in wooden chairs ranged along one wall. In the centre of the room there was a large table, behind which three men dressed in full military attire already sat. A single chair had been placed in front of the table and when Father was brought in through a door on the side of the room opposite us, he was taken to that chair.

When he was seated, one of the men at the table picked up a scroll and read, "Iain Alistaire Macqueen, you have herewith been charged with the grave offense, punishable by death, of desertion from Her Majesty's Navy in the year of our Lord eighteen hundred and forty-one. The Court is ready to appoint a Naval Advocate for you, Sir, should you require one."

"I do not require it," Father said.

"So be it. How do you plead to the charge, Sir?"

"I am innocent of desertion or of any other dereliction of duty while I served in the British Navy, Sir," Father said.

"The plea is 'Not Guilty.' We will proceed. Captain Allan, you are called to testify."

The captain stood and walked to the table. A scribe came around and held a Bible out to him. "Place your right hand on the Bible, Sir. Captain John Andrew Allan, will you swear to Almighty God on the Holy Bible that the testimony you are about to give this Court will be purely the truth and nothing but the truth?"

"On my oath, I do swear it."

The man who had read the charge said, "What is your association with Mr. Macqueen, Captain Allan?"

"Mr. Macqueen has been a passenger aboard my ship, the *Borealis*, on a passage from Liverpool to Fort Victoria. In the more than four months he was aboard I had the good fortune to be closely associated with him."

"Is the Court to understand your testimony on his behalf is to be based solely on that acquaintance, Captain Allan?"

"I'll turn the question back on ye, Sir. You are a navy man. Would any navy captain be expected to survive in his position if he couldna gain a true knowledge of any person aboard his ship in fewer than four days?"

"He has a point," the man in the middle said.

"Aye," Captain Allan said, "and merchantmen have nae the benefit of navy progression of training, or of navy discipline in handling a crew. Like as not *we're* forced to take the measure of a new man *before* our ships leave the dock."

"You have made your point, Captain," the centre man said. "Please proceed."

Captain Allan looked around the room. "Is it not the policy of the Court for the accuser to be present at a hearing? I dinna see Mr. Rake."

"Mr. Rake will not be joining us this morning," one of the tribunal said. "He has given us a sworn statement which has been read by each of us."

"I have not read Mr. Rake's statement," Father said.

"That will be your privilege after all testimony on your

behalf has been heard, Sir. Say on, Captain Allan."

Father had never been one to tell tales of his own child-hood or early adult life, and I now heard a story that I had never before heard.

"Mr. Macqueen is a gentleman and an humble man," Captain Allan began. "He wouldna relate the full details of the circumstances he was forced to tolerate under Mr. Rake, but I can assure ye, Sirs, his actions were estimable, especially when tis considered he was but a lad when the incident what has caused him to be wrongly charged with desertion took place."

One of the tribunal said, "There is no jury of laymen here, Captain Allan. Only officers, well versed in marine law. This is not an arena for emotional pleas. Kindly stick to facts."

Captain Allan's manner became official. "The facts, gen-tlemen, are well known to the Admiralty in London and will be substantiated by documents currently housed at the Admiralty. At the age of sixteen, Mr. Macqueen signed on HMS *Elgin* for one tour of duty. At the time, Mr. Rake were second mate of that ship. Before a fortnight passed, Mr. Macqueen had first-hand knowledge Mr. Rake were unjust with his power over those of lesser rank. Because Mr. Macqueen was an educated and articulate man, which I and you, gentlemen, know most of the sailors serving before the mast are not, the ordinary seamen of the *Elgin* began to look to him for guidance in the grievances they were piling up against Mr. Rake. Mr. Macqueen made a written list giving the details of injustices and brutality. This he intended to present to Captain Crane, a man well known in the navy for his ability to receive evidence and render impartial and correct judgements when he were sober." The Captain paused and then continued, "Mr. Rake found out aboot the list and Mr. Macqueen's intentions, and henceforth bullied Mr. Macqueen, using every excuse he could to administer punishment that was unwarranted."

"You were not aboard Her Majesty's Ship *Elgin* at the time in question, were you, Captain Allan?" one of the tribunal asked.

"I was not, Sir."

"Then your 'evidence' is merely hearsay, Sir, and inadmissible to this Court."

"Hearsay! I should say not, Sir, for every word I have said is documented in the testimony of those what served with Mr. Macqueen on the *Elgin*."

"Let the man speak," the centre officer said. "Say on, Captain Allan."

The captain told of Mr. Rake making life aboard the *Elgin* so intolerable for Father that Father applied to Captain Crane to be transferred to another ship. Captain Crane agreed, but before the transfer could be effected, Captain Crane died of what Captain Allan called "his affliction." There was a shuffle and the first mate of the *Elgin* was assigned to another ship, while Mr. Rake was raised, temporarily, to the rank of captain of the *Elgin*. Mr. Rake promptly cancelled Father's transfer. But Father, Captain Allan said, got hold of the original order and applied to the captain of another ship, which agreed to take him on if he could get his captain's approval.

To save face, Mr. Rake said he would agree *if* the second ship would provide him two men in the place of one. The captain of that ship, "a shrewd man ye will agree," Captain Allan said, "unloaded two crew members what had been dragged into service by a Press Gang and were rebellious and troublesome, to serve in the place of Mr. Macqueen." Captain Allan said when Father finally got to London, he presented himself in front of the authorities and gave them a copy of his documented evidence against Mr. Rake. As well, he informed the authorities of Mr. Rake's interference with his original transfer, which Captain Crane had approved.

An inquiry was called and a lengthy process begun of rounding up and hearing the testimony of all who had served on the HMS *Elgin* under Mr. Rake. The captain of the ship Father was transferred to was also questioned. While the hearings were taking place, Mr. Rake was taken on as second mate aboard another ship, but before he'd served there thirty days he was broken back to ordinary seaman because of his brutality. This, Captain Allan said, he had heard himself, because seamen were a small community, after all, and one of his own men had served aboard that ship.

When all the testimony had been heard, Mr. Rake was found guilty of tyranny, and any rise in his career came to an abrupt standstill. He was told his future in the navy held nothing more than continuous duty as an ordinary seaman before the mast, no matter how long he should remain in the service. "With that judgement before him, Mr. Rake resigned from His Majesty's Service," Captain Allan said. "I submit that Mr. Rake, seeking to secure revenge for the disgrace he brought upon himself, has falsely accused Mr. Macqueen of desertion. You need not take my word for Mr. Macqueen's innocence, gentlemen. But send for a dispatch from London giving an account of the hearings that found Mr. Rake guilty of tyranny and ye will have your proof."

It took less than a minute or two of conference before the centre man in the tribunal said, "Very good, Captain Allan. We will send for these documents. However, until we receive them, Mr. Macqueen, we shall require you, Sir, to remain in Victoria and to keep yourself at our disposal. If you will give us your word as a gentleman that you will abide by these conditions, we will release you on your own recognizance."

"Done," Father said. After he had put it in writing, he was told he was free to go.

I was barely able to restrain myself until we were outside that somber chamber to leap at Father in my joy and kiss his cheek, and then at Captain Allan for his part in it. I quieted, though, when Jock was brought into the building under guard.

Seeing our excitement, Jock smiled and came and shook Father's hand.

"I'm only sorry, Sir," Father said, "that your good conscience on my behalf has brought ye to this."

"And I am sorry, Iain, that it was my unthinking action of ordering the boat away from the dock that has kept you incarcerated these two days. I hope you and Tess both will forgive me."

"If you require forgiveness, Sir, then tis freely given. Twas nowt but what any man fearing the worst would do," Father said.

"Will ye ask for counsel, Jock?" Captain Allan asked.

"There is no need for it. I must own up to my guilt."

I could not believe Jock was guilty of anything, and I sought to put the blame elsewhere. "Twas Mr. Rake who pointed his finger and denounced ye both and the military that did the shooting with no more evidence against you than that. In Scotland, every man accused has the right to defend himself."

"Aye," Father agreed. "At least allow us to speak as character witnesses on your behalf, Jock."

"All right," Jock agreed. "It might do some good."

"But of what crime could the navy possibly hold ye to be guilty? Ye were but a lad of thirteen when you left your ship, and were ye not following the lead of those around you?" I cried.

"I was very near the age you are now, Tess," Jock said gently.

"Would you have others held responsible for your own acts?"

"Well I ... I dinna ken, Sir. I have not been in circumstances to be so tested."

"Time, Sir," the man at Jock's elbow said, and took him into the room.

"Best ye wait out here, lass," Father said. He and Captain Allan went into the room and I was left alone in the hall. There were two chairs by the wall to the left of the door. I sat. The thirty minutes Jock's hearing took seemed more like thirty years.

I could glean nothing of the verdict from Father's and Captain Allan's faces when they came out. "What is it?" I begged. "What's to happen to Jock?"

"We dinna ken, lass," Father said. "We maun wait."

A few minutes later, Jock, minus his guard, came out. I took this for a good sign but was immediately dismayed when he said, "I could have been ordered hung," and then I was greatly relieved when he added quickly, "happily that is not to be my fate. Thanks to you, Iain, and you, John, the navy will be content with a fine and a term in gaol. I've given my word I will present myself tomorrow morning to be shipped out for England."

A term in gaol did not sound a proper place for Jock to me. "Why cannot the navy be merciful?" I demanded. "Ye've done nae harm to anyone."

Jock smiled. "Ah, but there's merit in their pronouncement, Tess. I am told to consider myself lucky, and indeed

I am much luckier than the navy knows. I had need to return to England for a short time; now I'll do so at their expense. And again at their expense I'll be provided with a fine opportunity to catch up on my correspondence, and sleep, of which I've been much deprived of late."

I did not share his sense of merriment. "What of Mr. Rake? What's to be his punishment?"

"He is free to go his own way."

"How can he be let off free when he makes false accusations against others and leads a man to suffer for what was no crime at all?"

"It is sometimes the way of the world, lassie," Father said.

Determined not to be appeased, I said, "That is no excuse at all."

"No one is excusing it," Father said.

"Well, Jock," Captain Allan said, "there are things to discuss."

"I'm bound to the land until I sail, John. We'll have to stop at the Moses house tonight."

"Aye. Ye'll pay of course, as tis your folly what will cost us the price of a room," Captain Allan said. Then he turned to Father. "By the bye, Iain, the *Princess Royal* will stand in at Esquimalt the day after next and your brother, Hammond, is reported among its passengers."

"Uncle Hammond? But I thought he was coming on the *Leviathan*, Father."

Father said, "Something changed. Thank ye for the news, John." To my delight, he added, "If ye'll permit it, Jock, I'm certain Tess will agree that we'd like to accompany ye to the dock tomorrow."

"I'd be honoured to have your company," Jock said.

Shortly thereafter we parted from the Allans and returned to Victoria, where Mrs. Trump welcomed Father into her house, giving him another room that had "just come available that morning." The doorway was a bit of cloth hung over a hole in the boards of the wall that separated it from the room Father had to pass through to get to his room, and both rooms had several occupants each. In Father's room, six, all wearing their boots and guns, were crowded into a bed meant for one.

When he complained about it, Mrs. Trump said, "Now don't you worry about disturbing any of them other gents, Mr. Macqueen. They are gone out most of the night and they spends their days in a stupor. They aint like to notice you a bit."

"It's no disturbing them that worries me," Father said. "'Tis avoiding the spittle that comes in a stream from each man on the bed at various intervals."

Mrs. Trump laughed. "Just find a corner of yer own far enough from the bed and you'll be all right. Or you can try another house if you've a mind, but this one is the best there is. Aint no room anywheres in town."

Father opted for the parlour floor and a blanket from his trunk, which he kept in my room.

THE gig we had hired was rattling along the moonlit road with me, Father, Captain Allan and Jock in it. The landscape was so quiet it seemed nothing was stirring except us and the wind in the trees. Captain Allan said the *Borealis* was bound for Owhyee in the Sandwich Islands, then Singapore, Macao, Canton, Rangoon, Lisbon and many other ports of trade before it finally arrived back at Liverpool. Jock was to go on HMS *White Gull*, which had set a straight course for England.

In the harbour there was a good deal of action, most of which we could hear but couldn't see, it being too dark. Strident orders and "aye ayes" and the clanking of anchor chains echoed across the water as sailors scurried about on the decks and in the rigging of the ships. Sometime in the night more ships had arrived. Freight and people were being ferried back and forth. Both *White Gull's* and *Borealis'* boats were already waiting at the end of the little dock, which was almost obscured with piled goods. There were six marines in the *White Gull's* boat.

Father shook hands with Captain Allan and then with Jock. "I hope to see ye back in the colony ere long. God's speed to ye both."

"Aye, God and Neptune willing, the *Borealis* will be back two year from now," Captain Allan said.

Jock picked up my hand and kissed it. "When next I see you, Miss Macqueen, you will be a woman."

His merry-lighted eyes belied his circumstance, and looking into the depth of them I felt my own feelings rush and tumble in confusion and a blushing rise of warmth. I wanted to be annoyed with his teasing of me, but I could not. The two years and more he would be gone seemed a very long time to me. To hide my inner disorder, I joked back. "And when next I see you, Mr. Allan, ye will be a reformed man." At which he laughed heartily.

"I shall write to ye while ye are in gaol, Jock," I said.

"I'll welcome your letters."

Too soon the ships' boats pulled away from the dock. It was not long before HMS *White Gull*, smartly manned by career navy men, was leaving the harbour. It was still too dark to see that distance, but I thought I saw someone waving in our direction from her deck, and I imagined it must be Jock.

As we were getting into the gig a man approached us. I was surprised to see that it was Mr. Waddington. He touched his hat and inclined his head to me. "It is indeed a pleasure to see you again, Miss Macqueen. I hope you are well. And your father? Have you word of him?"

"This is my father, Mr. Waddington. Father, this is Mr. Waddington, the gentleman I told ye about."

"Ah," Mr. Waddington said, "then it is indeed a happy occasion. You have been reunited."

"Tess has told me of the kindness you showed her, Mr. Waddington, and I'm much obliged to ye for it and pleased to meet you," Father said. "If you dinna have transportation of your own, we would be pleased were you to accompany us."

"Thank you," Mr. Waddington said. "I am glad to accept."

The two men chatted amiably while I sat silent, being almost overwhelmed with the speed of changing fates.

❧

Father hired a cart and we drove again to Esquimalt, this time to meet the *Princess Royal*. Uncle Hammond had debarked and was hiring an express wagon when we pulled up. There were greetings and inquiries all round. I thought Uncle had the air of someone carrying a great burden, his round face pulled long and his movement heavy, but he said he was quite well. He signalled to an Indian, who lifted a trunk and carried it to our cart and loaded it. Uncle produced a coin which he tossed to the Indian, who bounced the piece in the palm of his hand and then bit it. His face split in a grin. He said something Uncle seemed to understand.

"What did he say, Uncle?" I asked.

"He called me a *Tyee*."

"What does that mean?" I wanted to know.

"That I'm an important man to them."

My reply to that was, "Oh."

"How was your voyage, Hammond?" Father asked as we bounced and jolted through and over the great ruts in the road.

"Intolerable. I had to cancel my passage on the *Leviathan* because it was run aground almost as soon as it was in the water and so is now in drydock being repaired. I was forced to endure the crossing on the *Nugget*, which was run aground by her incompetent master at the mouth of the Columbia. I shall sue both the *Leviathan*'s and the *Nugget*'s shipping lines for the fiasco. They have caused me a great deal of inconvenience."

"Was anyone hurt by the accidents?" Father asked.

"Fortunately for the *Nugget*'s captain, no one was in danger of drowning because the *Princess Royal* was in the area and was able to take us off her. But it will not save him from losing his captain's papers, I promise you. The captain of the *Leviathan* has already been dismissed. There's nothing but incompetence around. The imbecile I hired to look after my accounts here has made a botch of things. And the scoundrels who run the *Borealis* have cost me dearly."

"The *Borealis*. But that's the ship we came on," I protested, "and 'tis run by Captain Allan."

"Captain Allan!" Uncle Hammond almost spat the words. "He and his wretched brother. I'll do my best to see those two broken."

"I dinna ken what has caused your choler concerning them, Hammond, but I have known Captain Allan and Jock Allan for more than four months and they are fine, honest men," Father said.

"Honest men, Iain? Jock Allan is a traitor to the Crown. If that isn't enough, they've charged me hundreds of extra dollars to pay for their own abuse of power. Had I known their character I should never have engaged the *Borealis* to transport any cargo of mine. I'll not make that mistake again."

Father blanched. "Then ye dinna ken the truth of what caused the extra money to be spent, as I have not known until this moment all the things ye import to the colony. Twas Mr. Samuel and Mrs. Motherwell who were at fault, not John Allan. Ye can thank his actions, and Tess who sounded the alarm, for saving the lives of those ye refer to as yer 'cargo.' Whatever the extra cost charged to ye, Hammond, ye can be certain it was warranted."

"I fear your judgement, Sir, is as damaged as your own record. I am sorry to say I am sorely disappointed in you. Not only am I shamed to find the good name I have worked to build here sullied with charges levied against Macqueen as soon as you set foot in the place, Iain, but I must advise you the Missionary Society is extremely particular about the character of any it gives positions to. This disgrace ..."

I leapt in. "Father has brought no disgrace to anyone. He is innocent of any charge."

"You are rudely interrupting me," Uncle Hammond snapped. "The crime of desertion, Iain, is a heinous one."

"I've nae doubt that if ye've heard the charges, ye've also been informed the resolution of them is forthcoming," Father said.

"I sincerely hope that resolution will be satisfactory to my good name. As for your chances with the Missionary Society ... any hint of scandal is enough to withdraw a man's name from recommendation. I'll have a great deal of difficulty maintaining my own position in favour of you with them."

My father's voice was perfectly modulated when he said, "Dinna worry, Hammond. Ye'll no have the need to maintain anything on my behalf."

Uncle Hammond pursed his lips. "I shall be engaged for the next few days in seeing the goods to be delivered by the *Rose* to various locations are loaded aboard her, and that all the papers are in order. While I'm in Victoria I will be staying at the European Hotel. When the *Rose* is ready to depart, you and Tess will of course accompany me as far as Genoa, where you will, I trust, find my house more than adequate for your needs until you can find your own accommodation. I shall be continuing on with the *Rose* to the ports where I have goods to be delivered to make sure there are no further abnormalities in my accounts."

"I've given my word I'll remain in Victoria until the dispatch from the Admiralty in London has been received by the Navy here," Father said. "I'm certain ye'll appreciate the importance of my keeping that agreement."

"Quite," Uncle Hammond said.

Inside, I rejoiced. This must mean we would not have to live with Uncle Hammond. Knowing it was ignoble, I silently wished the dispatch from England would never arrive. That thought was pushed aside by another as I fully realized what Father and Uncle had said. It was Uncle Hammond who had brought the lasses to the colony. "Uncle," I said, "I have been trying without success to discover the whereabouts of the lasses since we arrived. Please tell where they are gone. I want to visit Gabby and Nadia."

"Gabby?" Uncle grimaced at the name.

"Gabrielle. She is the youngest ..."

"That will do. I am well aware of who she is. It is entirely inappropriate for a young lady of your station to associate herself with a person of hers."

"But I have promised ..."

"Promises loosely made are easily broken."

"I dinna want ..."

"No doubt they are in a place inaccessible to you. In any case, I should not permit your association with them. Reconcile yourself to that."

I bit my lip, then said, "I will not be reconciled to anything of the kind."

Over my head, in a mild tone, Uncle Hammond delivered his judgement of my behaviour to my father. He spoke as if I were not present at all. "Elizabeth's obstinate refusal to yield to the will of one in authority over her is an indication of how long she has been permitted to act without the proper control. If this indulgence continues, it will ruin her for society. It's a pity there are no proper schools for her in the colony, but until she can be sent abroad it will benefit her to be under the correcting influence of my household, Iain."

Father's reply was not what my uncle wished to hear. "I believe your household might benefit from having a lass like Tess in it, Hammond."

My nerves were shuddering at the mere thought of what my uncle's household might be like.

F ATHER left immediately after breakfast and was out when Mrs. Trump presented me with three cards requesting us to call. I knew nothing of this custom and was surprised to read that Doctor and Mrs. Sebastion Helmcken requested the presence of Mr. Iain Macqueen, 4th Laird of Lochaber, and his daughter, Miss Elizabeth Macqueen, at supper on Wednesday night. Supper to be sat at 6:30. RSVP.

The second note had been left by the Misses Penrice, asking us to luncheon, and the other was an invitation to join a riding party leaving from Craigflower at ten o'clock the following morning, and later to attend Colwood, the home of a Captain and Mrs. Edward E. Langford, for a party in honour of the arrival of the naval ship, *Princess Royal.*

"There's five Langford girls," Mrs. Trump said, "and if they aint been a magnet to the navy boys since the day they got here, honey don't draw bees. The youngest of them girls aint much older'n you."

The prospect of the double pleasure of riding and of meeting girls my own age put me in a fever of excitement. I could hardly wait for Father to get home.

Shortly after, the front door of the house opened and closed and Father stopped in the doorway to the parlour. Running to him and thrusting the Langford invitation into his hand, I started with the plea, "And there are these two other invitations as well. May we go, Father?"

He put them into his pocket. "I've nae the time now, lass. I will talk with ye at tea." He went immediately to the stairs and up them, giving me no time to voice my disappointment. A few minutes later he came back down and left the house again. I looked out the window to see him climb into a buggy with Uncle Hammond and drive off. Fighting back my disappointment, I stared out at the bright day. Suddenly I longed for the freedom of Dunharbar so intensely I could sit no longer inside a house. Making my own excuses to Mrs. Trump, I went to my room, collected a shawl, and slipped quietly out.

Fort Victoria was rowdy with the noises of the cutting and hammering of wood, accompanied with a vibrato of the loud shouts and curses of the builders. There were dozens of new buildings going up. To me, most of the completed construction looked rudely finished, and new framework made of wood appeared spindly. I much preferred the stone and brick of Scotland.

In front of the buildings there were wooden walks and

in front of them open ditches that ran with pungent brown-black sludge. In the middle of the streets, what had been a quagmire of mud a few days ago was now a swirl of dust rising from the wheels of vehicles, the hooves of mules and horses, and the feet of walkers. There were people everywhere. I wanted the country.

I set off toward the only road out of town I knew — the one that led to Esquimalt. Tramping north and east I came to a street labelled Yates Street and turned down it toward the water. In a quarter of a mile I came to Wharf Street, turned right, and followed it north and west till I reached the bridge that spanned the gorge separating Victoria from the Songhee Indians' reserve.

I crossed over the bridge and stopped. There were far more Indians here now than there had been even when we had arrived, their tents massed behind the long wooden houses down by the shoreline and on the slopes of the brae until very little ground was left that had not a shelter on it. Where there was not a tent or housing, the ground was covered with refuse of every description. I could hear voices coming from some of the tents, but there were only a few women and children visible outside them. Would they let me pass? *Dinna be silly*, I chided myself, *they've not stopped you before*. But I had never passed through their settlement on foot and by myself before.

I took a breath and proceeded to stroll along the road that bisected the settlement. Near the road, a group of children was playing a game in the dirt with sticks and stones. A little distance from them, some dogs slept curled up in the sun, while others fought over some of the bones that lay thick on the ground. Seated on mats outside a large tent not far away from the dogs, two old women and one young one were weaving baskets. The old ladies laughed with toothless, or almost toothless, grins. The young one kept her head down and went on with her work.

I had gone just a wee distance farther when some of the children dropped what they were doing and stood up. I walked faster and then faster still as they began to chant in melodic, high-pitched voices. When I reached the other side of the reserve I was panting and moving very fast, but my chest was less constricted with fear as I seemed to have left the children behind me and no one else had followed me.

I didn't go far along the road before I was beguiled by the pale gold sunlight filtering through dark green boughs and spilling onto sword ferns in the forest. I looked up, craning to see the tops of the huge trees, and felt as small to them as an ant might feel to me. Nothing at home compared to the size of them. A person sitting on a swaying, topmost branch might see a hundred miles out to sea. Or clear to the other side of the island. What boundless possibilities were up there in those trees? Fir and pine and cypress. Oak trees, too, grew here, their branches covered with the delicate green of new leaves. There was every colour green imaginable, and the colour and the coolness of the forest drew me in. The ground was soft and clean, carpeted with needles and moss. Happily inhaling smells of damp growth, of bark and sun, I followed a faint track. Water rushed and bubbled in the distance. A squirrel chitted. For the first time since coming to the colony, I felt at peace.

Walking uphill, away from the sea, I followed the path to where it levelled out and ran beside a burn. I stopped and sat on a rock and trailed my fingers in the clear, cold water. Minnows darted here and there. A little way upstream, a sunray slanted through the giant trees and turned a tarn into a pool filled with dazzling sunflies swimming on its surface and bouncing, fluttering high into the air.

From farther upstream came a faint sound of voices. Curious, I got up and followed the sound, climbing over and around downed trees, boulders, roots and other obstacles. In places, the footpath left the creek and I lost it and had to search to find it again. I heard a sobbing sound, and turned my head. Two Indians were standing in an open spot near an immense cypress tree. The girl was dressed in white women's clothing — a torn blouse that stretched tight over her bosom, and a long skirt. The man had on a breechcloth. The two of them were deep in con-versation. She was greet, the tears flowing freely down her face. I stood motionless, mesmerized by the scene, and then he turned his head in my direction. His black eyes, outlined with red, seemed to burn a line right through tree trunks. Their message spurred my legs. I ran, not stopping until I'd reached the Songhees' village again.

The children were ready for me, not merely standing and chanting now but coming at me, grabbing hold of my skirt and shawl, pulling me. The girl who had been with the old women came out and waved them away from me. She strode toward me, and stopping a foot in front of me, held up a finished basket with one hand while she pointed at my shawl with the other. *She wants to trade!* I thought, surprised.

She wore rings made of abalone shell in her ears, a silver ring in her nose, and several silver bracelets on her arms. In spite of her pointed head and her frown, I thought her bonny. I also thought her work must be worth far more than my everyday, rough shawl. The basket was exquisite, with tiny animals made from darker grasses worked into the light overall design. The weave was tight; the pattern intricate. The animals, I thought, were goats. I didn't move and she pointed again and pushed the basket toward me. I removed the shawl and held it out to her. She snatched it, tossed me the basket, and without a word went back to the tent and disappeared inside it. I walked slowly back to Mrs. Trump's.

"Law sakes child!" Mrs. Trump called when she spied me through the parlour door. "We've been worried sick over you. Come right in here and sed down!"

I went into the room where she and the two American gentlemen were seated. "Good afternoon, Mrs. Trump, gentlemen," I said.

"Good afternoon, Miss," the men said.

"Now have a cup of tea," Mrs. Trump said, "and tell us where you got to."

I set the basket down to take the cup she was offering. "I'm sorry if I've caused ye to worry, Mrs. Trump. I was only out for a walk. Look," I said, holding up my basket. "A lass in the Songhee village gave this to me in return for my shawl."

"Mercy! Ywal went all the way to the village by yerself! If yer father knew I'd allowed you to do thet, he'd skin me alive."

Remembering my own fright, and feeling somewhat ashamed of it, I denied it. "Tis no very far, Mrs. Trump, and I was made welcome there."

She shook her head. "The Indians will trade with anyone, but these are dangerous times. I'd surely 'preciate it if you didn't go off like that again without a word, I surely would."

I sighed, saying neither aye nor nay to her. Mrs. Trump had no husband, at least not one that was present. She must sometimes go out and about by herself, I thought.

Father returned at suppertime. During the meal I again brought up the subject of the invitations, which inspired Mrs. Trump to begin a lengthy description of the most prominent families in and around the fort. We all politely listened. When we had finished eating, Father said he would like a word with me in my room.

"Ye've had a pleasant day, Tess?" he began.

"I've had a wonderful day." Showing him my basket, I said, "Twas made by a Songhee. She exchanged it for my shawl and I dare say I got the better of the trade. Do ye fancy it?"

"It is handsome," he agreed.

"Aye," I said, swelling with pride. "I went past the Songhee village, and a little way down the road I went off it into the forest and climbed a hill." I hesitated, seeing now how pale and pinched his face was, and then I chattered on in hopes of cheering him. "The countryside here is truly beautiful, Father. Mrs. Trump says tis too dangerous for me to walk about on my own, but I dinna feel it so. At the Songhee village no one took any notice of me at all except the children, who only wanted to play, and the one lass."

"Mrs. Trump is a kindly soul," he said.

I knew the truth of this and agreed. "Aye."

"She has lived in the colony for a number of years. It would nae doubt be wise of ye to heed her advice." He studied me a moment. "I've asked a great deal of ye these past months, daughter, and I've more to ask."

I waited, almost holding my breath. Almost beginning to shake.

"I have secured permission from the navy to accept employment outside Victoria, and I have a position in the coal mine at a place called Coleville, which some call Nanaimo."

"What of your position as a missionary?"

"The Missionary Society has decided I will be better fit for service after I've spent a year or two learning the customs and the language of the natives. They are right in that." He paused and then went on. "The arrangements at Nanaimo are for a single man. I canna take ye with me. Your uncle will take ye to Genoa with him." I was hardening with refusal when he added quietly, "Hammond is the only family we have here and he is willing to provide fully for you, Tess."

"But ..." I began, and stopped. I dropped my eyes to the floor. Slowly I asked, "What length of time will it be before you and I are to be together?"

"I dinna ken. A few months, perhaps a year. Hammond has told me the *Rose* will be ready to sail a few days from now. I'll be travelling on it with ye and will see ye off at Genoa before the *Rose* goes north to Fort Rupert. In the meantime, I have accepted the Langfords' invitation, both for riding in the morning and for the party in the evening."

The pleasure I would have had from this last was undone by the former news. My mind was filled with a prayer we would not be apart for a year. We had been separated for months before, when Father had gone to the mines, so I thought I might handle a month or two. I looked at him, attempting to smile, but "All right" was all I could manage to say.

SIXTEEN

Uncle Hammond's House
Where Tess Meets the O'Reillys

F OUR days after my arrival in my uncle's house, I was sat in a low chair looking up at him in his seat behind his desk. Uncle had returned from his trip on the *Rose* that morning, and after I'd met and greeted him he had spent some time closeted with Miss Bigget. Their conference ended, Miss Bigget came and told me I was wanted in Uncle's study. I had gone directly. Uncle was examining some papers on his desk and I was becoming annoyed with waiting when he finally raised his head and said, "I trust you are comfortable in your room, Elizabeth?"

Miss Bigget had told me Uncle's ten-room, Elizabethan-style house was the grandest house outside Victoria. "Aye, Uncle," I replied, "'tis a lovely house. I've walked all round the property, over Octopus Point to Maple Bay. With the water on three sides and the high bluff behind us it is a very pretty, peaceful place."

He looked pleased when he replied. "The property is well

sheltered from the elements, and has good land. It will be very valuable some day." After a slight pause he added, "Miss Bigget informs me you have been bathing in the ocean."

My hair, wet from the early swim I had taken before he had been brought to shore in a ship's boat, was plaited and still damp on my back. I answered enthusiastically, "Aye. Tis wonderful, Uncle. The Pacific Ocean is very much warmer and gentler than the Atlantic and there is much to see on the bottom."

In the same placid voice, he said, "You have a penchant for indulging in an utter lack of restraint and decorum, Elizabeth, as I witnessed at Craigflower and Colwood. It is past time you were guided by a stern hand."

Caught off guard and shocked, it took me a moment to conjure up the memory of the delightful day and evening we had spent as guests of the Langfords the day before we left Victoria. I especially had had a wonderful time with Mary and Emma Langford, who were both very kind to me.

"Have you nothing to say for yourself?" Uncle asked in the same mild tone.

"I dinna ken what to say, Uncle."

"It is a parent's or a guardian's solemn duty to guard their wards against an aggregate of evil influences that cannot have any end but your complete moral perversion. My brother did not rebuke you when you tore up and down the green like a jockey, nor did he restrain you from dancing through the night, which enterprise is wicked. The result of his leniency is clear."

"Wicked? I have been told dancing is part of almost every gathering in Victoria. And as for riding, far from rebuking me, Father has always encouraged me to ride. Horse racing is common sport at home. Have ye never participated in it yourself?"

"Young ladies do not engage in sport."

"Captain Langford's daughters are admired for their horsemanship. I was honoured to be invited to join in."

"The willingness of the Langford women to make exhibits of themselves reflects the low society that family is from, and your recounting of injudicious comments made concerning the girls' ability to ride, indirectly praising yourself, is a sin of pride. It demonstrates that you have already been rendered callous to good impressions and hardened to correct religious emotions.

"Dancing, besides being a terrible waste of money, is an evil that has long been prohibited by the church. It leads to nothing but incorrect and even indecent emotion. You are too easily drawn into base entertainments by common people, Elizabeth, and I will not have any niece of mine behaving like a tart. Henceforth you will not collaborate in activities of this nature, nor will you bathe again in public. Is that clear?"

My astonishment and rising anger surfaced in an insolence that could well have been termed wicked. "At Mrs. Trump's and at the Langfords' people from all stations freely min-gled, and all were polite and civil to each other. Indeed, Mrs. Trump has said society in the colony is unlike the old country. That here there is a society of equality. But if I am to consider class in my associations and behaviour, if the Langfords are 'common,' are not we? In Scotland we were middle class. Here, ye are in trade and my father is a labourer, which at home are lower classes. And if I am nae of the upper class, am I not saved from the restrictions that govern the behaviour of those that are?"

"You are impertinent. I believe your sense of propriety has been strained by the change of climate, Elizabeth. You will obey me. You must have a tonic to balance your emo-tions and clear your thinking." He immediately went out and ordered Miss Bigget to give me one.

Miss Bigget stood over me while I drank a foul-tasting mixture. Within the hour I was perspiring heavily. Shortly after that my limbs were very weakened and my head began to ache. I was required to sit still for some hours before I felt it safe to stand up on my legs. I was not hun-gry for supper and the headache continued until the following day.

At breakfast Uncle and I dined in relative silence and then he went out, saying he hoped I had a pleasant day. I had wanted to ask him what neighbours were close by. Instead I sought out Cook, who was discovered in the summer house separating milk. Miss Bigget was there, too.

I came under the shelter of the three-walled room and addressed them both. "I wanted to ask Uncle if there are neighbours close by enough to visit," I said, "but he has gone out before I could."

"There's only Mr. Ordano within miles, and a few men who've come here to cut trees," Miss Bigget said.

"Aye, them what lives in squalor in the backwoods, where like as not a squaw lives with 'em, and the squaws is more'n servants to their masters, if ye gets my meanin'," Cook added.

I recalled Jock saying the Hudson's Bay Company encouraged its men to marry women native to the land, and he thought it was a wise thing. Cook clearly did not. A short distance away by boat was Salt Spring Island, which Father had said had the largest number of settlers in the colony next to Victoria and Nanaimo. I asked about the population there.

"They are young men sent out by their families to learn farming, but their only occupations are hunting, riding, gambling and lying about," Miss Bigget sniffed.

"Are there no women at all?" I asked.

"There are some families. Not many."

On hearing there were whole families a half-day from us by rowboat, I immediately suggested we go and visit, or send out invitations to them.

"They are not the kind Mr. Macqueen visits," Miss Bigget said emphatically.

"There's blacks living over there," Cook said, "and you never knows what the rogues will be up to. Thems as bad as Indians and Lord knows what grief the Indians cause us. All the tribes makin' their 'orrid noises up and down the straits day and night. Then the Yeukeltas and Haidas comes down from the north and there's nothin' but trouble. All them Indians're too close by half if you ask me, specially the Cowitchens under that greedy Chief Saw-se-a."

"They are unspeakable," Miss Bigget said. "If we did not bar the doors to prevent them, the filthy heathens would march right in and steal everything your uncle owns, and worse. We might be murdered in our beds."

The fact that my uncle employed several local Indians to clear his fields and do other work, and that we opened the door and went outside and walked around unmolested whenever we were so inclined, did not appear to be a contradiction to her beliefs.

At supper I asked Uncle about visiting our neighbours. "I have not the time for dillydallying," he snapped, and would discuss the matter no further.

Whatever had happened to cause him to want to be a world unto himself, I still yearned to mix with other people.

❧

After that, while Uncle was at home, I was required to occupy myself with handwork, handwriting, music, French, German and deportment. To otherwise engage my mind, he set me lengthy classical passages to memorize and recite from books I had not hitherto heard of, and which I forgot the title and the author of as soon as I had successfully passed his examination.

One happy subject I stumbled on by seeing some blueprints on his desk was his interest in ships. I found I could divert him to talking about the ships by asking mathematical questions, and when he talked about them he had a keen zest I did not see at any other time. He said he intended one day to own a shipping line of his own. I did not doubt for a minute he would do it.

He was not in residence at Genoa for many days together before business took him off on a voyage once again. Before he left, he gave written instructions of what I was to complete before he returned. When he was gone I finished the work quickly and had a good amount of time to myself.

I soon considered the saving grace of my tenancy at Genoa to be the fact that my uncle was rarely at home. His usual routine when he was home was to leave the house immediately after breakfast and not return until late afternoon, when he would summon me for examination of my work. He would then be in his study until supper. Most often he would take his evening meal by himself, but on the days he did attend the supper table with me, he ate in the nearest thing to silence he could achieve in the face of my prattling, and excused himself directly after supper to retire to his library. In the lengthening light of the early summer evenings I read books I borrowed from his library, and started letters to Father and to Jock. My loneliness for the company of others, and particularly for my father, grew.

When Uncle was gone and I was out, I explored the land. On the Maple Bay side, when the tide had ebbed, I could go along exposed beach for miles. There were vast numbers of birds, fish, seals, dolphins and passing whales, and I loved to watch the ever changing temper of the water. I thought I could understand why sailors left the land to go to sea, and my uncle's fascination with ships. Sometimes I saw Indians in canoes paddling by. I waved and they waved back. I thought it would be wonderful to be out on the water, paddling about wherever my strength would take me, but Uncle said I was not to even think about going out in a boat unaccompanied, and he had no time to muck about in boats.

So for the time being I stayed on the land. When there was no one in sight I went swimming. After all, Uncle had only said I could not bathe in public. However I justified swimming to myself, I began to be caught up in a deception to keep my uncle from knowing I was doing it. After going into the water I was careful to dry my hair fully before returning home, and if Uncle asked what I had done to occupy myself that day I did not mention having bathed.

When the weather was foul, I sewed, beginning to try to create the same kind of tapestries Mother had made. Uncle was very generous, supplying me with whatever threads and material I wanted for this. Or I went out to the barnyard and the stables. I had not done this many times before I asked Uncle's most trusted hand, Billy Trueworthy, if I might feed the animals. He was very happy to oblige me. Taking care of the animals soon became my chore, and some days I was able to have friendly talks with Billy, too. He loved to tell tales about mysterious creatures of the sea that had been seen by his own ancestors.

Three weeks after my arrival, Miss Bigget told me she and Cook and Billy were going to meet the HBC steamer, *Otter*, to pick up supplies. I was delighted and announced I would go, too. When we climbed into Billy's boat, it was a beautiful sun-filled day. The ocean was mirror-like. And Uncle was away for a few days on business.

By the time we got to the Cowitchan Bay shore, off which the ship would anchor, people from every settlement around were there. Whites, blacks and natives had made the crossing from the outlying islands, and for the first time in many weeks I was treated to a festive air filled with laughter and chatter. Children dressed in white shirts and pinafores were running between and around the adults, who stood together in groups, while out in the bay Indians pounded the sides of eleven large canoes with the ends of their paddles in perfect unison, and whooped a long and complex chant. Other Indians walked among the crowd on shore offering strings of fish and baskets of clams and oysters for sale or trade.

We stopped a little apart from everyone else, close to the shore edge. I found myself flanked by Cook on one side of me and Miss Bigget on the other, both of whom were large women. I felt hemmed in. Miss Bigget took on the role of our spokeswoman, acknowledging "How dos" with a curt nod and a crisp "Good day," but that was all. She did not invite anyone to join us or make any introductions. Becoming impatient, I excused myself from the servants and made my way a short distance up the beach.

A small Indian standing near the water's edge alerted us to a change when he pointed to the horizon and called out, "Boat!" I strained my eyes in the direction he had pointed. Able to see nothing but the gently rolling sea, I marvelled at his excellent vision. It was at least ten minutes before the column of smoke curling upward and being left to trail behind the Otter's stack was visible to me.

The steamer, accompanied by canoes filled with more natives, came very quickly into the bay. Close by I heard a voice saying, "... all the news from home and your brother coming to visit! I do envy you, Mrs. O'Reilly!"

I looked around and saw two women standing a little in front and to one side of me. I started toward them. But then I stopped, not wanting to intrude on their conversation.

"I was up all night with the promise of it," the woman who had been spoken to said. "And you have a box and letters to look forward to, Mrs. Erin."

I wonder if I'll have a letter from Father, I thought, and then dismissed it. It was too soon.

Mrs. Erin said, "Have you seen herself, Mrs. O'Reilly?"

This custom, where married women unfailingly addressed one another as "Mrs." even if they were good friends, was much more closely kept in the colony than it ever had been at home. I had seen the strict formality observed in Victoria as well as now.

"Who?" Mrs. O'Reilly asked.

"Miss Macqueen. Not saying a word to the likes of us, she isn't. Too good for us, she is. What airs. Thinks herself Miss Queen of Sheba! And her uncle what he is, bringing females here to serve in sin, and her father nothing more than a labourer."

"Ye do not consider the sins of her relatives are her fault, Mrs. Erin?" Mrs. O'Reilly asked.

"The sins of the father are visited on the child," Mrs. Erin answered.

"Well, I know of no sin her father has committed," Mrs. O'Reilly said. She turned a quarter turn and saw me. "Oh, dear," she said.

I felt the red heat of confused embarrassment rise in my neck and cheeks.

Mrs. Erin then turned and also saw me. "Excuse me," she said to Mrs. O'Reilly. "There's someone over there I want to have a word with." After a short nod and brusque "How do" in my direction, she quickly moved away into the throng.

Mrs. O'Reilly recovered herself first. "I beg your pardon, Miss. I am Mrs. O'Reilly and I do think you must be Miss Macqueen." She had a sleeping bairn in her arms.

"Aye. I am Elizabeth Macqueen and I'm pleased to meet ye, Mrs. O'Reilly." There was another awkward silence. "Tis a bonny wee babe ye have," I said.

"She's a good baby," Mrs. O'Reilly said, smiling.

I smiled back. "She looks an angel. The noise doesn't seem to bother her a bit. Tis very exciting when the steamship arrives, isn't it? So many have come for it."

"Oh my, yes, everyone comes out on boat day. Tis a grand time. We get our supplies and catch up on all the news." We saw that people were debarking from the *Otter's* boats and Mrs. O'Reilly waved. "There's me brother, Mr. Beckley! Don't go away, Miss Macqueen, will you. I'll be right back." She bustled off through the crowd.

For a few minutes all else was lost in the flurry of activity accompanying the landing of supplies and people, and then Mrs. O'Reilly appeared again in front of me with a man in tow. "Miss Macqueen, I'd like you to meet me brother, Mr. James Beckley. James, this here's Miss Elizabeth Macqueen."

Where Mrs. O'Reilly had a fair complexion and blue eyes, Mr. Beckley had a dark, severe appearance with steel-grey eyes that were deeply recessed under bushy brows. His face was clean-shaven, but had the shadow dark men with heavy growths of hair sometimes wear. I had a vague feeling of having seen him before.

"How do, Miss Macqueen," he said.

"James and three more of me brothers have a sheep farm near Fort Victoria, Miss Macqueen," Mrs. O'Reilly said.

"Oh," I said. "How do you do, Mr. Beckley. I've recently come from Victoria. I was lodged at Mrs. Trump's Boarding House. I wonder if we could ..."

A barking voice surmounted the general din and immediately the crowd stilled. The ship's officer in charge of the mailbag had begun to call out names. Everyone wanted to hear his or hers pronounced. I was pleasantly surprised to hear my own quite near the first.

Excusing myself, I hurried forward. In exchange for the packet I was given by him I gave him two, one for Father and one for Jock. I had learned about the boat-mail service when in Victoria, and I told him my father would pay for my letters out when the *Otter* stopped at Nanaimo and delivered him his. My letters were accepted.

The packet I received was a slender bunch of letters tied together with string. I could see the topmost was a single page folded and sealed with wax, addressed to me on the back in Father's hand. There looked to be three more of these, but among them was one envelope. The name of the sender written on the top left corner of the back of this was J. Allan. *Oh!* He had written first! I wanted to find a quiet spot and read immediately what Jock and Father had sent, but Mrs. O'Reilly, smiling widely, caught my eye. Another man had joined her and her brother. My letters would have to wait.

"Miss Macqueen," Mrs. O'Reilly said, "this is me husband, Mr. O'Reilly."

"Welcome to the colony, Miss Macqueen," Mr. O'Reilly said.

He was a short man, as wiry as his wife was plump. He had a full grey and silver beard and moustache, and a head that was bald, when he lifted his hat, except for a silvery fringe that ran over and between his ears, touching the nape of his neck at the back. Where he and Mrs. O'Reilly were identical, was the happiness they reflected in their faces. Looking at them, anyone would feel joy.

"Mr. O'Reilly and I have had a thought twould be a nice celebration of yours and my brother's visits to the area to have you and your father, and your uncle of course, round for lunch. It would give us a pleasure if you all would consent to join us," Mrs. O'Reilly said.

It was a dream come true. "Oh, I do thank ye for the invitation. I should like it very much and I'm sure my father would accept were he here. Unfortunately, he is in Nanaimo. I'm afraid my uncle is away just now, too, and I dinna ken when he'll be returned." I hesitated. "Uh ... I ... if it's na too forward of me, I was planning on an outing tomorrow morning. Perhaps I might ..."

Mrs. O'Reilly beamed. "Tomorrow would be wonderful, wouldn't it, Mr. O'Reilly? The weather is forecast to be fine. My brother and Kieran, that's our eldest, will come over in the skiff and pick ye up and bring ye across for lunch, and return ye home in the afternoon. We'll expect you, won't we, Mr. O'Reilly?"

"We will," he agreed.

Her enthusiasm stretched my own mouth in a wide smile. "I am looking forward to it already. Is it closer from Maple Bay to your home?"

"Yes," she said, "but tis no trouble at all for James to come to Genoa, is it, James?"

He started to shake his head but I said, "I should like the walk to Maple Bay."

"Maple Bay it is, then," she agreed.

Mr. O'Reilly and Mr. Beckley excused themselves to see to some goods now landed on the beach that they must load into their own boat. Mrs. O'Reilly and I talked about time and tides and eight o'clock was set for the pick-up. A few minutes later Mr. O'Reilly came back, commenting on the strengthening wind. It was time for them to go, he said.

"Goodbye, Mr. O'Reilly, Mrs. O'Reilly. I do look forward to tomorrow."

Miss Bigget appeared at my side.

"Good afternoon, Miss Bigget," Mrs. O'Reilly said.

Miss Bigget acknowledged both the O'Reillys with a short greeting and then said to me, "Billy has finished loading the supplies, Miss Macqueen, and we are ready to leave."

I was still caught up in the excitement of meeting people and did not want to leave here, but the O'Reillys were going and I supposed I must, too. "Please give my goodbyes to Mr. Beckley, Mrs. O'Reilly, and tell him I will look for him."

"I certainly will, Miss Macqueen," Mrs. O'Reilly said. Miss Bigget was already walking away. Reluctantly, I followed.

⚓

In my room, I settled myself on a pillow on the floor, my back against the wall. Four letters from Father; one from Jock. I ripped open Jock's.

My Dear Tess,

Just now we are lying hove to about a quarter of a mile off the starboard bow of the Trincomalee, a ship lately out of Leith, bound for Esquimalt. Captain Negie has been taken aboard to speak with her captain. As a consequence, we are afforded some leisure, and I can think of no better way to spend it than to write you a letter.

I hope you and your father are both well. Happily, the Captain is allowing me to fill my days by working alongside the able seamen. He is a very fair fellow, and the officers have taken their lead from him in how they carry out their duties, and so everyone on board is generally in good temper and the work is done with speed and efficiency. The weather has also been excellent and we have been running ahead of a fresh breeze, doing from twelve to fifteen knots.

There is a rumbling among the marines that we have been hailed because the White Gull is to be rerouted. They have been at sea two years and some have sons and daughters they have never seen, which is a pity, and they hope the rumour is false. I of course have a personal interest in see-ing which way it goes.

9:40 a.m. I was called up on deck for a task and have just returned to this. Lieutenant Palm, a marine who has become a friend to me, has told me he thinks White Gull will be sent to India to help put down the Sepoy uprising. He said the war against the Sepoys has been won by Britain, but some believe it is necessary to tidy up the affair by taking Lucknow and making certain there will be no fur-ther thought of mutiny on the part of the Indians by killing all who had any part in it. In spite of wanting to get home, the other marines and crew who heard Palm say this cheered the idea.

I did not endear myself to them when I asked which of them would not defend England were Indian soldiers to swarm over her soil and claim it for their own. Some took my stand for irrefutable proof I am a traitor and a coward, and were determined to deal me instant justice for it. The Lieutenant stepped in, saying Lord Canning deplores the continued slaughter and the looting of Indian possessions currently being carried out by Britons in the name of divine justice, and he has called for mercy. These men call the Governor "clemency Canning" — with an unfavourable meaning to "clemency." But they have served long with the Lieutenant, and respect him to such a degree his intervention gave them pause, and certainly saved me from a beating.

Palm has just come to tell me the White Gull has been

ordered to reroute, though only Captain Negie knows to where. Thus I may not be in England for a while and I will send this with Palm, who is taking the quarterboat to collect Captain Negie. The Trincomalee will deliver it to Esquimalt, where it can be delivered to you, and you will be prevented from addressing any letters you write to me to England. I will write you again as soon as I am let know where I will be. Keep well.

Yours, Jock

I was very disappointed knowing the letters I had just sent to Jock would not reach him, and I was afraid for him. Where would he end up? I knew of the brutal Indian war. Mother and Father had talked of it, and when a peer who was visiting us said Britain was in the right, Mother said that British women and children had certainly not deserved to be slaughtered at Cawnpore, but that the politics of Britain, believing she has a right to take over other lands because we are supposed to be superior governors to the peoples who occupy the places we invade, were wrong in the extreme.

"Yer perspective is a woman's," I remember Lord Courtenay saying.

"Aye, my Lord, it is that," Mother agreed, "but how many Britons live and die in disease and filth? In Scotland and England were not tens of thousands made homeless so a few aristocrats could own large tracts of land?" She answered it herself. "I well know they were, my Lord, and I'm ashamed to say my own family had a part in the land clearings."

Lord Courtenay had allowed her that, but said it did not change that Britain was a superior society to most of the world, if not all.

Mother said she wondered how Britons could feel so superior to others when so much British wealth was funded by the obscene trade in human lives that flowed from her own seaports at the same time as our ships patrolled the oceans to keep other nations from doing the same. Lord Courtenay had changed the subject then.

I later asked Mother what she had meant about our family having a part in land clearings, and she told me the story of how crofters had been dispossessed of their lands so people of the upper class could use it to raise sheep, which a great deal of her family's wealth had come from, and that it had caused the crofters untold misery. I asked what she had meant by the obscene trade in human lives that Britain was part of, too, and she said twas slave trade she was speaking of, and many British fortunes had been established by it, and no one could describe the horrors of people being bought and sold like sheep.

I shook my head with the memory, and then I took a sharp breath. Wasn't the same thing happening on Vancouver's Island? Were not the British and the Americans taking it from the people who lived here? Would these Indians rebel, too, and kill all of us as the Sepoys had killed the Britons at Cawnpore? No, I told myself. On the *Borealis*, the men talked of treaties with these Indians. The British are buying this land, not taking it. It is not the same. I wanted to believe that, so I firmly put the question out of my mind. Hoping Jock would write again very soon and say he was in England, not India, I turned to Father's letters.

The dates were written on the backs to give me their order. I opened the first.

My Dearest Daughter Tess,

I will let you know immediately that I am getting settled into the company faster than I anticipated. I worked only a single day as a miner before I was appointed an oversman. My stellar rise is due not so much to my qualifications as to the temper of the manager of the Company mines. During a dispute, Robinson picked up the smithy's hammer and bashed the former oversman's head with it. The action resulted in McGregor — the oversman — being sent to Fort Victoria, and my upward move to fill his place. Such methods of arbitrating grievances are often put into play here, as are fists and knives, and I have been warned I can consider myself fortunate Robinson has taken a liking to me, and so I do.

The promotion provides me with both an increase in wages and better quarters, and this has given me hope I will be able to bring ye to join me sooner than I expected, although I cannot say yet when that will be. In the interim

I am thankful ye are being cared for by your uncle, and I have enclosed a note to be passed to him.

I have not the time for a lengthy description of life here, but I ken ye will be interested in what details I can supply. I will write as often as I can and enclose what other details I have the time for.

There are a number of experienced men here now, including twenty-four from Black Country, but most have come to mining by the route of being first fur traders, and next failed prospectors, and these have brought the disappointments and habits of their former professions with them. They are frustrated by the time it takes to acquire the skills of miners and they are unused to living in close connection with other men and of having to accommodate such physical restraints as that puts upon them. So a measure of my time is spent in sorting out their many quarrels. Most, though, know how to work hard, and I am confident they'll settle down when they can feel they are as good at mining as they were at getting furs.

A cause for distrust and anger among both experienced men and new is a widely held view that the supervisor works for the HBCo entirely at their expense, but they are being convinced a little more each day that I am concerned with their welfare as well as my own. However, they are correct that everything here is done for the profit of the HBCo, and tis fact that mining coal will never pay what getting furs put in the purses of those whose former trade that was, unless they get themselves in a position to own the mine. There is talk of striking for higher wages, but, through Robinson, the Company claims it is making nothing at all from this enterprise. Whether that is true or not is not for me to tell yet.

Nanaimo is a very small settlement, and a hard one at the present time. Due, in part, to being required to purchase supplies from the Company Store, where prices are exorbitant at best, the families are so hard-pressed they dinna have even enough left over to buy seeds to plant in their poor gardens, which are dug in soil made cantankerous with coal dust. Most distressing is the lack of education of the bairns. The wee lassies and laddies are kept busy fetching water from the spring and with other duties from early morning to late at night. From the time they are ten, the lads sit astride the troughs of the breakers, breathing coal dust and with the din of the machinery assaulting their ears for twelve to fourteen hours a day, while they pick the slate from the coal. Their ambition is to graduate from picking slate, which leaves their fingers in a perpetual state of open sores, to being door boys and then mule drivers, then labourers, and finally, if they've lived through all the rest — and many do not — to miners. The Indian bairns are worked as hard at loading coal and cutting trees and hauling goods to and from the vessels that stop. I am reminded that there are no laws against child labour in the colony.

In spite of all I think this will rapidly change, because this country is so rich in resources that any man will be able to *make a good living here when the hard work of settling has been done. Now the whistle has sounded and I maun back to work.*

I Am Your Loving Father, Iain Macqueen

Nanaimo did not sound a nice place, but it was where I wanted to be. I looked for more news of his advancement or other mention of how long it would be before I could go to him, but found none. The remaining letters described more of the doings of the people and the mines.

The plight of the children Father wrote about put me in mind of Gabby and Nadia. I wondered where they were and how I might again connect with them, but there were no answers to that.

I put the letter Father had sent to Uncle on the desk in his study and returned to read and re-read the letters, as if, if I read them enough and memorized the details of them, I could be present somehow with the writers. When it was too dark to see to read, I fell asleep.

❧ SEVENTEEN ❧
Breaking Uncle's Rules
Where Tess Learns Gabby Has Been Sold

FOLLOWING a breakfast of Cook's good pork pie and fresh milk that I had myself earlier obtained from Belle, the cow, I informed Miss Bigget I was going out and that I would not be back for luncheon. I did not wait to hear her advice on the matter, though it looked as if she would like to give it.

Coming to the top of the brae above the south beach, I saw that a rowboat manned by Mr. Beckley and a small boy had already come in, and was nearing the shore. Through the early morning mists, the water was smooth as glass, flowing a gentle rising tide, and the boat glided into shore. I ran down to meet them. "Dinna get out," I said, stepping into the water and quickly climbing in over the gunwale. When I'd settled myself on the bow seat, Mr. Beckley pushed us out with the end of an oar. "I'm Keewan," the small boy said. "I'm four and I can row. I have me own boat Daddy made me. This is Daddy's boat."

His bright face was the mirror of his parents', filled with joy of life. I laughed. "Hello, Kieran. I'm Tess. Will ye show me your boat?"

"Yes," he said. "It's at home."

Mr. Beckley told the boy to come and sit beside him. "All right then, boyo, let's see what you can do." He told him to take the oar. Kieran had considerable strength for his age, and Mr. Beckley moderated his, and we skimmed toward the channel. After inquiring after my health and that of my family, Mr. Beckley asked, "How do you like it here, Miss Macqueen?"

I looked around me and smiled. "The scenery is breathtaking. 'Tis beautiful and fresh."

"Yes," he said.

"What about you, Mr. Beckley, do ye enjoy Victoria and farming?"

"It's a hard life, but it suits me. Although I've four grown brothers, and with all of us under one roof it makes the house small. I'm thinking I'd like it better out, where there's more room."

I laughed. "Aye. I've nae lived with that many grown men, but I had three brothers and they seemed to fill Dunharbar up."

"Are yer brothers here, too, then?"

"No, they've passed on. My mother and youngest brother were taken by the flu just before Father and I came to the colony. My other brothers died before that of measles."

"Ah, a terrible thing. I'm sorry to hear it."

"Aye. I dinna think I'll ever get used to their being gone."

"Will you and your father be settling here?"

"I canna say for certain where we'll be settling. Just now Father's in Nanaimo and I'm to join him there."

"If I'm not prying, Miss Macqueen, what attracts him to Nanaimo?"

"He's working in a mine."

"Has he thought of farming? There's good land on the island for farming."

"I canna say whether he's thought about farming, Mr. Beckley. He was educated as an engineer and was the manager of my grandfather's mines in Scotland. When Grandfather died Uncle Hammond inherited everything and Father then looked after it all for him until last November, when my uncle sold the property where we lived. Uncle Hammond thought Father ought to come to the colony to be a missionary. That appointment hae been delayed and in the meantime Father's found work in Nanaimo."

"Your uncle has been out here a good many year, has he not?"

"Aye. He came to the colony ten years ago. Are ye acquainted with him, Mr. Beckley?"

"I've never met him, but I know his name. He supplies goods to most of the stores on Vancouver's Island and the small islands. He's well known. I hope you and your father will end by settling in the country, Miss Macqueen. You will make a fine addition to the island."

"Thank ye, Mr. Beckley. Tis flattery of ye to say so."

"There's no flattery about it. If men are to make their homes out here, there's got to be more women."

Roundly put in my place, I couldn't help laughing. And it hit me then where I'd seen him before. "Mr. Beckley, when Mrs. O'Reilly introduced us I had a feeling that perhaps we'd met sometime in the past. We hae not, at least not formally, but Father and I arrived on the *Borealis*, the same ship that had a group of Russian lassies aboard it. Were ye not on the dock at Esquimalt the day we landed?" His dark frown made me hesitant, but I was determined to pursue my idea. "I ask because I am a friend of two of the lasses who were on the ship, and I've been unsuccessful in finding out where they are. I thought because ye were there when they came ashore, and ye live in Victoria, ye might have heard where some of them at least are employed."

His frown deepened, but there was recognition in his eyes.

I looked at him sharply now. "If ye ken anything at all, Mr. Beckley, ye would be doing me a favour by telling it. Anything at all about the smallest, who is named Gabrielle, and a girl about my own age whose name is Nadia."

At last he said, "I've heard Rory took a small girl."

My growing excitement at being this close to discovering where Gabby was, was curtailed by a vague fear. Something in Mr. Beckley's manner signalled a warning. "Who is Mr. Rory? Can ye tell me where I can find him?"

"You'll have a good deal of trouble to find him, Miss Macqueen. He's a trader what moves about fast and hard."

"A trader? Do ye mean he has a ship like the *Borealis*?"

"No, he's got no ship. He runs traplines in the interior of British Columbia, but he comes south and over to Vancouver's Island to hunt otter, seal, beaver and the like, and to gather things to trade with the Indians up north."

I was puzzled. "What employment could such a man have for a wee lass like Gabby? She's nae got the size nor strength for trapping and hunting."

He studied me a minute before answering. "He won't keep her. He'll sell her."

A fork of lightning crackled through my brain. I protested loudly against the pain of the illumination. "Gabby canna be bought or traded! She's to be employed and when her passage is paid back to Mr. Samuel she'll be free to go wherever she will! She canna be sold, Mr. Beckley … Mr. Beckley?" I insisted when he didn't respond.

"I'm sorry to give you bad news, Miss Macqueen."

My feelings and thoughts became a muck of growing despair. I tried to sort them out, to think of something I could do, but no clear thoughts would come. I was roused by Kieran.

"I'm tired," he said, letting go of his oar.

"You did well, boyo," Mr. Beckley said, and Kieran grinned.

I wanted some activity. "May I try?" I asked.

Mr. Beckley looked surprised but agreed, and Kieran and I changed places. I watched Mr. Beckley and tried to keep pace with him, and succeeded after a short while to feel I was pulling all right. We talked minimally of Mr. Beckley's experiences since coming to the colony. I was trying to be cheerful, but I could not rid my thoughts of Gabby, and my heart was heavy.

At last we came to a bay where Mr. Beckley put the boat up on the beach, and after Kieran proudly showed off his little boat, which was crafted beautifully and seemed just right for a wee boy, we walked a pleasant trail through the woods to a clearing. There was a ravine with a bubbling burn running through it, masses of wildflowers, including maidenhair ferns growing among the stumps of the cleared land, and a house built with logs. There were corrals and other buildings, too. I could only guess the work it had taken to make all that was there. Kieran ran ahead.

Mrs. O'Reilly came out to greet us with the same wide smile she'd shown me the day before. "Welcome, Miss Macqueen. Come in, come in." She ushered me into the house. Mr. Beckley came behind me.

The room we stepped into was a kitchen, dining room and sitting room all in one, with the furniture denoting where one area ended and another began. The kitchen had a stove, a wooden box with a lid, and a Hosier cupboard with doors and drawers. There was a large bowl of water on the Hosier's porcelain-topped counter and Mr. O'Reilly was standing in front of it washing. The bairn Mrs. O'Reilly had been holding in her arms when I'd seen them at Cowitchan Bay now occupied a cradle by the stove. It was wide awake and cooing. I noticed something I hadn't seen then, when Mrs. O'Reilly's stomach had been covered by her arms and the wee girl. There was a third child coming, which at the moment was a large round ball protruding under Mrs. O'Reilly's skirt.

The long table in the dining area was made of planks covered with a cloth, and twas already set with places and bowls and platters piled high with food. The seats were two long benches, one on either side of the table. "Please sit down on the inside bench, Miss Macqueen, you next to her, James, and we'll eat while it's hot," Mrs. O'Reilly said.

Mr. O'Reilly settled himself on the outside bench, along with his wife and Kieran, who had pillows under him so that he could see over the tabletop. Mr. O'Reilly delivered the blessing: "Lord, bless this food and the sweat that watered it. Thanks for good comp'ny. Amen." We tucked into soup and halibut, hot roast chicken, bowls of steaming potatoes, peas and turnips. There was a large jug of milk, a plate of fresh butter and a breadboard with a loaf of warm bread sliced upon it. Beside the breadboard was also a saucer full of soft goat cheese.

"You must have spent the entire morning cooking all of this," I said. "Tis wonderful."

"We are blessed," she replied. "Mr. O'Reilly were so fortunate to have gotten this land. If one is willing to work, it will provide. We're looking forward to many more settlers coming, aren't we, Mr. O'Reilly?"

"That's a fact," Mr. O'Reilly agreed.

"Won't happen if Governor Douglas don't start cooperating," Mr. Beckley said. "The Governor has to make it easier for folks to come. Has to start keeping some promises, too, like the gunboat he promised to send up here regular to keep the Indians in line."

"Well, now," Mr. O'Reilly said, "way I see it, the more that do come, the harder it'll be for the Gov'nor to keep on being king of his little kingdom, and bein' as the Gov'nor aint a stupid man, he aint goin' to make it too easy too quick."

"Are the Indians so troublesome the settlers need a gunboat?" I asked.

"They're peaceable enough so far," Mr. O'Reilly said.

"These ones been paid for their land yet?" Mr. Beckley asked.

This brought a cluck to Mr. O'Reilly's lips. "Nope. I 'spect the ship bringing the cash had only one sail and when it got to Fort Vancouver it were likely so full of rot it had to be entirely rebuilt."

Acting the straight man, Mr. Beckley said, "Why would you think that now?"

" 'Cause that ship is the slowest boat on record to get from England to Vancouver's Island," Mr. O'Reilly droned.

Mr. Beckley laughed, but Mrs. O'Reilly said, "Tis criminal and doesn't it put us all in a bad light." Then, as if to put me at ease, she said, "But there's no need to worry about the Indians, Miss Macqueen. They 'bout scared me half to death our first year here, coming round and looking in every window like they do. Sometimes they walked right into the house. They touched everything, even bit things to see what they were made of! Made me suck in my breath so that I looked as if I were wearing a corset, I were that worried, until I saw that the more I remonstrated with them, the more they did it, and even though they kept their faces all drawn down fierce-like, they couldn't shut the laughter out of their eyes. They like to laugh as well as we do, the Indians do; better when the joke's on us. After I stopped reacting to them, they started making noise to give me warning they were coming, and they don't come into the house anymore without they're invited."

"Do they do that to all the settlers?" I wanted to know, and added, "because I haena seen any come to my uncle's house."

"Well, I think they do it most when someone's first come. But if a settler shoots at one or more of them, they'll usually stay away, or at the least they'll take care not to get caught creeping around a house that's shown its unwelcome strongly enough. All they really want is a bit of food. They don't have anything like flour, you know, and they love it. Flour and molasses. There were times I had to take to hiding both or I'd have lost it all! But they don't steal it. They trade fish and other things, or they take crates of apples or chickens to other farms for me."

"They'll do that?"

"Oh, aye. They'll deliver things all up and down the straits; even over to British Columbia and Washington and Oregon. First time I weren't sure how it would turn out, but they brought back every cent I was owed and they've done the same every time since. It can be costly when a dozen of them go along in the canoe to watch over the chickens, but usually it's just one or two."

Then she asked me questions. How was my trip over? What did I think of this new country? Would I be staying long with my uncle? Had I met any of the other settlers? Would Uncle and I be attending the summer solstice picnic on the island? Mr. O'Reilly said I'd likely like it better were I given a chance to catch my breath between questions, and Mrs. O'Reilly took his gentle ribbing with a soft laugh.

After lunch, Mr. O'Reilly and Mr. Beckley excused themselves to get on with some building they were doing. The baby had fallen asleep in her cradle and Kieran was curled up on top of the wooden box in the corner of the kitchen, breathing rhythmically. Mrs. O'Reilly and I cleaned up the dishes and went out to stroll around the farm. I admired the work that had been done. Shortly after that it was time to go, and Mrs. O'Reilly said another boat was going to Cowitchan Bay and would pass Genoa and had offered to take me. They were Negroes, she said. Right neighbourly people, and she'd trusted her children with them many a time. Would I care to go with them?

I thought of all the work Mr. O'Reilly and Mr. Beckley had to do and of how long it would take Mr. Beckley to row to Genoa Bay and back for my sake. It seemed a terrible waste of valuable time. "If they are known to you and ye think it is all right, I'm very happy to," I said.

At the beach, with Mrs. O'Reilly saying, "Come again. Come anytime," and waving, and me answering, "I shall," and a sleepy Kieran rubbing his eyes with one hand and waving with the other, I climbed into a boat with four men and two women. Having two sets of oars and two strong rowers, our passage was much swifter than coming had been, but there was time for the usual questions and answers to be repeated. They spoke of a school they had started on Salt Spring Island, which was open to all the children, and they seemed warm and gracious people.

When we reached Genoa, of their own accord they let me off at a spot well below and out of sight of Uncle's house.

❧

Uncle arrived home two days later. I was out walking when he came. As soon as I returned to the house I was summoned to his study. I was glad to go, intending to ask him what, if anything, he knew of Mr. Rory and Gabby.

As soon as I entered his room he said, "Sit down,

Elizabeth." I did and he said, "Miss Bigget tells me you accompanied her and Cook to Cowitchan Bay when the *Otter* came in."

"Aye. Father enclosed a letter for ye in a packet he sent to me. I put it on your desk. Did ye see it?"

"Yes. Miss Bigget also tells me that while you were there you became acquainted with Mr. and Mrs. O'Reilly and Mrs. O'Reilly's brother, Mr. Beckley, and went to luncheon with them the following day," he barrelled on.

"Aye. Mrs. O'Reilly asked that you and I and Father all come and when I explained ye and Father were away she still wanted to have me. I had a wonderful time. I'm sorry ye were nae there, Uncle. Ye would ..."

"I begin to fear your mother has failed to teach you any manners whatsoever. Well-bred young ladies do not speak to gentlemen to whom they have not been properly introduced and they do not go calling without the permission and supervision of their guardians."

I seethed. "I will nae hear my mother's name taken in vain. She is niver to blame for my faults."

"Your faults, Elizabeth, are numerous."

"Perhaps they are, Uncle. However, in this matter I dinna see any fault at all. Mrs. O'Reilly introduced me to Mr. Beckley quite properly, I assure ye, and there can be nae harm in anyone visiting an entire family. At Dunharbar I've been trusted to visit cottages on my own since the age of seven."

His face was livid, but his voice was low and dangerous. "I exercise some care in choosing those with whom I associate. In the future you will visit no one in my absence, and you will refer all invitations to me, to be answered by me."

"But the O'Reillys are lovely people and I would like to know all the neighbours. What reason can there be to shun them?"

"I do not account for my actions to you."

My own contempt matched his. "My mother would niver have shunned anyone without reason. Tis her philosophy I prefer to yours."

"For as long as you are under my roof," he thundered, "you will abide by *my* philosophy! And you will obey my orders!"

I stood up.

He turned and stood staring out his study window with his back to me. Without turning around, he said in a level voice, "A nature such as yours, that allows itself to be influenced by all that is around you without the ability to screen out undesirable elements, is easily overtaxed, Elizabeth, and your health thus easily put out of balance. You have some small eruptions on your chin, which along with the willfulness and choler you continue to display are evidence of a system that is sorely out of balance." He pulled the bell chord. "What you need is a purge." Miss Bigget entered and he said, "If you'll be so kind as to bring Elizabeth some Mezereon, Miss Bigget, I think her spirits will be much improved by the medicine."

As soon as Miss Bigget left the room I said, "I do not require a purge."

"If you do not swallow it, I will be forced to take other steps to insure you do not become ill. My brother has left you in my care and I will not have you fall victim to a disease that is established for want of the most assiduous attention to your welfare on my part."

I took the dose Miss Bigget brought, and was bent double with cramps within the hour. My night was largely passed in the outhouse, where I shivered uncontrollably with rage and with the weakness and chill that accompany being purged. Happily, the symptoms abated by the morning and though I was somewhat light-headed when I sat for breakfast, my strength was already returning. The broth Cook served me tasted very good. In an effort to avoid another quarrel with my uncle, I kept my eyes down, determined not to speak unless spoken to. We ate in silence.

When he had finished eating, Uncle wiped his mouth with his napkin and said, "I have written a letter explaining your present situation to your father, Elizabeth, and sent it with Mr. Beckley, who I've heard is planning to be aboard the *Rose* when she makes her next voyage northward."

At this, my head shot up. "What situation?"

"The delicate state of your health, my dear."

"I hae always been fortunate to have the most robust constitution, Uncle, and I am enjoying excellent health. Ye will give my father cause for worry where there is none."

"It is unfortunate that I must contradict you, my dear, but it is my opinion your constitution has suffered a breakdown and it is my intention to alleviate unnecessary worry on your father's part by keeping him informed. He will be comforted to know you are being cared for."

My head was spinning. I could not credit what he was saying. "But it isna true!"

"You see, you are distraught again."

Laying my napkin on the table, I said, "If you will excuse me, Uncle, I hae had quite enough to eat."

"Certainly. The lessons you will complete today are on the writing desk in the library."

I went to the desk and sat. Pushing the lessons aside, I took my notebook from the pocket of my dress. I would write my own letter and ask Mr. Beckley to deliver it also to my father.

My Dearest Father,

Uncle Hammond told me he has written you saying that I am ill, or on the verge of it. I wanted to write immediately to let ye know I am enjoying the same good health I have always had and to dissuade ye from believing anything he says.

I'm sorry to say that Uncle and I are getting along poorly. It seems I can do nowt that disna cause his bile to rise, and when he tries to correct me, it usually ends with the two of us quarrelling. Even when I am trying to comply with his endless rules, there is fault to be found with me. It is a very

unhappy house here, Papa, and, I think, an unwelcome one
for me. I am praying for your advancement and the time
when I can join ye to arrive very soon.

I knew I could not send it. Father was doing all he
could. Receiving this letter would increase his distress. I
must make an effort to understand my uncle. Why did he
persist in believing I was ill when I was not? The eruptions
on my chin were as nothing to me. I had had them before
and they had gone away leaving no untoward effects. It was
true that in the past year I had often been almost overcome
with feeling I was falling into a chasm so deep and black
and filled with emptiness I thought my heart would break
from the strain of it, but tonics and purges could never
cure me of that. Nothing could cure me of that because
nothing could fill the terrible emptiness left where my
family had been. As for the choler Uncle complained of ...
I sighed.

My own patient mother had at times been vexed by my
tendencies to passion and to contrary opinion; my father
much more often. However, they had never thought it a
sign of ill health. They had said it was my stubborn nature
and counselled me to put more effort into resisting
indulging myself in rash action and arguing. Remembering
this, my conscience pricked me. Where my uncle was concerned I had not only *not* resisted behaving according to
my stubborn nature, I had grown ever more defiant of his

wishes and at the same time ever more willing to gratify my own. I was nothing like a dutiful niece. How could I pacify Uncle's notion of me and so have at least a peace between us? I sighed again. I had no idea because I simply could not contemplate agreeing with him. I would have to ask for Father's help. I took up my pen again.

My Dearest Father,

I hope ye are continuing to be well and that we will be reunited soon. I miss you so very much. I have written you and Jock and sent the letters via the Otter, which I expect ye will have got by now. I'm hoping to have this one ready to send with a Mr. Beckley, who is the brother of one of Uncle's neighbours. Mr. Beckley is going on the Rose to look at land on a more northward part of Vancouver's Island, and Uncle Hammond has also given him a letter for you. Tis Uncle's letter that I write about first.

Uncle told me he has expressed concern for my health to ye. He is quite overprotective of me in this regard, Papa, and except for suffering the effects for a few hours of a tonic and a purge he gae to me, I'm very well. So please dinna worry at all about my health; it is excellent, as it has always been.

It was a pleasant surprise to discover a letter from Jock among yours, though the news in it was not what I wanted. I am enclosing it so ye can read it in case ye have not received the same. I daily pray the White Gull is not gone to India, and for Jock's continued safety, as I know ye will.

A few days ago I had the good fortune to go on an outing and to meet the O'Reillys, who are Uncle's neighbours mentioned above. As well, I was introduced to Mrs. O'Reilly's brother, Mr. Beckley, who has come from Victoria to visit them. The O'Reillys live on Salt Spring Island and kindly invited Uncle and you and me to luncheon with them the following day. As neither you nor Uncle were here, I accepted the invitation on my own behalf. Uncle did not approve of this, but I was very happy in the time I had with them.

Their farm is one hundred sixty acres of land. They say it is easier to clear and farm than that on the east coast of Vancouver's Island, but they have put a great deal of work into making it provide them with a living. In only a few short years they have developed a field for growing corn, and another is producing more potatoes and vegetables than they can use, so that they market some. As well, they have apple trees, and keep ducks and geese they are raising for sale, and have about one hundred fifty chickens they keep for eggs and meat for themselves and also sell some. For milk, they keep goats instead of coos because Mrs. O'Reilly says goats will browse all manner of brush and brambles and thus they help to clear the land. Of goats they have a dozen nannies and one buck. Male kids are killed for meat at about six months of age or castrated and kept as wethers to help clear the brush. The O'Reillys use pigs to dig out roots, moving the pen whenever an area has been sufficiently churned up.

The day of my visit Mr. O'Reilly and Mr. Beckley were putting up a new goat house and pen so Mrs. O'Reilly will be able to separate the kids from the nannies in a few weeks and she will have milk to sell, too. She thinks it will sell very well just now because there is such a shortage of coo's milk on Vancouver's Island, everything being taken to supply the hordes passing through the fort on their way to and from the gold fields. If so, the money twill bring can only be a boon to them. Just think of it, Papa, all that work and only the two of them to do it! There are few servants in these parts and the O'Reillys dinna even think of having them. I'm glad Mr. O'Reilly has Mr. Beckley's help at least for a little while.

I dinna think Mrs. O'Reilly can be more than nineteen or twenty years old but she has already two bairns and is in the family way again. But with all the work of the farm and the children to tire her, ye will never meet a more cheerful person. Mr. O'Reilly is older, and a dry wit, and I think ye would greatly enjoy knowing him.

Mr. Beckley is older than his sister and seems a kindly man, as ye will see when ye meet him. I asked him if he knew anything of what had become of Gabby and Nadia because he had been at Esquimalt the day we landed. He said a small girl was taken by a man named Rory, who is a trader. Mr. Beckley disna think Mr. Rory will keep her, and though he didna say it outright he hinted she may be traded by Mr. Rory to the Indians. Gabby was the only small girl on the ship and I am convinced tis her he's speaking of. The idea she could be bought or traded by anyone to anyone is outrageous. It canna be possible, can it, Papa? I intend to talk to Uncle Hammond about it, but as he is ill inclined to talk to me about anything other than what is required of me, I do not think I shall have success in receiving information from him. I would like it very much if you will write and ask him about it. Will ye? Mr. Beckley had no news of Nadia, but she and Gabby are in my daily prayers.

I would take great comfort in a continued friendship with the O'Reillys, but to my sorrow Uncle Hammond has forbade it. He says he disnae wish any association with any of his neighbours save the doctor, and in this and in the matter of my health he and I are much at odds. I confess, Papa, I do provoke him with my outspokenness. Because ye are adept at keeping the peace between quarrelsome men, maybe ye can tell me how I can better live with my uncle. I will do my utmost to follow your advice, except, I beg ye dinna tell me I am to agree with him in his ideas.

I think of ye many times each day and look forward to the time we will be reunited. In the meantime, I pray to God to keep you safe and well. Please let me know also if ye will write to Uncle about Gabby, as I fear for her.

Always your loving daughter, Tess

By the time I had finished the letter, Uncle had gone out. I concluded it would be best to find Billy and ask him if he knew of a way my letter could be taken to Mr. Beckley so he could deliver it to Father. I was closing up the desk when the knuckle of my middle finger bumped against the catch that released the secret drawer that is to be found in all writing desks. Inside was an envelope addressed on the back to Father in our Scottish solicitor's hand. Curious why Uncle hadn't sent it with his letter to Father, I pulled it out. The seal had been broken and so I thought it must be something Father had given to Uncle, and I was going to put it back when my curiosity turned to unbridled nosiness.

I opened the envelope and took out two separate items: one a letter written by the solicitor and the other a copy of Grandfather's will. The solicitor wrote this was the will left in his keeping by my grandfather and that he had seen nothing of the version that had been produced a few days after Grandfather's burial until it was sent to him by the English firm. He wrote that he had wrestled with his conscience regarding the question of sending the original to Father, as the other had in fact been declared Grandfather's Last Will and Testament, but that he had decided in favour.

Footsteps precluded further reading. I hastily replaced both items into the envelope and the envelope into the drawer and left the room, meeting Miss Bigget briefly as I passed through the parlour on my way to my own room. When I left the house a few minutes later I did not see either Miss Bigget or Cook.

❧

Misunderstanding my request, Billy told me some of his acquaintances were leaving for Salt Spring Island and would take me with them if I wanted to leave right now. I was delighted. "But will they bring me back?" I asked.

"Yyuh," he said. "Them come back. Work."

"When?" I wanted to know.

"When water change direction," he said.

About five hours, I reckoned. It would be enough time. Happily I went skipping down to the water in time to occupy a canoe with eight Indians. I was amazed at how fast they were able to get across the channel.

Mrs. O'Reilly and Kieran were in the cornfield working. "What a nice surprise," Mrs. O'Reilly said. She stopped hoeing and wiped her sweating forehead with the back of her long sleeve.

"How do, Tess," Kieran said.

"How do to ye, Kieran," I replied. "Look at ye with a hoe just your size. Did your daddy make that for ye, too?"

His chest puffed up with pride. "Yes! I'm helping Mama." He went back to cutting at the weeds with a flurry to show me.

"Aye," I smiled and turned to his mother. "My uncle has told me Mr. Beckley may be leaving on the *Rose* and I've come to ask if he'll take my letter as well as my uncle's to my father."

"He and Mr. O'Reilly are over to the Davie place for a

barn-raising. They won't be back till this evening, but of course he'll take your letter. If you'll leave it with me, I'll see he gets it."

"Thank ye," I said, handing it to her.

She wiped her forehead again from the heat. "You'll have some lemonade and lunch," she said in a tone that had no question in it at all.

"Me too!" Kieran said.

"Yes, you too," Mrs. O'Reilly laughed.

During luncheon I explained Gabby's probable fate to her and said I was dreadfully anxious to discover her whereabouts. Mrs. O'Reilly tried to comfort me by telling me that in this country native tribes betroth their children to form an alliance between two tribes, sometimes when the children are still on the cradle board. She said that when the time comes for the girl to be sent to her husband's home, goods are exchanged, and it is a marriage contract, not the "sale" of a youngster, for it to be done that way. "If Mr. Rory has been long in this country, mayhap he is practising the Indian ways, and the wee girl has gone to a home," she said.

I knew well enough Gabby's prospects in this country were for a hard life, but I did not think the age of seven was a suitable one for marriage no matter what the local customs were, and said so. I asked her to ask Mr. Beckley if he would kindly pass on to my father any further information he might gather, and she said she would.

After lunch Kieran and I went back to the corn while Mrs. O'Reilly tended to the wee one and other chores. Kieran worked with a burst of competent energy, moving sideways through the rows as he snagged and disposed of weeds. And then he disappeared. I waited a few minutes for his reappearance and then went looking for him. I began to call his name. I was beginning to get worried when I heard a tiny snigger and a small boy jumped out from behind a stump yelling "Boo!"

"Oh!" I said, my hand flying to my chest. "Ye scared me half out of my wits!"

Clearly pleased with himself, he sang out, "Got you!"

I drew myself up, monsterlike, and he dropped his hoe and ran zigging and zagging through the corn. He was fast and when I caught him we collapsed on the ground in a heap of giggles. He was an imp, reminding me so much of Colin for a moment that my heart caught in my throat. We had a game or two of tag and settled back to work. An hour passed more quickly than I wanted, and before I knew it I had to say goodbye.

I was home only minutes before Uncle, who, at supper, asked where my lessons were.

"I didna do them," I answered.

"I see. Miss Bigget said you were away all day. Where were you?"

I was reluctant to answer and did so haughtily. "I went to visit the O'Reillys."

228 ~ JOCELYN REEKIE

t "In direct defiance of my orders."

I knew I should be sorry for disobeying him, but I could not feel sorry at all and so I tried to defend myself. "I went to ask Mr. Beckley if he would take a letter from me to Father as well as yours, Uncle."

"Did he agree?"

"I didna have an opportunity to ask him. He and Mr. O'Reilly were away at a barn-raising."

"Give me the letter, Elizabeth."

"I've nae got it."

"Where is it?"

I took several moments to reply. "It is my own private correspondence, Uncle."

"Am I to understand you are refusing to give me the letter?"

"Aye."

He was surprisingly calm when he said, "You have disobeyed my orders in every respect and you dare to sit there and defy me further. There are consequences for such undesirable behaviour, Elizabeth. Take the lessons with you and go to your room and complete them. Bring them to me in my study when you are finished."

I went. It took until long after dark to finish all Uncle had set me, but he was waiting when I went to his study. When I had recited the passages he'd set to his satisfaction, he said, "Go to bed now."

I had expected at the very least a lecture, but it did not

come. His manner remained as calm as it had been earlier and I felt a flood of relief that there would be no unpleasant scene. "Aye. Good night, Uncle," I replied.

"Good night."

I woke in the night, used my chamber pot and went back to sleep. When I got up in the morning I couldn't open my door. I shook the knob and tugged at it but it was stuck fast. Finally I knocked on the wood and waited for a response. After knocking a second time and still getting no response, I started pounding and calling out for anyone there. Soon I heard footsteps on the other side.

"I canna open the door," I said, feeling somewhat sheepish. "'Tis jammed."

"Move away from it and I'll open it," Uncle said. I moved back. There was a grating sound and a click. The door swung inward and Uncle stepped over the threshold. I looked at him and at the door.

"But I couldna budge it, no matter how I tried."

"It was locked," he said. He handed me a sheaf of papers. "These are today's lessons. You will be brought bread and water presently. You will remain in this room with nothing but bread and water for your fare until you see fit to repent your sins and change your ways."

I was dull with incredulity and stared at him dumbly. He stepped back through the door and pulled it closed. Too late, I ran, but the key was already turning in the lock. I had never in all my life felt as cold with fury as I did that moment. It froze me into utter helplessness. My legs gave way. I sank down beside the door and sat there growing numb and stiff, slowly sinking into a suffocating, killing sea.

⚜ EIGHTEEN ⚜
Imprisoned
Escape

I DIDNA know how long I'd sat when I came back to myself. I got up and went to the window. The bottom half of the window slid upward and was held up with a stick propped under the frame, but the opening was very small — a hand-span high by two feet wide. The whole window was only two feet by two feet square. I tried every way I could to squeeze through, but nothing I did could flatten my bones or suck my flesh in far enough to make me small enough. I wished I was a mouse or a rat, which I'd seen squeeze themselves through impossibly tiny holes. Or a being with all kinds of magical powers, like in olden times. *I'd be powerful enough to change Uncle into someone nice.* Wish as I might, nothing changed. I was me, Uncle was Uncle, and I was trapped. I stood staring at the barnyard and the forest beyond it.

I was still standing there when the door opened and Uncle came in carrying a glass of water and a plate with two slices of buttered bread on it. He held them out to me.

I didn't budge. "You canna keep me here like this," I said.

Setting the water glass and plate on the floor to the right of the door, he said, "Have you completed your lessons?" His voice was sticky, like syrup.

I glared at him. "I will not be kept locked up. My father will be reekin' when he hears of this."

In the same syrupy voice he said, "I will return in several hours to see about your lessons, Elizabeth." Saying it, he stepped back over the threshold and pulled the door closed after him. Again I was too late getting to it.

"You canna do this!" I shouted at the wood and pounded on it. "Uncle! I'll not let you do this!" I still could not believe it was really happening. *He'll never bully me into obeying his bloody rules! I'll never do anything he wants. I hate him!* I ranted in my mind. *Think!* I commanded myself. *There must be a way to get out.* I went back to the bed and sat on it.

When the door opened again I was standing close to it, ready. It was Cook, not Uncle, bringing more bread and water. I knocked against her and heard the sound of breaking crockery as I charged out and turned left toward the front door. Looking over my shoulder instead of ahead, I ran straight into Uncle. He grabbed my arm and hauled me back into my room, waving at Cook, who was picking up the last pieces of a shattered plate, to be gone. As soon as he released me, I ran out again. I was quicker than he, but when I got to the front door of the house I found it was barred shut and he caught up with me and took hold of me with a grip that made me gasp. I struggled but could not get free.

"You'll not survive one day on your own in the wilderness, my girl. If the bears and panthers and wolves don't get you, the Indians will," he said, his tone never changing from the sickly sweetness of earlier. Again he deposited me in my room, this time forcing me to sit on the bed. "Have you finished your lessons?" he asked.

"I'll nae do lessons while ye keep me locked up like a gyte," I said through clenched teeth.

Saying nothing more, he released me and went out, closing the door and locking it yet again.

The next morning Uncle set a jug of fresh water, a plate with bread on it, and more papers on the floor to the right of the door.

"I need to use the outhouse," I said.

"There is a pot in your cupboard. Have you completed your lessons?"

I refused to say anything more and resolved not to eat.

In the evening another slice of bread was put on the plate to the right of the door. "Have you finished your lessons?" Uncle asked. The sound of his voice made me grind my teeth. I stared at him, wanting to take his throat and shake it to make his normal sounds come out of it. To pummel the sticky sweetness off his vocal cords. I did not reply.

For five days it continued the same. Fresh water, fresh bread, the uneaten bread retrieved, more papers and the question, had I finished my lessons. I never answered. I drank the water but would not eat. Water to wash in was not brought, and though I saved a little of my drinking water each day until I had enough to at least wipe myself down, the room was hot and became fetid with my own odour. I paced continually and did whatever exercise I could think of to keep up my waning strength.

The sixth day I knew there was no help for my situation. Uncle would keep me here for as long as it took to get his way. I sat to do the lessons he'd brought each day. It took two days to complete them all. When he asked his usual question on the eighth day, I held out the papers to him. He took them, closed and locked the door. He returned several hours later. "Have you discovered the error of your ways?" he asked.

I stared at him. It was another of his tests and I understood that if I didn't answer he would continue the regime. "Aye," I said, "I've been mistaken."

"Give me your word you will not disobey me again," he said.

I chewed my cracked bottom lip. "Ye have my word I will nae disobey you again."

"Water will be brought you to clean up. You will join me for supper."

The following morning, after Uncle had set me the day's lessons and left the house, I dressed in my favourite Hieland summer clothes: sleeveless vest with buttons shaped like wolf heads — the Macqueen family crest — short skirt, soft slippers laced up around my ankles and a plaid of the finest, lightest wool pinned to my shoulder, and went toward Maple Bay. I hadn't gone one mile when Billy and another Indian materialized beside me, took hold of me and brought me back. I had seen the second man before, from a distance. He had a regular head, not a pointed one like Billy and most of the others I'd seen so far. And he carried himself differently. More like the Indians I'd read about. When I'd mentioned him to Cook, she said he was not a local Indian. He came from somewhere north on the island, and west. He hadn't been here long and she didn't trust him at all. "Them northern Indians like to collect up scalps," she said. The good thing about him was he seemed to understand when she and Miss Bigget told him to stay clear of the house and yard. The only native they trusted near the house at all was Billy. Now I was reminded of where Billy's loyalties lay. I felt utterly betrayed. I had thought of him as a sort of friend, but I would not be able to ask him to help me get to Nanaimo. He worked for Uncle.

Uncle was in the yard. He said something to Billy in his own language and when the Indians had gone out of the yard he said to me, "Go to your room."

Without a word I did so. I heard the key turn in the lock. I did the lessons and waited. At suppertime Cook brought a tray to me in my room and when she went out the door was locked behind her.

After waiting for everyone in the house to be asleep, I put Mother's lucifers, a flint, my notebook and a lead, and a second, longer plaid into pockets I had folded in my plaid. I thought about the two silver cups I had brought from home. Their handles were shaped in the family wolf-head crest, and together with the buttons on my vest, they were the only tangible ties I had with my heritage. I decided to take them, and wrapped them in my second plaid. I retrieved my knife from the bottom of my trunk and shoved it securely through my belt. Lastly, I pulled a wine-skin and a waterskin from the trunk, emptied the water glass into the waterskin, and slipped the thongs over my head criss-cross so one pouch hung against each hip.

With every ounce of strength I had, I swung my straight-backed chair. Its thick legs shattered the entire window. I picked up my metal washbasin and with it bashed out the bits of glass that still clung to the pieces of casing. My locked bedroom door and the sleep induced in my uncle by strong spirits were now a blessing for me. I got my right arm and leg through the window, ducked my head, and pulled my left side out. The door banged open, but I was already a little distance away from the house racing full speed for the forest when Uncle's shouts cracked across the night at me. I paid him no heed at all.

Twas a night with a full, bright moon and I was grateful for it. It let me see clearly, but it would also make me visible. I had to take a route that would confuse anyone who came after me.

A little way into the forest I climbed a tree. The trees were huge, and closely spaced, and I was able to keep above the ground, going out on a thick branch of one tree as far as I could and stepping or lowering myself onto a branch of another. The first time I had to jump, a flying squirrel gave me the courage to do it. Somewhere behind me I heard voices, but they were muffled by distance. In time they faded away entirely.

When I'd gone far enough that I thought my footprints would not be seen, I went to the ground and doubled back to Uncle's farm, being careful to keep to footing where my footprints wouldn't show. I had planned this part of my escape with long hours of thought. Mother said we most often miss what is right under our noses, and so I went to Uncle's barn, gathered some hay, and crawled into Belle's manger. The cow didn't flicker an eye at the intrusion. I piled the hay on top of myself and slept.

I was wakened by Cook's voice and the sound of a slap. "Get on over there, Belle." The three-legged stool was put down beside the cow and milk began hissing into a pail. "Come on, you miserable old coo, let your milk down now. Missy always got at least a pail and a half from you. Hold back and Mr. Hammond turn you into table meat. He's mean mad. Niver seen him madder. He catches Missy, he'll not let her loose again. You wanna be roast of beef, eh Belle?"

Belle tongued up a mouthful of hay and stood munch-ing. There were more splashes, some glop-glop sounds as the milk deepened in the pail, and a few final splots. Then the tie-rope smacked the stall wall. "Back up then, you," Cook ordered, and Belle's hooves thudded in the dirt that was the floor of the centre aisle. I held my breath.

The handle of the milk pail squeaked. Cook's footsteps followed Belle's. Slowly, I climbed out of the manger and crept to the door in time to watch Cook go around the house to the summer kitchen. That was where the separator was, and separating the milk and cleaning the separator afterward took at least a half hour. I knew Miss Bigget would be busy, too, cleaning Uncle's rooms while he ate his breakfast.

I went to the well, where there were two buckets. One was used to bring up water; the other held a gallon can of milk from the day before, and blocks of cheese and butter that were kept fresh by the cold water. I pulled the second pail up, filled my waterskin with milk and my wineskin with water, and cut a large chunk of cheese, which I tucked into my plaid.

Keeping as much to the trees as I could to avoid being seen, I struck off again for Maple Bay. What I wanted was to find an Indian travelling up the passage by canoe — one that I could bargain with. The way Mrs. O'Reilly told it, the Indians would do things for whoever could pay them. I would have to find one who wasna associated with my uncle. It would have to be an Indian because I could be sure no settler would dare to take me where I wanted to go without my uncle's permission.

But how to know which Indians I could approach? I had thought Billy would be safe. I shook my head. However all that might be, right now I had to hide till nightfall, or I wouldn't get any farther than I had yesterday.

NINETEEN
Running North
A Hieland Vow

IT had worked to come back to my uncle's barn for the night because it had not been expected. Now I maun find somewhere else to go. *The beach*, I thought. A hole covered with seaweed in such a manner searchers would not think to look twice at it.

In Maple Bay, with my hands and a thin, flat rock I scraped out a shallow berth. I piled up rocks, put some driftwood around and over them and arranged seaweed over the top of that. I crawled inside. Twas cramped, but relatively cool, the only real bother the sandflies that bit at me. I drank some milk and ate some cheese and tried to ignore the stinging bites. In time, I fell asleep.

When the sun went down and the moon rose up, I awkwardly inched my way out of my hole, almost crying out with the pain of moving my stiffened limbs. The tide was a low one, but it was nearly in. The only sound was the waves whooshing as they curled and broke on the beach. Walking below the high-tide mark so my footprints would not be seen, I followed the coast northward. Where the tide ran up to the treeline, I was forced inland and the going was thick with brush, brambles and trees. In many places I had to climb up, over and down rocky outcrops. Often I had to wade waist deep, or swim, around a point of land I could not climb over.

A skittering nervousness inside me was fuelled with worry about the wild animals Uncle had said would rip me limb from limb, and the Indians. I hid at every sound I couldn't immediately explain. The night stretched long ahead of me.

When the sky turned the dull grey that signalled the dawn, the tide was again a long way out. I dug clams. During the night I had drunk all the milk I had, so I filled the skin with sea water and dropped the clams in to let them clean themselves of sand. I went ashore and into the woods to make a firepit in the forest floor, reasoning with myself that the overlapping branches of the trees would help to hide my smoke. When the roasted shells popped open, I fished them out of the coals with a stick. The moist meat and juice were delicious.

I found a burn not far away — Cook and Miss Bigget called them "creeks" and "streams," and they were plentiful in this country — filled my wineskin up with water and drank my fill. Then I climbed a tree to where two large branches formed a fork and wedged myself in, and slept. When night came I climbed down, stamped for a while to get the pins and needles out of my feet and legs, and returned to the shoreline to walk.

The second morning I scrambled up an outcrop that formed the southwest arm of a little, horseshoe-shaped bay. Twas a bonny place with a grassy bench of land backed by a high rock wall. Near where the land on the northeast side turned to solid rock, a waterfall spilled over the cliff. The falls had dug a pool in the grassy land, and the pool in its turn overflowed and ran down the beach in a stream of cool, clear water to join its father ocean.

Out in the bay several seals were basking on a rock in the morning sun. When I started down the arm toward the beach, some plunged and some slipped into the glistening sea until all had disappeared from sight except one small pup that was left behind. It mewed pitifully. Crying for its mother, I thought. "Dinna be fretted, wee fellow," I said. "She'll come back for ye." I hoped it would be true.

Something, somewhere on the promontory I'd come down, moved. I whirled and scanned the ridge. Nothing. Was my imagination playing tricks? This bright, pretty place was suddenly turned dark and mournful as a Hieland moor with moving shadows and the continuing wailing of the wee seal pup. Twas as if spirits roamed. I swept the top of the bluff with my eyes, but there was nothing to be seen up there. The hairs on my neck pricked. *Dinna be so silly*, I chided myself, and started for the waterfall. At least I could have a drink and refill both my skins with fresh water before going on.

On the bench of land my feet crunched down on hard, lumpy things buried in the grass. I probed and found an undercarpet of broken shells and bones that went right from the front edge to the back. Refuse left by someone who had sometime lived here. I looked closer and saw patches of ground where tents might have been. On the *Borealis* Jock had told me that single families in tribes owned rights to rivers, streams, inlets, plots of land and bays, where they went at different seasons of the year to harvest things like clams, abalone, camus bulbs, seaweed, berries, crabs and various kinds of fish. Was this one of those family villages? If it was, when would the occupants be back? Perhaps soon. I ought to leave. But twas a protected place with a ready supply of water. And perhaps the people would be going north. I had been on the move all night. I was very tired. I decided that in spite of my unease it was a good place to rest.

I crouched beside the pool and spied a raccoon coming down the southwest arm. I breathed a sigh. The mystery of the moving shadow was solved. The raccoon was travelling on three legs, carrying salmonberries in one of its front paws. Several times it stopped, sat up on its hind legs and snuffed the air. When it was close to the bottom its wee eyes glared at me. Apparently deciding I was no threat, it proceeded to the stream, where it et the berries one by one. Finished, it started up the beach toward the pool. I didna move. By now it seemed completely unafraid of me, but it kept at least one eye on me at all times. After patrolling the rim of the pool, it plunged a paw into the water and flipped a small silver fish onto the grass. I marvelled at the ease with which it had done that.

My own empty stomach growled, but I knew I wouldna be able to take the raccoon's catch from him. If I tried, he would simply grab it in his teeth and run. I sat stock-still and watched him cut the fish into strips with his razor-sharp claws. His filleting was expert. He cut the cheeks out of the face but left the eyeballs in. He speared the pieces of cut fish on the claws of his right hand and then ate them daintily but fast, saving the cheeks for last. When he was finished, he washed his hands and face.

While *he* had been eating I had moved, slowly, to sit on a flat rock near the stream. I had picked up a largish stone. The furry little bandit's belly was very round; his movements far more sluggish now than they'd been before his feast. His eye caught the glint of light the sun bounced off my knife. Curious, he waddled toward me; came too close. I threw the stone hard enough to stun him. And then killed him quickly with my knife.

I made a fire on the beach below the high-water mark and roasted the meat on a spit made of driftwood. The skin might come in handy, I thought, but I didna ken how to treat it properly. If I left it as it was, it would soon smell very bad. I scraped it as best I could, then weighted it down in the salt water. Leaving it to soak, I et, buried the remains of my fire, found a shady spot, and lay down to sleep.

I woke when the sun was behind me in the western sky. The tide had flooded and was retreating again, but there had not been much change in water height. The water in the bay would still be warm to swim in. The seal pup was gone. Did I dare stay here longer?

Maybe Uncle's given up looking for me, I thought. *He'll have made a proper show of duty, but he disnae care much for me; so perhaps the duty of trying to find me has been served by now.* The thing that would make him continue in it would be Father, but did Father ken I had run away? I doubted that he did. So, I reasoned, I can stay here the night and start travelling by day, when it will be easier because I'll be able to see where I'm going. In truth, I knew I was just too tired from running to go on.

Stripping off my clothes, I waded into the water and sank down into a crouch. Rolling forward, I flattened out and swam just above the stony floor. I came up to gulp some air and dove down head first to stand on the bottom on my hands. I arched my back and let my feet fall over my head. Came up on my back, spouting water out my mouth. I closed my eyes and floated, bobbing up and down in the gentle, soothing waves. At last I began to feel quiet inside. I rolled over and swam back and forth between some rocks, then headed back to shore.

In the shallows I put my feet down and stood, watching the clear, cold water run down my arms, belly, legs. In the twilight thousands of tiny droplets glistened quicksilver on my skin, reminding me for a moment of my mother's love of wearing precious gems against her own soft skin. Her beauty was such it could not be diminished by the hard fire of the everlasting stones. A warm breeze blew off the water onto the land, drying me, and I smiled with the thought it might be Mother's lips blowing me a kiss. Feeling comforted, I walked up the beach.

I was almost dressed when, out of the corner of my eye, I saw an Indian on the same arm I and the raccoon had come down. My mind screamed, *Run! Get away!* But I stood there as if held to the spot by some unseen force and watched while he descended and strode to a spot on the bench of land where he stooped and laid what looked like rolled skunk cabbage leaves on the ground. A little distance from them he plunged the spear he carried into the sandy soil. Squatting, he pointed at the cabbage leaves, which had fallen open to reveal two large fish inside them.

He was not wearing the shirt and trowsers I'd last seen him in, but I recognized him. He had been with Billy Trueworthy when Billy had returned me to my uncle. Which meant my uncle had sent him after me. How long had he been following me, watching me? Why had he let me come so far? How could I get away from him? He rose and came toward me. I wanted to scream. I wanted to close my eyes and pray. I wanted to bolt. But I did none of those. Trembling, I willed myself to stand where I was, keep my eyes open, watch him.

He came close enough to touch the wolf's head buttons on my vest. He took one near the bottom, rolled it between his thumb and forefinger. I could hardly breathe. Then he walked back to his spear. My legs went weak and I was taking in air in fast little gulps as if there wasn't enough of it in the world to fill my lungs. I touched the button he had touched. In a voice that sounded to my ears to be as quivery as my legs felt, I said, "The wolf's head is my family crest."

"Cook fish," was his reply.

Standing still, unwilling to move lest I fall down, breathing hard but deeper now, I forced myself to look directly at him. "Ye want me to cook it?" He made a gruntlike sound. No servant I had ever known would have dared to order me about. But his manner told me clearly that though he might work for my uncle, he was not a servant. His manner also indicated he would wait. His distance made me feel a little braver. "I'll nae cook for you," I declared.

"You cook," he said. It was evident he meant it. I was too afraid to resist further, but I took time to put my light plaid on. With shaky hands I fastened one end to my shoulder with a brooch and pulled the loose end over my vest and wrapped it securely round my middle, tucking the end into a wrap to hold it there. Then, being careful to keep my knife out of sight, I took the lucifers from my bundle and rewrapped the rest of my things in the longer plaid, which I tied closed.

There were two salmon, about five or six pounds each, I judged. I would need wood for a fire and some sticks to skewer them on and set them over the flames. First I needed a firepit. I set about digging it, keeping my eyes on my work now rather than on him, but I had observed him well enough.

He looked not far above my own age. Fifteen, sixteen, I guessed. A laddie still. Somehow that thought was heartening. The hair on his head was thick and straight, falling to his shoulders. Although he had worn no jewellery when last I'd seen him, now he had on Indian earrings — shells dangling from his lobes. He also wore a necklace that looked made of teeth strung on a leather thong, and a stout knife with a tidy hole through its ornate handle hung on another thong around his neck. He was fairly small in stature, but his muscles were well defined, showing clearly under his burnished, dusky skin. I had noticed his maleness, too, and saw him see me do it. He made no move to cover or hide himself in any way, nor did he preen. He appeared to be completely at ease with his nakedness. Unwillingly, I envied him that naturalness.

When I used a lucifer to start the fire, he came and held out his hand. I gave him one and he struck the tip against a rock as I had done. It flared to life and he dropped it into the fire, then held out his hand for another. I was surprised to discover my fear thawing with his display of childlike wonder at the fire-lighters. It was what I'd felt when I had first seen them. But I shook my head. "Waste," I said, and was grateful when he did not pursue it.

I picked up a fish and he made a motion with his hands for me to put it down. When the fire had burned to coals, he showed me how to cook them Indian-style. He took the cabbage leaves to the stream and wet them, used some to wrap the fish, laid these on the coals, and covered them with the rest of the leaves. He found two hollow bones in the grass and pushed them through the upper layer of leaves. Then he motioned for me to help him cover it all with sand. We piled on a layer, being careful not to cover the ends of the bones. He took one of my skins and poured fresh water into the bones until the steam misted upward through the sand. Then he settled down beside the cooking fish to wait. He showed no desire at all to talk.

The silence was not easy for me. I could not ken his thoughts, but I was thinking of being taken back to my uncle's house. My eyes darted here and there, searching for a way out, but I knew that if I ran the Indian could easily run me down. He had the advantage of knowing the country while I did not. I would have to wait for a better chance.

When he decided the time was right, he scooped the sand away. As he unwrapped the fish, all my thoughts turned to food. He stabbed both fish with his knife, took them to his place beside his spear and laid them down. Squatting, he ate, rapidly slicing off large pieces of flesh and gulping them down noisily. He gave no sign he intended to share his catch with me. I began to shake again, with anger, and with fear. Had he learned this practice from my uncle? Did he mean to starve me as punishment? I stepped toward him, intending to face him down, but he abruptly got to his feet, pulled his spear from the sand, put the thong of the waterskin he still had over his head, and went to the northeast arm. Without a backward glance he climbed the rocky incline. In a few minutes he had disappeared.

I didn't know what to make of it. Was he gone for good? Should I run? He had found me here. Could he not find me anywhere? He'd left a little less than half a fish uneaten. I grabbed it, gobbled it down, and the question of my escape was settled when he came around the corner of the bay in a dugout canoe. I had missed my chance. I was filled with self-disgust. There was no way to escape him now. *Daft! Ye're daft and spineless, lass! Is this what yer mother raised ye for?* I ranted in my head. Which was useless, too.

He beached the canoe, got out, waded into the water and swam. He dove down out of sight. I'd nae miss a second chance. I grabbed my bundle and sprinted for the boat. But before I'd run five steps, he was up, waving the raccoon skin I'd sunk. So now I knew. He had been watching me for some time before he'd shown himself. My cheeks burned hot with what he maun have seen. He came up the beach, the sparkle in his eyes belying the solemn look on his face. With a shock I kenned he was laughing at me. This redskin was nasty. Nasty and sneaky and ... and I would nae go back! I broke. Got to the canoe and took hold of it and tried to push it off the beach. It was a good deal heavier than it looked. I grabbed the paddle and whirled to face my uncle's henchman, determined to strike him if I had to, to get away.

He stood out of reach of the paddle's length, not looking at all afraid of me, or it. "We go now," he said.

I tried another tack. "I am travelling to Nanaimo, to meet my father," I said. "I would like it would ye transport me there."

He just looked at me.

"Coleville," I tried. "Some people call it that. North," I pointed. "I want tae go north."

He stood, unyielding.

"My uncle will be glad of it if ye'll take me to my father," I said, believing it was true, "and my father will reward ye well when we arrive."

"Water good to go now," was all he replied.

I was desperate. I dug into my bundle and pulled out a silver cup. I held it out to him. "This is for you, if ye'll take me where I want to go."

He dropped the raccoon skin into the canoe, took the cup and examined it, running his fingers over the wolf's head handles. He bent and opened the tight-fitting lid of a wooden box that was under one of the cross poles that served as thwarts. From inside the box he lifted out a wooden dish, also with a lid. The dish was highly polished with the soft patina that time and use impart to wooden things. Both the box and dish were decorated: indented carvings on the box, a sculptured carving on the handle of the dish lid. The images on his things were not lifelike, as were the drawings and sculptures I was used to seeing. These were filled with geometric shapes that evoked a feeling in me of seeing something from the inside-out. It was an eerie, haunting feeling, and I thought both box and dish were beautiful. He put the cup inside the dish and stowed them both back inside the box.

Bringing me back to my unfortunate reality, he motioned for me to get into the canoe. I didna ken what else to do, and resigned myself to it. Wearily, I climbed over the gunwale and made my way to the opposite end, where I set on the pole that had been wedged crosswise between the sides. I sat facing him. Balancing on that skinny seat was much harder than he'd made it look, and I had to drop the paddle I still held and clutch the boat rim to steady myself while he pushed us off the beach and leapt aboard. In what seemed one motion, he had his paddle in his hands and was stroking so strongly and swiftly we left a wake as we glided through the water. Soon we were out of the bay and into the channel, heading east, edging south. My chest ached and heaved. Hot tears threatened to run down my cheeks, but I fought to hold them in.

I thought back to the cold November day when Father and I had killed the stag. Was it only eight months ago? A deep lament, like molten lava, bubbled up in me. I hated this place, I hated this Indian. Most of all, I hated my uncle. *If twere nae for you, Uncle, Father and I would be together at Dunharbar. We'd have Nanny and Cook, and our friends, and Sampson still. We'd be near Mother. Mother, and Wallace, and Earl and wee Colin.* Oh, Mother! The pain hardened into icy gall. *I hate you, Uncle, and I make a solemn vow that I shall repay your treachery, even if it takes the remainder of my life!* It was a Hieland vow, backed with all the vengeful feeling of an ancient people who had, in the past, acted with swords first, words last. Then I was spent. My churning, changing emotions had exhausted me. Overwhelmed with tiredness, I fell asleep.

❦ TWENTY ❧
En Route

I WOKE curled up in the bottom of the canoe. The sun was up. Twas a beautiful, hot summer's day, but I was stiff and sore from being poked by what occupied the planked floor between the seats: the paddle I had held, a cedar mat, some rope, a large, finely woven basket, the Indian's spear ... and a gun. Not a musket, which I had seen some Indians carrying, but a repeater rifle. He saw me eye the gun and kept his eyes on me. I struggled back onto my seat. Behind me was a round water cask, very like the ones carried in ship's boats, and the thought of drinking water, and the sound of rushing water, made me realize how badly I needed to urinate. I pointed toward the closest shore. My captor shook his head.

He was swirling his paddle backwards and forwards, sculling, holding the canoe outside a narrow channel that had big rocks at one side of the entrance. Tons and tons of water were pouring through at a great rate, creating an overfall about four feet high. That was the rushing sound.

Minutes later, I could see the overfall was flattening out, although the current wasn't running any slower. A few minutes after that, he was paddling through it hard. I held on, but I felt my body thrill. If this had been another circumstance, I would have liked the speed and skill I was being shown. As it was, I hoped we'd be overturned, the Indian would be drowned, and I'd somehow manage to hold on and upright the canoe.

But we made it through entire. We rounded a point of land and were in another narrow channel of water, flanked on both sides by islands and islets. I sorrowed anew inside myself. Meeting Her Majesty's ships, or any ships, in waters such as this was impossible. I would have no opportunity to call to whites for help. For the moment, though, that was overshadowed by my urgent need. Again I pointed to land. "Prithee, go there," I beseeched.

A short time later we entered a quiet bay with a wide, gravelly beach, the land rising steeply behind it. The usual tree cladding came down to the water's edge on either side of the beach, and climbed the hill behind it. When the canoe was close to the beach, I jumped clear and ran for the trees. As I relieved myself and my body relaxed, it came to me the forest was thick. I might be able to hide here. If I could hide long enough, the Indian might get tired of looking for me and leave me here. *Then what?* I didn't know. I'd think about that later. I looked around. He hadn't followed me, or at least I couldn't see him.

Stealthily, I moved uphill, trying to make no sound. The incline was steep; the hill high, and when I got to the top of the island I looked toward the channel we'd been in. It took a minute for me to understand what I was looking at. Facing the direction we had been moving, the sun, risen now to a point somewhere near eleven o'clock, was on my right and towards my front. The morning sun. So, we had been going northward, north and east, not south. North toward Nanaimo, east because that was the way the channel ran. I raced back to the beach, not wanting to waste any more time ashore. But the Indian was gone. With him, my belongings. I was dazed.

I could think of nothing to do other than to climb the hill again to where I'd seen some bushes loaded with huckleberries, and gorge myself on them. I ate my fill and went back to the beach. I sat, trying to decide what to do. I was still pondering when the Indian came gliding back. I hastened to meet him, helped him pull up the canoe, and maun have smiled my welcome at him because he grinned back at me. I wasna going to tell him I'd thought him gone, or that I had been so mistaken of the direction we were going. I was to learn how often the dictates of the tides, and channels and waterways neither I nor any of my countrymen who had not plied these waters for a lifetime could know anything about, would confuse me about where, exactly, I was headed.

He retrieved some fish from the bottom of the boat and dropped them on the ground. I flitted to look for wood to cook them with. There were no skunk leaves to wrap them in, so this time I skewered the fish and roasted them on a spit.

As he had before, the native took all of the cooked meat, moved aside and started to eat. I did not know it was a custom of his people for men to eat always before the women, and I thought it rude. I was used to being served first. I walked over to where he was. "I would like some, too," I said.

He seemed surprised, but he cut off some flesh and handed it to me. The meat, I noted, was far less moist than it had been when cooked his way. Between mouthfuls, I asked, "How many days is't to reach Nanaimo?"

He shrugged.

"Have you been there?" I wanted to know. "Dae ye ken how far it is?"

"If wind, water, good — four sun, three moon. No good, maybe seven sun. Maybe more."

I had no idea how long he had worked for Uncle Hammond, though I thought it maun be a long time as he understood English so well, and that thought, together with Mrs. O'Reilly's stories of how reliable the Indians had been about delivering her goods and returning with her money, gave me fresh alarm. "Did my uncle hire ye tae come for me?" I asked.

He grunted rather than spoke. "No uncle."

The weight of the world was lifted off my shoulders, but it was fleeting relief as a new suspicion flooded in.

"Then how came ye to find me?"

"I go home," he said. "You Indian village, where I stop."

"Do ye mean that was a village site of your people?"

A single grunt, which I could not determine as yes or no.

"Where is yer home?" I asked.

He waved his hand northward, drawing himself up as he did so. "Matlinniaht territory. I a'xoe, son of koa'yauc, son of nepitm'a, son of ..." He continued on for fully ten minutes, reciting names with sounds so strange to my ears I could not follow them, but I understood he was reciting his lineage. I was astounded. I knew the lineage of my people was written in our family Bible, but I could not have recited it earlier than my great-great-grandfathers. The Indian went many times further back than that. When he had finished, I tried to repeat the first name he had said, but I could not make the sounds he had made.

He repeated it for me. "A'xoe. English, young seal."

"I am pleased to meet ye," I said. "My name is Elizabeth Macqueen. I am called Tess."

I thought he would stay here then awhile to rest, but he had finished eating and was already heading toward the canoe. He had paddled through the night and through the morning, and I did not know how long he'd been awake before that. I had heard stories about the Indians' ability to go without sleep for several days at a time. I was to learn this one could go without food and water, too, far better than I.

❦

We had travelled for two days and nights, stopping only twice, briefly, for food and rest. I had joined in the paddling and in spite of blisters on my soft hands, and aching back and shoulders, had learned to stroke with some efficiency. It was more difficult than it looked, perched on the narrow seat, especially when we moved against the tide. But I needed to do something other than simply change position, sitting first on the pole and then on the cluttered floor of the canoe when my buttocks hurt. To my surprise, Young Seal was a patient teacher. He said nothing when I dipped my paddle into a swell at the wrong time and hindered him, and nothing when I got it right. He simply let me learn.

He was not talkative, but I wanted another activity to take my mind off my painful body, and I kept pressing him for words. He had a good memory and a better ability to pronounce my language than I his. He said his words were Chinook jargon, the language used for trade between the Indians and the whites all over the colony, and I thought twould be a most useful language to learn. However, he only spoke when spoken to and I found the conversation difficult to carry.

❦

We were still among the islands and I was marvelling at a particularly inviting-looking bay with a flat, accessible, sandy beach, and behind that a flat bench of lush grass, part of a larger island, when Young Seal touched me on the back with the tip of his paddle. I turned to look at him and he motioned for me to stop paddling. I lifted my paddle and laid it across the gunwales and waited. A moment later I saw a small, black-tailed deer step out of the trees and into the long grass seventy-five feet or so from the ocean's edge. The animal lowered its head to browse. Without thinking, I let go of my paddle, reached for Young Seal's gun, slowly eased it up to my shoulder and aimed. The instant the deer raised its head, I shot. It fell quivering, and then lay still.

Young Seal's brow creased. "*Tenas le bal kloshe,*" he said. He was smiling. By his tone and the individual words I recognized, I knew he was pleased. I puffed up inside, proud as any peacock, but I said nothing. My mouth was already watering for the venison.

While I gutted, skinned and butchered the meat, he built a firepit. The next lesson I got was how long it took a deer to cook this way. We had long since cut off pieces of the outside flesh to eat, but I had not been raised to waste good meat, and so wanted it cooked through. After two days and nights in the confines of a canoe, I also yearned for rest. Young Seal was content to whittle and sleep. In the morning, before the sun was up, we et the rest of the still-roasting deer. Young Seal buried the firepit, and we were off again.

By mid-morning the following day, strong northerly winds were whipping up the ocean against the flooding tide, creating short, steep seas. Ahead was another pass between two islands where I couldna believe the speed and height of the water pouring through it. Young Seal said something and motioned with his hand in a way that gave me to understand we maun wait. We turned back the way we'd come.

The wind and water became fickle. Confused by hidden rocks and shoals, seas came at us from all directions. A whirlpool opened ahead of the bow, just catching a piece of it before we could reverse our strokes and get clear. The bow was whipped to the right so fast it took several seconds for me to comprehend we had been spun round. I was now peering into the dizzying swirl on the port side of the canoe, whilst on the starboard side waves came at us broadside. Certain we were going to be pushed over the edge of the whirl, pulled vertical, swamped and drowned, I turned in terror to look at Young Seal, while I plunged my paddle deep and pulled long. The muscles of his neck, shoulders, arms and body bulged with his effort as he dug and stroked. While I stared at him, a huge wave rolled toward us. In the instant before it hit, Young Seal lifted his paddle clear of the water, turned it sideways and neatly sliced off the top half of the wave. In the same motion his paddle was returned to work at the side of the canoe. The wave hit, rocking us, but his action had diffused its power and we shipped less than a quart of water over the side.

"*Winapie!*" Young Seal yelled behind me, and I held my paddle still. "*Klatawa! Klatawa!*" he shouted, and I paddled for all I was worth. We moved past the whirl.

"Ye've a great bag of tricks, laddie," I grinned at him.

The wind picked up and Young Seal started chanting. When a wave larger than the rest came at us, his chant became a yell and he blew and spit against the wind, as if he was in contention with some evil spirit of the storm. He turned toward the nearest land.

At the entrance to the bay he was heading for, a sandbar and a maze of rocks made the waves rear up. We rose on the back of an advancing wave and were carried over the reef. I churned my arms as fast as I was able as we raced down the cresting water, to beat the curl before it broke on our backs. In waist-deep water Young Seal leaped out of the boat, grabbed hold of one side, and ran its head onto the beach. The wave smashed, throwing spray into our stern, and then its foaming fingers raked the sand as they retreated back into the surf with a whoosh.

When I'd caught my breath, I saw we were not alone. Up the beach to our right, four canoes had been pulled high and dry and turned up on their sides. Under the cover of each huddled several Indians, all of whom were watching us. "Haida," Young Seal said. "*Peshack,* enemy."

We could not leave, but it seemed to me more dangerous to stay. Young Seal handed me the gun and while I stood guard he pulled the canoe up to where it, too, could be rolled up on its side. He did it so the opening faced his enemies, and he used the paddles to prop it in place. We crawled under it, knowing our backs at least were protected by the thick cedar hull. Young Seal took the gun and I took my knife out of my plaid. For the rest of the day we watched the Haidas watching us. No one made a move.

When night fell the wind still blew at gale force levels and it was raining hard. The rain formed a curtain that made it impossible to see more than twenty-five or thirty feet ahead. I couldna see the Haidas and their canoes but I could feel them. I stared in their direction, unwilling to trust my ears to pick up any sound of an advance against the background of shrieking wind and slamming seas. My eyes burned and my body cramped with the tension. I wriggled from time to time, trying to ease the cramps. Young Seal sat cross-legged and was still. He motioned for me to go to sleep.

I lay down, pillowing my head on one arm. In my other hand, I held my knife. I couldna sleep, but perhaps I dozed. Sometime later he touched me, handed me the gun, and while I sat up he stretched out and closed his eyes. In seconds, it seemed, came soft snores punctuated with a gentle little whistle every few breaths. I was so tense I almost giggled at the sound. In time I slumped, but thoughts of never seeing my father again kept me awake.

The storm blew itself out overnight. Before dawn I could see the stars winking in the sky. The sea had dropped back down; the watch-dog waves were gone. The Haidas began to stir. I saw their dark shapes emerge from under their canoes. Without my saying or doing anything, Young Seal came wide awake. He sat up, took back the gun and duck-walked out in front of the canoe. He sat there, cross-legged, holding the gun in his lap. His enemies didn't even glance in our direction. They went about getting ready to leave, dropping their canoes onto their bottoms, pushing them into the water, and reloading them. With a few shouts, they had paddled over the reef, and were gone.

Young Seal said, "This best slave-hunting season. Many tribes hunting for women, children to take to village. Warriors make trouble. Caught, killed. One warrior in canoe, sometimes taken for slave." I wished he hadn't told me.

Much later, I would learn that my uncle had put the word out I'd been taken by Indians. He had issued a warning that when it was discovered which tribe had taken me, that tribe would be punished, and that if I had been harmed there would be dire consequences. Anyone involved would be hunted down and hanged. Queen Victoria's gunboats would destroy the village of the perpetrators. A description of me had been dispatched on every ship.

The Indians' information network was vast and incredibly fast-moving; their ability to match descriptions with people they saw uncanny. With threats looming large, no tribe would risk touching me, and so my uncle's lie was what had saved Young Seal and me in this, the peak season of raiding and trading by tribes that were out looking for new slaves.

"Will they come back?" I asked.

"No."

I found myself reluctant to leave this place, though it was far from comfortable. But leave we did.

At the pass we'd turned back from the day before, the tide was right and we had no wait. We were soon through. On the other side, Young Seal moved us far out into the straits to avoid the shoals and jagged shores of any land. I petitioned God to let no other canoes come this way.

IN the morning Young Seal told me we would hunt deer on several small islands, because he desired to have something to trade for goods at the Nanaimo settlement. He said we were very close to Nanaimo, and my impatience at the idea of our arrival being delayed was palpable. Appearing not to notice it, he went on to say it was the habit of the women of his tribe to keep what they received when they traded things they had made, or food they had killed or dug to trade with whites. Other food, he said, unless eaten on the spot, went into household stores, with part going to the chief. He said our catch was all for trade, and some of it would be mine. My displeasure at the dallying was a little appeased.

We soon discovered that I, having more acquaintance with guns than he, was the better shot. But he knew where to find the game, and how to come upon it without it knowing we were there. He could also gut in half the time I could. We formed a partnership. Before sunset we had half a dozen deer heaped in the canoe, parts of bodies spilling over the gunwales. Young Seal answered my question about what it was he wanted with a list including flour, biscuits, potatoes, molasses, a tin pot, bullets and blankets, but I didn't know what I wanted yet. I said I would see what Father needed before I decided.

With the last light blazing on the water, we entered a bay on the northeast edge of a large island Young Seal said the English called Gaviota. Named for the birds, he said. There were hundreds of them. Gulls and cormorants circling in the sky, bobbing on the water and roosting on the cliffs. Many kept watch over our progress, with a greedy eye on what lay in our canoe.

We were tired, and after pulling the boat up on the beach and lighting fires at either end to keep scavengers away, we stretched out on the sand, he with nothing between him and nature, me covered with my plaid, and were soon asleep. Young Seal had said there was a village on this island, but the Indians were not enemies of his.

In the dawn light, I saw several carvings in rocks — figures chipped out of the rock faces. I was curious who had done them and what they meant and I asked Young Seal if he knew. He told me many tribes made pictures such as these. Some had been done in a time no one remembered, and some were newly done. When I asked him what they meant, he shrugged. "Maybe say this Indian territory," he said, and I thought they did that all right.

I was very impatient to get where I was going, but we must stop and fish on the edge of rips. However anxious I was, by now I knew trade goods were very important to him, and he would do what he maun to get them. I was amazed at the little time it took him to handline forty fish, which I helped him land. Then, truly laden, we were off again. The gunwales barely skimmed above the surface of the water and there was very little room inside the boat for us. I had more cause to be amazed as he showed his skill at handling such a load.

In less than half an hour we had rounded the northern tip of the island and Young Seal swept his arm and pointed. "Nanaimo," he said. We were coming at it from the east.

❧

No one seemed to take any notice of us as we slipped toward the town. Nanaimo was a cluster of soot-covered buildings on a stump-filled rise of land, surrounded by a dark forest of immense trees. At the back of the town, behind the forest, a mountain so high it had pockets of clean, white snow partway up it, even in summer, reared. Most of the buildings were very small; some were a little bigger. One looked like the bastion in Fort Victoria, though this one had eight sides. It was a bastion complete with cannons inside it, I would learn, bastions being considered necessary in every settlement for the protection of the settlers.

Fifty yards to the left of the bastion there was a boardwalk built on stilts out over the water, with more buildings built on the boardwalk. One of these had a high fence in front of it and a jetty in front of the fence with a float attached to the jetty. A Red Ensign flew here, and the front of the building that could be seen over the top of the fence bore the legend COMPANY STORE. Young Seal steered for the float below the Company Store.

Toward the north end of it, the harbour was alive with Indian canoes filled with women and lasses ferrying coal to four ships that lay at anchor not far from a jetty that came off a tremendous pile of dirty mining refuse. The slag spilled down the slope and right into the water below the building Father had described in a letter as the head of the mine called Number One. To the right of Number One and below it, down at the water's edge, a rackety steam engine huffed and chugged its white smoke into the air from under cover of another log shack. This was Number Three Shaft, where Father worked.

Number Three was wet enough to require an engine to pump the water out of it. He'd written me about it with some humour, saying the machine was expensive because "where the horses didna demand any great wage, the machine operator does." He'd said several shafts had closed but there was no threat of shortage of work for miners because a new fifty-four-inch seam had been dis-covered, and the powers in San Francisco and south of there were asking specifically for Dunsmuir coal, which was as good as Scottish coal, Father said. I remembered he had written that there was a rivalry between Mr. Dunsmuir and Mr. Robinson, and Father thought Mr. Dunsmuir would come out on top. Thinking of Father being now so close at hand, my mouth was stretched wide with my happiness.

My heart was thumping with excitement. I kept turning my head, hoping to catch sight of him, though I knew that by this hour he would have been down in the mine for almost a day of work. There was no one visible except the man in charge of weighing the coal at a weigh station near Number One, the Indians who carried the weighed coal in packs on their backs down to the jetty where they put it into baskets, the Indians in the canoes who took the baskets to the ships, and the men on the ships.

All of the Indians I saw here had the cone-shaped heads, and they were dressed similarly to those in Victoria, in torn blankets or shawls pinned over what looked to be very old cloth skirts and trowsers. Indeed, Young Seal now had on a blanket, too.

By now I kenned there were many different tribes that reshaped their infants' heads, forcing the foreheads to slant backwards and the crown to be thrust into a point by keeping the infants on a hard board and applying a pad and hard pressure on the forehead with tight binding. Sometimes a rock was used for weight. It was a look the adult Indians prized, but I thought it like the Chinese practice of binding feet, and cruel. I could see no beauty in it. I was glad Young Seal had not suffered this fate of having his head squeezed, and he had told me his tribe did not do that.

He had told me more of his customs, and I had been amused when he'd also said he'd come to the south end of Vancouver's Island to be among the white men because his tribe wanted to learn all they could about the whites. But he was deadly serious. Knowing our ways, our beliefs, was the only way the Indians would survive us, he said, and it made me very sad to think they believed we would do them so much harm. I'd made up my mind to speak to Father about it. Perhaps as a missionary he could allay their fears.

I started to jump out of the canoe almost before we got to the float, but Young Seal stopped me and I sat back down. Twas another of his manners. Women did not go first into any situation. Twas he who went and knocked on the gate of the fence, while I waited in the canoe. It took some time before the gate was opened and a man came out, guiding a wheeled box made from bent twigs down a track that led onto the jetty. He wheeled the box right onto the float and then he peered into the canoe. "All right," he said. Young Seal got back into the canoe and began to throw the fish into the box while the man counted. The man had not so much as glanced at me, as if I didn't exist.

"There are forty fish," I said, "and six deer."

The man stopped counting and stared at me.

In the face of his apparent shock, I introduced myself. "My name is Elizabeth Macqueen, Sir, and I wonder if ye are acquainted with my father, Iain Macqueen?"

I was affronted when he turned without a word and ran back up the jetty and through the gate, but it was barely minutes before he returned with another, older man lumbering beside him. The first man was babbling, "She ain't Injin, Mr. Horne, she ain't Injin. She's that girlie what was taken, the Macqueen girl."

"Hush up," the older man snapped. "Are you daft as well as blind, man? Any man can see she aint dressed like a Injin. Don't stand there like a nincompoop, get her out of there," Mr. Horne ordered, and then he shouted for someone else to come.

I was handed out of the canoe and instantly surrounded by arms coming at me from both sides. They partly pushed and partly carried me up the jetty, through the gates, across the beach that was the yard below the store, into the store, and straight through into a bedroom at the back where I was sat on a bed. A woman who was in the family way came and sat beside me and picked up one of my hands, and the men went out. All the while I was being hustled away from the canoe I heard a commotion behind me of men who had arrived quickly, shouting, but it was a mixture of sound and I couldn't sort the words. I had no chance to turn around to see what was happening because

I was kept going forward and held onto very tightly. No one had paid any attention at all to my protests.

"Miss Macqueen," the woman said, "I'm Mrs. Hawkes. Are you all right, lass?"

I was alarmed with the kind of attention I was getting and with not knowing what was happening to Young Seal. "I'm very well, thank ye, Mrs. Hawkes. I'm anxious to see my father and Young Seal —"

"I'm acquainted with your father, Miss Macqueen. I'm afraid he isn't here. He left for Genoa as soon as he got word you'd been abducted."

An acute sense of shame swelled my throat and I cried, "Oh no!"

"Are you quite sure you're all right?" she asked. "You haven't been hurt in any way?"

"Hurt? No no, Young Seal kept me clear of any harm. What's happened to him?"

"Is that the Indian you were with?"

"Aye. He brought me here. I wasna abducted, Mrs. Hawkes. I came of my own accord and partway in the journey I came upon Young Seal and hired him to bring me the rest of the way. No one kidnapped me or has hurt me at all."

She still showed the look of grave concern and I lowered my eyes to hide my returning sense of shame. How much to tell a stranger? I couldn't tell her I'd run away from my uncle.

"Please rest here, Miss Macqueen," she was saying, when the door to the room opened and a man with a doctor's bag came in.

"Miss Macqueen," Mrs. Hawkes said, "this is Doctor Benson." He was a very big man with a head covered in a mass of grey hair that was tossed every which way. His square face wore a heavy beard salted with grey.

"All right, let's have a look at her, then," the man said. He picked up my hand and felt my wrist, then patted the back of my hand. His hand was as warm as he was rotund. "Strong as a horse," he said. "Have you talked to her, Mary?"

"I have. She tells me she's unhurt and that she wasn't abducted. She made the journey on her own."

The man's eyebrows went up. "Does she now tell you that?"

"I've come to join my father, Dr. Benson," I repeated and, in a much lower voice, said, "I ... uh ... I left my uncle's house against his wishes, but I was not taken anywhere against my own."

There was a rise of commotion that floated in through the window and I felt my neck prickle. "What are they doing? Young Seal ... do they think *he* abducted me? I maun go and — "

"I'll go and see," Dr. Benson said. He turned and I got up and was right on his heels. "No, child, you stay here."

"No, Sir, please," I pleaded, and neither he nor Mrs. Hawkes did anything to stop me from coming.

The noise was issuing from the bastion. Dr. Benson and Mrs. Hawkes went through a gate at the back of the store and started on a dirt path that went down a ravine and up the other side of it, winding around and between the stumps. A small crowd of men had gathered outside the bastion and were standing in bunches of twos and threes on the grass, while more miners drifted toward it from the little cottages behind and to the right of Number One. Dr. Benson went past them and knocked on the door, and when a man opened it he went past him into the ground floor of the bastion. Mrs. Hawkes followed him, and I followed her.

Besides the man at the door there were five other whites and Young Seal, who had his hands trussed behind his back and was being held bent forward over the barrel of a cannon by two men. A man with a cat-o'-nine tails in his hands stood to one side of and slightly behind Young Seal. There were welts on Young Seal's bared back.

"Stop it!" I yelled. "I hired him to fetch me here! I wasna kidnapped. Don't ye touch him! Ye've no cause!"

Whereupon the man who'd opened the door said to another, "There yer be, Stuart, wi' egg on yer face as what yer bloody haste gets yer and I want it know'd I were an unwilling part of this here jury."

The man he'd addressed drew an old paper out of a pocket of his coat, unfolded it, and read: "In accordance with the laws of Her Majesty, Queen Victoria, Queen of

England in this her twenty-first year of reign, God save the Queen, and whereas there is new testimony taking the part of the heathen named Axel previously found guilty of misdemeanours against Her Majesty Queen Victoria ..."

"What?" I demanded. "He has committed no misdemeanours unless safely transporting a British subject from one place to another be one."

"He has resisted arrest and injured a man in the process," the man said.

"It was false arrest and he had every right to resist," Dr. Benson said quietly. "Let him go immediately, Stuart." The two men holding Young Seal down let him up and moved away from him.

The man who'd read the paper turned it around and held it up so Young Seal could see the writing. "See this official mark?" he said to Young Seal, pointing to the mark of a shipping company that was above the body of a letter. "Mark of Tyee Queen Victoria. It means yer free to go, but if yer cause trouble of any kind she'll send the gunboats after yer. King George boats come if yer make trouble," he repeated, "and shoot and burn yer village. Ye know it's been done before. If ye make trouble, ye'll have a taste of British justice." He refolded the paper and put it back in his coat pocket. He walked to Young Seal slowly, saying, "Stand still now, while I untie yer." Young Seal maintained an absolutely smooth countenance but there was a murderous look buried in his dark eyes.

When he was freed he stepped toward the man. The man jerked back. Young Seal spoke in a low, threatening voice. "Paper not from white Queen. British justice not Indian law. This Indian territory." Saying no more, he walked past his tormentors and out of the building, not looking back or acknowledging anyone in any way.

I had never been more ashamed. "Did you suppose ye could fool him with a false document? Tis you, sir, who should have a taste of justice."

Mr. Stuart bristled. "A child has no place in here. Get her out."

"Please come with me, Elizabeth. You'll stay with us until your father gets back," Mrs. Hawkes said matter-of-factly.

I had not finished what I wanted to say to these men, but I went.

There was muttered conversation going on among the men and the few women who had joined them. I caught snatches of sentences. "Injin lover ... His squaw ... Alone with a Injin ... Can't hardly tell her from a Injin ..." I winced, and must have shown it, because Mrs. Hawkes said softly, "Hold your head up, Elizabeth, or you'll give them the false idea they're right. That's the way."

"I'd like to say goodbye to Young Seal, Mrs. Hawkes, to thank him. And what will be done to compensate him for being punished wrongly?"

"Nothing, I'm afraid. I'll accompany you."

At that moment I thought as little of Nanaimo and its settlers as I ever had of Mrs. Motherwell, Mr. Samuel, Mr. Rake and my uncle. My disgust covered up the kindness that was being shown me like a heavy, smothering blanket. I understood the murderous darkness in Young Seal's eyes.

In the store Mr. Horne said Young Seal took payment for only some of the deer and fish.

"Aye, Mr. Horne," I said, "he is honourable, and he told me what I killed are mine. Dae ye ken if he'll be returning here?"

"Ha," he snorted unflatteringly. "Savages is here one minute, gone the next. Can't never tell when they'll stay, when they'll go, or when they'll come back."

"Dae ye wonder they're evasive when they're treated as he was?"

"Don't matter how they're treated, Miss," Mr. Horne said, "they're a slippery lot. You've not been among 'em long, I'll wager."

"Nay, I have not," I agreed, "but I was with Young Seal the best part of five days and in all that time he was never less than gallant, which is much more than can be said for the white people here who would beat him for no cause."

"Likely weren't a lick amiss, Miss," he said. "What goods do you want for settling up?"

"I dinna ken. I'll wait until Father is here to make a selection."

"Right. It'll be marked in the book. Mind, there are strict limits to what you can take in trade."

"I'm certain Father will be aware of what those are," I said, and turned away. I hoped Young Seal had not left to go back to his home, though why he would stay where he'd been assaulted I could not think. But I was not to see him again.

Mrs. Hawkes and I went to the coal jetty and got a ride out in a canoe to HMS *Daphne*, which was due to head south on the next tide. I made arrangements with the captain to take the news of my safe arrival to Father in Genoa, and then Mrs. Hawkes took me back to her home and made me tea.

In the two days I stayed with her family, I learned that she had become the settlement's nurse because of her abilities. Dr. Benson called on her, settlers came to her directly to have their wounds dressed, and even the Indians came to her for advice about medical matters, especially venereal disease. In all cases she dispensed medicines, bandages and advice with a calm, forthright, caring manner that I greatly admired.

During the day, the three Hawkes children who were school age attended school in the cabin that was the teacher's house as well as being the school. Mrs. Hawkes said the teacher, Mr. Bryant, lamented that not many children came to school, and that he worked very hard to get them there. Those who did attend did not often pay their fees and he had almost no supplies. She said the parents of the Indian children who went to school had asked Mr. Bryant when *they* would be paid because their children were going there, and so Mr. Bryant lived in poverty that would have been unrelieved had it not been for the support his uncle, George Robinson, gave him. As Father had written, poverty was indeed a hard fact of life for most of the settlers here.

I wondered if someday I would attend the school. Each night I prayed that Father would let me stay. Right now I was happy helping Mrs. Hawkes care for the children that weren't in school, and processing the garden vegetables that had come ready.

~

Father came, unannounced, on the third day. I was stirring clothes in a tub in the Hawkes' yard. Sensing someone coming up behind me, I turned just as he reached me. I dropped my stir-stick, wrapped my arms around him and hugged and hugged. I inhaled the smell of him and rejoiced in the feel of him. "Oh, Father, I ..."

"There's nowt to say now, lass, except thank the Lord ye're safe. Good morning, Mrs. Hawkes. I was told by Robinson Tess was here and have come to fetch her and to thank ye and Thomas for looking out for her."

"It was our pleasure, Mr. Macqueen. I'm happy the captain was able to deliver the message and you're quickly home," Mary Hawkes said. "But Tess has been so helpful I don't know what we'll do without her."

"Message?"

"The one I sent with the captain of the *Daphne* telling ye I was safely come to Nanaimo, Father. Ye did receive it?"

"Nay. I didna linger in Genoa. When the *Sarah Stone* got that far and we hadna spotted ye on the water and your uncle said ye'd been seen by some Haidas being held by one of their enemies and heading north, I turned right around and came back in the *Sarah Stone*. We maun have passed by the *Daphne* in the straits, maybe at night, or missed her while we searched every bay and cove we could."

I was more than a little apprehensive learning that his distress had gone on so long. While he and Mrs. Hawkes exchanged news of people, I tried to bargain with God. "Please God, let me stay here with Father and I'll never do a rash thing again. Cross my heart!" It was of course a lie, even if I did think I meant it heartily.

"I'll go to work now," Father said. "Ye don't mind keeping her for a little longer, Mrs. Hawkes?"

"Not at all."

He left then, and returned before supper. I didn't know what to expect, but for a brief time I had felt the warmth and laughter of an entire family again and I knew I would sorely miss being with this family. There were tears teetering at the edges of my eyes when I hugged the Hawkeses goodbye.

Father led me to another, older cabin that was closer to the beach and near Number One. "Number Three adits run right under these cabins," he said. "Mr. Robinson has given me this one to use while you're here."

"Am I to stay?"

"We'll talk on it after supper." Inside, he showed me the supplies he'd moved in and said, "Cook us a meal, lass." I did what I was told and prepared pork pies with cabbage. After the few dishes were washed and put away, we lit the lamp and sat on the stumps that served as chairs at the small plank table, facing one another.

"Did ye receive my letter?" I asked him.

"Aye, lass. I can read between the lines. It was a trying time for ye with your uncle, but ye were wrong to leave Genoa the way ye did. Ye have given us both cause to be worried grey. It's by luck and the grace of God that ye have come here unharmed, nowt else."

I did not know how to put into words the shock and terror I had felt at my helplessness in my uncle's hands. At last I said, "I was frightened, Papa."

His face blanched and he took a breath. "I dinna believe yer uncle would do owt to willingly hurt ye, Tess, but he was much misguided in his treatment of ye. I've nae doubt he learned a few things from you about children that he'll not soon forget. Pray for both yer souls, lass.

"I've thought hard on it. I'm sending ye to Edinburgh." He held up a hand when I raised my face to protest. "Hush and hear me out now. You'll live with your Uncle Liam and Aunt Hester for the next two years. They offered to take ye before we left Scotland, but my thinking was drawn inward to my own need to have ye with me and I refused them." He looked at me with unswerving conviction. "This is a wild place, Tess, but twill be a good place to live in time. I am no miner in my nature. I am content on the water and in one thing I've decided your uncle is quite right. I will be a missionary. I intend to have a good boat built when I have the money. It will be finished when ye come back and are ready to help me with God's work."

"I could better help were I to remain and learn the customs and the language," I said bitterly. I had always loved my mother's brother's family, but the prospect of leaving Father again seemed more than I could bear. "Father," I implored, "I love you. I want tae stay with you!"

His face came as near to crumpling then as I had ever seen it. With softness and a small quaver in his voice he said, "Tis for yer good that ye go to Edinburgh. Yer aunt and uncle will see to it your schooling is furthered, and you'll have the influence of a good woman to follow." He touched my face. "Tutoring I canna gie ye and that ye are in need of yet, lass."

I saw the awful pain behind his eyes. He loved me. That was certain. I bowed my head, fighting to keep my own tears back, knowing there was no more I could say.

❧

I remained in Nanaimo for three weeks before Father and I returned to Victoria, he to see me on my way to round the Horn and cross the Atlantic once again, this time aboard the *Princess Royal*. Father, rarely demonstrative in public, held me for a long time and kissed the top of my head. "Ye're fourteen years old now, lass. A woman. I know ye'll account yourself as one with your aunt and uncle."

If twas a plea, it was well done, and I couldna disappoint him. "I will," I said, "though I shall think of ye every day and wish I was here with ye."

A longer silence ensued, which I broke with, "Will ye look for Gabby while I'm gone? And if ye find out she's a slave, will ye buy her back and take her out of it? I've left the second silver cup. Ye could use that. She could be a housekeeper for ye, couldn't she, and ye could let her go to school with Mr. Bryant, couldn't you?"

"Ye'll be bargaining to your last breath, lass," he laughed. "I will ask wherever I can and if I discover her whereabouts I'll write ye."

"But if she's a slave ..."

"Aye. If she be and tis possible for me to do it, I'll take her out of it," he promised. I asked him to send me word of Nadia, too, if he learned anything about her.

The ship's band struck up "Auld Lang Syne." It was time for those going ashore to go. Father walked away proud and straight and soon he was watching us move toward the harbour entrance.

I stood at the main deck rail, squeezed between several other passengers, until we were out of the harbour, tears streaming down my face. The band was still playing "Auld Lang Syne."

❧ EPILOGUE ❧

IN January 1859, a fortnight from our destination, HMS *Daedulus*, homeward bound for Britain, caught up with us. We and they sat hove to for two hours while the captains had a tête-à-tête. *Daedulus* had mail taken on board in Victoria to deliver home, and our captain returned to the ship with letters for some of the passengers — including one sent to me — and four copies of *The British Colonist. The Colonist* was started in Victoria in December 1858, by a man named Amor de Cosmos. The papers would be passed around for all. I read Father's letter, dated October 20, 1858, first.

My Dearest Daughter Tess,

I am sending this in the mailbag of the Daedulus, with the hope it will reach you before Christmas. If't does not, I pray ye have spent a pleasant Christmas out of storms and well feasted at the captain's table, and that ye are well. I am happily fit, and so is your uncle, who sends you his regards.

All of your acquaintances here have begged to be remembered, most particularly the Hawkes family and Dr. Benson, who have said their letters to ye will be on the next ship going home, and so I shant tell you much of their news, except Mrs. Hawkes was delivered of a lusty baby boy two days ago and he is named William Thomas.

News ye will want to hear immediately is that Gabrielle is safe. She was discovered on a beach in Bute Inlet, after word of a skirmish between two tribes there reached Fort Victoria. The report was brought by a group of friendly Indians, who told a story of a clash when one tribe, seeking to avenge murder committed against several of them five years ago, attacked the other. The friendly Indians had apparently witnessed the fight, and said the tribe that was attacked had a small white girl with them, and that she disappeared into the forest during the battle.

Hammond was in Victoria when the news arrived, and he immediately got up a rescue party that went over to Bute to look for the girl. They found Gabby a little way from the beach, frightened, but unhurt. They brought her back to Victoria and your Mrs. O'Reilly said they would like to have her, so she has been taken in by them and she helps Mrs. O'Reilly with the children when she is not in school. I think that is a Christmas present ye will enjoy having. Another is news from Jock, who has sent us black humour from the Old Bailey in London, where he is now. He writes that they mine for gold teeth in the prison and that therefore he is very glad his teeth are nowt but ordinary white ones. It could be your aunt will escort ye to London in the high season, and ye'll have occasion to visit him and offer him some small comfort. I am enclosing his letter with mine for you to read all he has to say. I have no news of Nadia, but with news travelling as it does, I believe we would have heard if anything bad had happened to any of the lasses and hope ye will take comfort in that.

I heard from friends in Victoria that Mr. Samuel has been charged with unlawfully selling wee Gabby. I queried Hammond about it and he replied it was Mr. Samuel who was responsible for where the lasses were placed. Mr. Samuel gave Hammond false information about their placements and so your uncle dismissed him, and Samuel was subsequently charged. Apparently Mr. Samuel is denying his responsibility in the matter, but I have no doubt he will receive his just rewards.

There is some concern in Victoria right now about the fate of lasses who have been and will be brought to the island. In an article in the Colonist, Mr. Waddington says he intends to launch an investigation into the practice of importing white girls and women into the colonies to subject them to degrading occupations. He writes there is now in England a Society to help women emigrate and find placements as domestic help or work in what capacity they are suited. He adds there have long been groups of women in England established with the aim of having wage positions other than Governess available to middle-class females who desire a life independent of marriage, or who maun live independently because they are widowed or do not find husbands. There is a goodly number of the latter because the ratio of ladies to gentlemen in England is at least four to one. I mention this because your mother, who was herself raised in a free-thinking home, took an interest in affairs concerning women, and I have seen the same interest budding in you. Ye will be interested to know also, that because there is now a committee in Victoria to study importing large numbers of female emigrants to the colony, your uncle has said he will no longer be in that line.

Miss Bigget has accepted a proposal of marriage from Mr. James Beckley and has gone off to Victoria. Your uncle has not been able to replace her and he is unhappy about that.

I've hired an Indian boatbuilder, and have been amazed to witness his skill in measuring with nothing but his eye for a gauge. Tis not often I'm let watch him work, as he much prefers to do his work in complete secrecy. I believe tis a test of faith for me, while for him it may be a way of protecting his methods from being usurped by others. I have every expectation the boat will turn out beautifully.

I send you my love and am Your Loving Father,
Iain Macqueen

I was delighted to hear about Gabby, and equally happy to know that Jock was safe in prison. It could not be more dangerous than India. I was also glad for the news of people I'd come to know in Nanaimo. Father would be spending evenings visiting them. They were decent, kindly people, working to make a new start in a hard life. As for my uncle and Mr. Samuel, I was unwilling to trust either. I had witnessed Mr. Samuel's ability to lie to evade blame on board the *Borealis*, and I could not believe Uncle Hammond had no hand in what had happened to Gabby. The letter I had seen in Uncle's desk, referring to my grandfather's will, also came to mind. *Well, Uncle,* I thought, *I've made a vow that will not be dismissed, and one day I will act on it. You too may yet receive your just rewards.*

The British Colonist was printed December 18th, 1858. I was interested to read in it there was a kind of government being formed in the colony that some thought would eventually take the colony out of the hands of the Hudson's Bay Company's stewardship, and put matters of policy in the hands of the settlers. The editor, Mr. de Cosmos, was openly calling for more settlers when he wrote:

> Our vast industrial resources lie hidden from the world; and the means necessary to make millions [of] homes and happiness are untouched. Our fisheries remain but to be developed to prove a mine of untold wealth. Our inexhaustible coal mines — more valuable than diamonds — are scarcely opened. Our lands — the patrimony of the people — are still in the possession

of the Indian, or exposed to the clutch of the land-grabbing. Our vast forests — instead of making ships and homes — are unexplored and undisturbed. Our Indians — in place of being gathered into reservations — roam at large, a hindrance to settlement.

I hung my head with the hard thought of European, Asian and other nations' intrusion into this new land, and of Mr. de Cosmos writing of it and behaving as if it was ours by God. Young Seal's people had reason for their fear. I wanted to shout, "The land-grabbers, Mr. de Cosmos, are all of us." But I knew there would be no reversal. My people would stay in Young Seal's land, and I knew, too, that I would go back.

❦ ACKNOWLEDGEMENTS ❦

No matter how isolated a writer thinks she is, it takes a cast of dozens to produce a book. To everyone who participated in the production of *Tess*, both before and during it, a heartfelt thank you. First thanks must go to my family. To Bill for all the years of unconditional support, and for great suggestions for storylines when I ask for them. To Stephanie for her boundless enthusiasm for my work, her shrewd judgement, and most important, for being who she is. Many of her traits are visible in Tess Macqueen. And to Chris, whose unfailing courage and spunk have surfaced here in Jock and Gabby.

Friend and writer Audrey Nelson, has read my "stuff" and provided me with inspiration for years, as has friend Carol MacRae, who also read the earliest draft of *Tess*, and asked the right questions at the right time. Special thanks, too, to writing colleagues: Heather Kellerhals, Jeanette Taylor and Annette Yourk, for our years of sporadic but timely meetings, and for valuable feedback in the early stages of *Tess*. Editor Joy Gugeler read a one-paragraph idea I had about a book I might write someday, and told me the time was now, and that she wanted it! For her faith in my ability to pull it off, I will remain grateful.

Thanks to Rowan Kehn, and Elise and Etienne Coté, who read early drafts of the book and gave me insights into how younger readers received the story. In my research efforts, Barbara Van Orden and Sherrie Fudikuf of the Vancouver Island Regional Library, Quadra Island Branch, were helpful beyond the call of duty, as were Linda Hogarth and Sandra Parrish of the Museum at Campbell River Archives. Knowledgeable sailors Shirley and Frank Wallace gave me hours of their time explaining the routes and waters of the Inside Passage. Elaine Price of the Laichwiltaich people shared her expertise about canoeing in the Strait of Georgia. Writer Janice Kenyon provided information about the Mersey and Scottish castles. Writer Hilary Stewart loaned me several books and talked about North West Coast First Nations' life. Staff members of the BC Archives and Records Service, the Vancouver Island Regional Library, The Nanaimo

Archives, and the Hudson's Bay Archives, along with researcher Leona Taylor, and writer/historian Dr. Richard Mackie, provided information pertaining to life on Vancouver's Island in the 19th century. Scottish lass Eileen Mackay kindly read the completed manuscript with an eye (and ear) to the Scottish Hieland dialect, and loaned me her Scots Dictionary. Any mistakes are totally my own.

Among the more than forty books and the many archival materials I used to discover the tone and details of life on board ships, and in the British colonies and other parts of the world in the late 1800s, the following sources were most heavily mined for information: Terry Reksten's *More English Than the English*, (Orca, 1986) and *The Dunsmuir Saga* (Douglas & McIntyre, 1991); Philip Drucker's *Indians of the Northwest Coast*, 1963 edition; Richard Henry Dana Jr.'s *Two Years Before The Mast* (Reader's Digest, 1995); *Lady Franklin Visits the Pacific North West 1861 & 1870: Excerpts from Letters of Miss Sophia Cracroft, Sir John Franklin's Niece*, edited by Dorothy B. Smith (Victoria Provincial Archives, 1974, Memoir No. XI); and *The Russian Question* by Aleksandr Solzenitsyn, translated by Yermolai Solzenitsyn (Harper Collins, 1995).

Near the end of the process for *Tess*, writer/mountain-climber Heather Kellerhals-Stewart, writer/naturalist Ian Douglas, writer/historian Jeanette Taylor, writer/anthropologist Joy Inglis, and former librarian Hilda Van Orden graciously agreed to read the manuscript and allow their opinions to be quoted.

And in the final leg, editor Barbara Kuhne gave me her perceptive and thoughtful insights with a masterfully sensitive touch, and we completed three rounds of editing almost painlessly. (Well, on my part it felt pretty painless; as for Barbara, you'd have to ask her.)

Finally, a warm thank-you to all those writers' groups members, and other friends, who have accompanied me down my writing road for so many years with their advice and support, and to Raincoast Publishing staff for their work on *Tess*.

PHOTO: STEPHANIE CHRISTENSEN

❧ ABOUT THE AUTHOR ❧

Jocelyn Reekie lives on Quadra Island, British Columbia, where she is at work on a third novel, writes picture books and performs as an actor and comic.

OTHER RAINCOAST FICTION
FOR YOUNG ADULTS AND TEENS:

Adrift by Julie Burtinshaw
1-55192-469-2 $12.95 CDN • $7.95 US

Dead Reckoning by Julie Burtinshaw
1-55192-342-4 $9.95 CDN • $6.95 US

The Outside Chance of Maximilian Glick by Morley Torgov
1-55192-548-6 $12.95 CDN

Stickler and Me by Morley Torgov
1-555192-546-X $12.95 CDN

Spitfire by Ann Goldring
1-55192-490-0 $9.95 CDN • $6.95 US

My Brother's Keeper by Marion Woodson
1-55192-488-9 $9.95 CDN • $6.95 US

Wishing Star Summer by Beryl Young
1-55192-450-1 $9.95 CDN • $6.95 US

The Accomplice by Norma Charles
1-55192-430-7 $9.95 CDN • $6.95 US

Cat's Eye Corner by Terry Griggs
1-55192-350-5 $9.95 CDN • $6.95 US

Raven's Flight by Diane Silvey
1-55192-344-0 $9.95 CDN • $6.95 US